Praise for
The Road Not Taken

"The compelling story, told with effortless grace, of a suburban woman driven to become a warrior, a hero, a priestess."

—*Ms Magazine*

"Susan Rubin's *The Road Not Taken* offers a magical tale of transformation and joy. A pleasure to read."

— Alicia Hoge Adams, Artistic Director, Bootleg Theater, Hollywood

"*The Road Not Taken* by Susan Rubin is a unique work of magical realism, filled with fantastic imagery, irony, and amazing ideas. *The Road Not Taken* sits next to Isabelle Allende and Neil Gaiman on my reading table. If you want to take a unique journey, filled with humor, fantastic imagery, ideas, and irony, grab a copy."

— Luisah Teish, author, *Jambalaya*

The Road Not Taken

Susan Rubin

Harvard Square Editions
New York
2020

The Road Not Taken
by Susan Rubin
Copyright © 2020 Susan Rubin
Cover design by J. Caleb Clark ©
None of the material contained herein may
be reproduced or stored without permission
of the author under International and
Pan-American
Copyright Conventions.
ISBN 978-1-941861-68-4
Printed in the United States of America
Published in the United States by
Harvard Square Editions
www.harvardsquareeditions.org

Chapter One
Give My Regards

I FELT MANHATTAN welcome another spring. The weather had gotten warmer. Winter's shadow was still in the background, but I could feel the vernal equinox coming and it made me yearn—as it always had—for something I couldn't name. I looked at the slice of skyline sticking up above the other buildings: the Empire State and Chrysler Buildings. The first spring storm had washed them clean and shined them up.

I was enjoying the whiffs of international foods, the vast mix of human beings. On Lexington Avenue I heard a siren, a profanity screamed at a jaywalker, cars, buses, people laughing and talking. Up the block two cabbies cut each other off. One, dark in a turban the other screaming loudly with a German accent. Their words were hard to hear from the distance I was, but one exchange came through clearly.

"F*cking towel head! Out of my way."

"You move before we blow up all of you Nazi shits!"

This interchange made me wish for the less contentious interior of Bloomingdale's.

The double doors felt lighter than usual. Inside, distinct smells hit me immediately: perfumes, expensive ones promising to make me instantly alluring. The noise in the store was completely different too—controlled. People murmured to each other but spoke loudly to the salespeople.

I searched the various cosmetic counters until I found Clinique which offered this month's Gift with Purchase. The customers here had a serious purpose: something free to go with something they needed for their face. These gifts came with a seasonally appropriate bag for carrying your makeup.

My purchase would be two lipsticks. That's where the gaggle

of women stood, lined up but still managing to look in the mirrors on the counter. One woman broke the rules and smeared a color directly onto her mouth. You're supposed to use the sample stick on your hand. I couldn't take my eyes off her, which was embarrassing. Her sampling of the lipstick was not a felony, just a breach of protocol. I forced my focus to a mirror further down the counter where I clearly saw a reflection of myself. Impossible. I was three feet away and not facing that mirror.

I stared at the person who was reflected there—a woman who was my height, and weight, same hair color, and as she turned, I saw my face on hers, my exact replica. Was I hallucinating? I was so stunned I forgot she could see me as I looked her up and down. She was wearing the 'one of a kind' black wool coat I had on, the French scarf with its flamboyant reds and oranges, and the same sweater and pants. My face registered my shock. The Me-like thing approached and spoke.

"I know it's disorienting, but I promise, I mean you no harm."

I was relieved a hallucination could be so pleasant. I mumbled back at her. "Uh huh."

"I like your outfit."

"Thank you. I like yours, too."

I stood like a zombie taking her in. Earrings, same as mine, hair—same cut and highlighted color as mine, eye liner—could've come right out of my makeup case. We were the same 5' 5" and probably weighed within a gram of each other. The only difference was the plum color on her lips. I was wearing coral to match my scarf. Hers looked better. I knew I would sound stupid, but I decided to remark on this to see how she would respond. To see if she was a living creature.

"Your lipstick is better with this outfit. I think I'll change mine."

She smiled. Then she turned her back and began to head for the exit. I followed her, but she was making a fast move to the double doors. She stopped abruptly at a jewelry counter. I stopped too. She picked up two identical bracelets on the bracelet rack. They were *faince* and gold *vermeil*. She handed them to the salesperson and paid for them. I watched closely, but she never looked at me.

When she had bought the bracelets, she put one of them in her Gift with Purchase bag inside her purse. The other one she held in her hand. I thought she was about to put it on, but she turned to me very suddenly, handed me the second bracelet, and left the store without another word. I watched her jump into a cab that squealed away from the curb.

I ran out of the store and waved both arms frantically at the next empty cab. It passed me by, leaving the stink of exhaust in my face as it drove off. I saw that it had no passenger, but I had no time to be upset before another cab appeared. I gestured a little less frantically so as not to put him off, but this cab also passed me by. I still had the bracelet in my hand. I quickly put it on. Maybe the two cabs had thought it was strange, me waving a bracelet at them? Or, was the derangement I felt visible to all the cab drivers on Lexington Ave? Suddenly the charm of the street was mired in the stench of steam coming up from the subway grate.

When the third cab came by, I put one hand up and waved at it demurely as the Royals wave in England. This was the right move. The cab stopped at the curb directly in front of me and the back door flew open. I hopped in. "Do you see that cab up ahead, sir? The one like a van?"

"Yes, Ma'am."

With no further instruction he took off in pursuit of Her cab. He swung into traffic so quickly that I almost slid to the floor. I managed to brace myself as he drove by putting my hands down on each side of myself on the seat. I felt something under my right hand. I looked down and found a plain white envelope taped there, addressed to me.

I ripped it open and found a ticket to the Metropolitan Museum of Art with a post-it on the ticket that said "meet me." "Excuse me, sir," I said. "Please take me to the Metropolitan Museum."

He said nothing but cut all the way across Lexington to catch the right turn that would take us to Madison and uptown to the Met. I looked at the driver more closely now. His neck was thick, huge really, and a color you could only describe as bronze. I couldn't see his license with the photo of him, but he was covered in a thin coating of sand-colored dust. I closed my eyes to see if I could find some normalcy inside myself. Instead, after years as an oncologist's wife, I came to the understandable conclusion that I had developed an aggressive brain tumor.

"We're here."

The cab pulled up in front of the museum. I paid him and ran out of the car and up the big staircase to the entrance. I could see Twin Me inside the massive lobby heading to an exhibit up the stairs. I had to run to catch up with Her but I didn't want to encounter Her directly, so at twenty feet behind Her I slowed down.

She was entering one of the Met's Impressionist Painters rooms. I kept up my surveillance from a safe distance. She walked fast through some of my favorite artists and headed to a painting by the Netherland's greatest gift to the world: Vincent Van Gogh. My heart pounded as I stood behind Her. I had always been scared of this painting. It was his bedroom in Arles. I had seen it many times and gotten away from it without daring to look deeply into the room with its single bed, small wooden table, window, and door.

This time I couldn't ignore it. I looked down and tried to gather myself into one piece because the experience of the last hour had shattered parts of my well-built insulation and I felt very strange.

Twin Me turned, and came to stand by my side. "Look at it," she said. "You never really look at it."

"I know that."

"Why not?"

"If I knew that, I would be able to look," I said.

"You do know. You know exactly why it scares you."

"How the hell do you know how I feel?" I didn't mean to sound so angry.

"I know you." She was particularly coy as she said this.

"I need to go now." I pivoted away from her. I could not endure a pompous stalker.

"I thought you might," she said. "Classic avoidaholic behavior."

"What did you say?!"

"Do you want me to take you inside the bedroom?"

"No," I said. " 'Take me inside?' Are you insane? Having a little joke with me? And where do you get off with your witty diagnosis of me?"

She ignored my questions. "Come on," she said. "People are getting annoyed that we're in their way. Let me just go in and you can follow." Without giving another glance to see if I was behind her, she stepped directly up to the painting and in the blink of an eye, she was no longer on the outside. Luckily no one but me saw her little stunt: She just stepped onto the wooden floor in Van Gogh's bedroom, scrambled quickly out the little door and vanished from sight.

Still angry, but totally mesmerized, I followed the woman into the painting: I just stepped up and into the canvas. Before I could worry about falling down or being arrested, I was in a sweet-smelling bedroom in the countryside of France many lifetimes ago. I wanted to get out of sight and find Her so I went through the little door she had gone through seconds before and there she was, standing in Van Gogh's kitchen chatting with some woman in French.

They turned their heads to me and we all greeted each other amiably. Twin Me was laughing and telling a story to a dumpy, quite pretty housekeeper who was preparing food, probably his dinner. Twin Me asked the young woman if she could borrow something, I wasn't familiar with the word she used.

The housekeeper smiled and said, "Yes, of course, keep it for as long as you like. We have others."

Twin Me took a small knife off the table and wiped it with a clean cloth. She wrapped the little knife in the cloth and put it inside her cosmetics bags from the Gift with Purchase exchange that seemed hours ago. She thanked the housekeeper and took off back the way she had come.

I said *"au revoir"* to the housekeeper and followed this mysterious incarnation of me out of the kitchen, back through the bedroom. I followed her when she put her foot back on the floor of the Museum and stepped out of the painting.

And there we were.

"Let me see the knife!" I said.

"You don't believe I have it?"

"No," I said. "I don't believe anything. I have no architecture left to my reality. Thanks to you."

She opened her pocketbook and pulled out an ancient kitchen knife in a piece of cloth. She thrust it at me. "All yours."

"No," I said. "Thanks. You were the one who took it. You should keep it."

"You asked to see it! Go ahead—look."

I reached out, she handed it to me. Its diminuitive wooden handle was very weather beaten, but the blade looked sharp. The knife smelled slightly of something? Cheese? Onion? Something delicious. I put it inside my own handbag and turned to speak to Her.

Her vanishing act was becoming disturbing. I looked for her in the rest of the Impressionist exhibit, but she was gone. I headed for the exit not bothering to watch for Her. I was still trembling inside from stepping into Van Gogh's house. If he had actually been there I would have died from shock. So if she needed to run off now, good, because I needed to touch base with reality. I ran down the museum steps onto the street.

The sky was spectacular—a blue that cannot be replicated, with puffy white clouds hanging there just for decoration. I had never felt the pull of spring so strongly. I decided to walk the four miles downtown to where I live.

Chapter Two
Remember Me

MY NEW APARTMENT on Thompson between Bleecker and Houston is always bright and sunny. That was one of the reasons I had paid the exorbitant price it cost to move back to the city. My husband, a noted and respected oncologist had fallen down dead in his exam room two months ago. It was completely unexpected: he was deeply concerned for his cancer patients—compassionate and proactive. Who would've dreamed he would keel over from a massive heart attack while giving a patient her prognosis?

But life is like that: abrupt.

I sold the enormous house in Connecticut we had lived in. Of all the years I had spent shopping to keep the house looking grand, there was nothing in it I wanted. I called Human Rights Call, the organization my parents had run when they were alive, and gave them every stitch of furniture, every painting, every expensive appliance. I gave it in my parents' name, and once they had stripped the house down to its empty shell, I walked out the door without ever turning to look back.

I gave a big chunk of money to my one child, and moved to a duplex in the West Village. This was where I had started out. Being suddenly alone with enough money to make choices, I had found myself wanting to go home.

Or at least to live in a building that looked like home. There is really nothing left of the culture I grew up around. The great leather goods shops now housed Comme Des Garcons or some other generic, expensive store, there to serve the Russians who had bought up most of the West Village. Not a great idea—these fancy shops—since Russians prefer to shop in Moscow—New York was merely a place to dump their vast accumulation of rubles. They were never in their places as they had homes everywhere and they were not as in love with MacDougal Street as I am.

I went into my kitchen to put the knife down. I was hungry so I opened my refrigerator but found nothing. I do not eat at home. I am not really living here yet. I am still getting over the change from my married suburban existence to this new life I am facing. I had liked my husband very much. We had argued about almost nothing since I couldn't articulate a strong position on his major interest: new chemotherapy drugs. In the early years the sex was good. Not astounding. Not the kind of sex that wars are fought over. But it was reliable, and pleasant—that was a lot.

Things got less frisky when my daughter was born. My husband really loved having a little thing growing up around us, but in truth, he was never there. It was me, with the baby—then the child, the housekeeper, and drinks with my friends a couple of nights a week. I did not find my little girl intriguing. I was perfunctory as a mother, but very good at doing all the motherly things. Luckily, my child seems unaware of my maternal apathy. Which is wonderful. I would hate to have scarred her with my lack of delight in her—a good thing that my husband was a doting father and very sweet husband. But he wasn't around much. And now, he was gone.

I found an old piece of manchego cheese in the back of the refrigerator and pulled it out. Cheese. Perfect. I took the little Van Gogh knife and washed it. Then I put the cheese on a little board, took the knife in hand and began to cut.

At the exact moment the knife hit the cheese the phone rang, the land-line, which is quite loud. My hand slipped off the cheese and instead of cutting the manchego, the knife took a nice swipe at my left hand. I dropped the knife and rushed to get my hand under some running water. It was a very small but deep cut and it bled a lot. When I looked at the knife, it had nothing on it. No blood. Strange.

Once I had cleaned my cut and put a bandage on, I got nervous. What the hell was happening to me? Where did this knife really come from? Was my delusion of having "stepped inside" a painting a symptom of the onset of dementia, an ominous sign of a meningioma attacking my brain? I tried to look it up on my phone on WebMD, but the print was so small that I gave up, grabbed my bag and ran down the steps to the street. I walked to Carbone's, a fine food and drink spot on the corner of Bleecker and Thompson. I walked in.

The restaurant was not quite open yet. But they knew me, so they shoveled me into a seat, brought a basket of bread and offered me a glass of wine. I stuffed down a big piece of bread, and said "yes" to the wine, which was odd. In all our years together in Connecticut, I served my husband wine with dinner but never drank any myself. I knew that the wine would pull away the veil I lived under. I had no desire to see myself: suburban mother, wife, party giver. I loved my husband and my child but knew they were not part of my reason for being alive. The wine ran the risk of making me feel a desperate dissatisfaction I could do nothing about. So I only drank at parties where I slogged down something strong and became a different person.

I left the table at Carbone's to go to the bathroom, I took my purse but left my coat so nobody would come in and take my table.

In the tiny bathroom, I looked in the mirror. I looked strange to myself: Maybe from the cut? Had I lost enough blood to make my face look unfamiliar, to make my hair look like it was not my own? I washed my hands and went back to my table.

Twin Me was seated there, across from my coat. When I approached her, she was ordering a glass of pinot noir and tossing back a big piece of bread. I tried to be casual. "Hello. Care to join me?"

"I already have." She smiled.

"Do you live near here?"

"Sometimes." She was annoyingly enigmatic..

Her wine arrived. She took it with her left hand—her bread

was in her right. There was a bandage on her hand exactly where mine was. "I cut myself"

"Yes, I see," I said. "I cut myself as well." I showed her my left hand.

"Hmm. An evil-intended knife?"

"You gave me the knife," I said. "So you should know."

"Asking if I'm evil intended?"

I took a swallow of my wine. Then another.

Twin Me repeated herself. "Are you asking me if I am evilly intended towards you?"

"I didn't ask you anything," I said. "But I have no real idea what's going on."

She stared at me. "Really? Still? No idea at all?"

"No. Maybe the wine will give me some insight."

"It won't come from the wine." She smiled again.

That annoyed me. "Are we twins?" I asked. "Do you know something about my genetics that my parents never told me while they were alive?"

"Twins?"

"Yes. Look at us. Dressed identically, hair identical—faces too similar. Almost identical. You don't notice this or find it curious?"

"I know who I am," she said. "This is your mystery to untangle."

"Maybe I'm having a prolonged hallucinatory response to being widowed?"

"Is that what you think is going on?"

I was feeling the wine way too fast. "I'm going home. I feel a little off. Are you going to be waiting for me when I get to my apartment?"

"No."

I stood up, put money on the table and started to leave. Then I turned back. "Will I see you tomorrow?"

"Yes. I want to take you back to the Museum."

"To return the knife?"

"No. "

"Another parlor trick?" I asked.

"You do look a little pale," she said. "Maybe you lost some blood with your cut. I will be at the Main Entrance tomorrow at noon."

"All right. I'll join you. Will you tell me tomorrow what is going on?"

"You'll want to figure this out for yourself." She sipped her wine.

*

We were already inside the museum lobby by 12:01. She had greeted me with a perfunctory hug, like we were old friends—which we were not. I hugged her back. Now she was walking quickly through the Egyptian cases on the main floor. I am a great fan of Egyptian mythology.

From the speed at which she was moving, it was clear she was on a mission. She didn't break her pace or stop to look at the display of spectacular objects of jewelry and art from the Pharaoh's tremendous collection. She headed straight to the Temple of Dendur.

I had been there but had never actually gone inside the Temple. It is a transplanted Pyramid brought to the museum one stone at a time from Egypt—they had even brought over the interior hieroglyphics that stood in profile inside the narrow halls of the structure. The Temple would have been lost when the Aswan Dam was built. It would've been drowned by the new river. Instead, it was given to the museum as a gift. I stepped up to the entrance to the Temple.

"Come on," Twin Me said.

"Why? What's in here?"

"A story. You will get into this."

That was what I was afraid of. Egyptian mythology had gotten to me at a deep subliminal level since I was a child. I wrote my senior thesis on mummification, which annoyed the hell out of my social-science teacher. But too bad; I had no understanding of death. My favorite uncle had died quickly of cancer and that being my first encounter with the Inevitable Thing We All Face, had left me scared. Nobody in my family had time to explain anything to me, and I didn't ask. He was there, then he was dead in an open casket with his favorite smoking pipe on his chest. We didn't believe in god, so there was once an uncle, and then there wasn't.

If anybody asked what my interest was in mummification, I would've told them about the Boris Karloff movie and how fascinating it was to me. And maybe that was what got me into Egyptian images of the dead and the not so dead. Maybe.

I looked up to find Twin Me staring impatiently. "Let's go," she said. "They close the temple in one hour."

"Okay," I said. "I'm right behind you."

She took a sharp left around a narrow corner and I followed her. Immediately the light changed, and we were in a musky, arid space no longer the hallway we had just been in.

It was hot: very hot and dusty. I let myself slide to the floor. She watched me with a mix of amusement and irony on her identical-face-to-mine. "Spacetime jet lag."

"What?" I asked.

"The way you feel. Don't be surprised, you just traveled 5,000 years back. That's one of the astrophysicists' newest pronouncements: we can only travel backwards on the space time continuum. But still, it's a shock to the system."

"Where are we?"

"I don't answer questions like that," she said. "Look around."

We stood on an unending plateau of desert. As my eyes adjusted to the dust and to the 5,000-year journey I had just made. I began to see large shapes around me. Pyramids. Huge pyramids. We must be at Giza in Egypt. But how?

"See her?" Twin Me pointed.

I caught sight of a smallish woman coming towards us. She was bronze-colored, just like the cab driver who took me from Bloomingdale's to meet my Fate. I don't mean the subtlety of saying somebody was very tan, or dark-skinned. I mean she was bronze from head to toe. As she came into focus the first part of her I saw were her eyes. Large, dark, almond-shaped and lined in thick black that crisscrossed at the outer end of each eye in exactly the way I had seen on the hieroglyphics. She approached Twin Me.

"Is this her?" The Bronze Woman pointed at me.

"Yes. It worked out quicker than I anticipated. She's quite adept at following a trail."

The Bronze Woman spoke to me this time. "Are you all right? Would you like a glass of water? Beer?"

I looked around. There was absolutely no source of water or beer, but I was parched. "Yes, water please. Thank you."

She turned her back to me, knelt over, and picked up a pitcher and a goblet that had not been there three seconds ago. Turning back, she poured liquid into the goblet and handed it to me. "You'll like this."

I took a sip. It was not water. It was not anything I had ever tasted before. I gulped down the whole thing. Delicious. And given the circumstances, obviously magical. Or maybe this was all part of the lunacy setting in on me—I didn't care. The minute the liquid hit my blood stream everything was much easier.

"Why am I here?"

The Bronze Woman turned. "You haven't told her anything yet?"

"No," Twin Me replied. "She'll see it all now that she's with us." She laughed. It made her look really pretty. My father used to tell me my best look was when I laughed. Twin Me and the Bronze Woman kept talking.

"I hope so. I don't get to make all that many selections," Twin Me said.

"Somebody's coming," I said.

Neither of the other women turned to look. But they both nodded their heads, "yes".

This time, the newcomer was a man. He wore only a loin cloth, like a linen kilt, and he was almost unbearably handsome and well-made. His black hair had been pulled back and tied in a braid which hung over one of his muscled shoulders. Also, bronze. His neck was the size of the cab driver's, and this man too seemed to be dusted in something.

When he was very close to us Twin Me spoke to him. "Welcome."

He pointed to me. "She will be Isis?"

"Yes," Twin Me said.

"She knows the story?"

"I think so." Twin Me turned to me. "You studied Egypt didn't you?"

"Yes."

"Tell me who he looks like to you."

"Is this Osiris?" I asked.

Osiris smiled. "I am. Have you seen Set?"

Twin Me answered him. "No. He's late as usual. But he's anxious to participate, so he will show up."

"Has she been given anything to eat or drink?"

This time the Bronze woman handed Osiris the pitcher and a goblet, which as before, she seemed to pull out of thin air. He poured himself a drink and finished it in one swallow.

I had been drinking the "water" for quite a while before I noticed the changes in me: I was no longer dressed in what I had put on this morning. I was in a gown of very fine gold-weave. It was barely a gown at all, sleeveless, quite transparent, low neckline, high slits up both sides which exposed my thighs. I looked at my leg and saw it was bronze. I felt my hair; the chic cut had been replaced with long black curls. I was wearing ornate earrings made of *faience* and gold.

I walked to an elaborate mirror that was lying flat on a gorgeously tiled table. I climbed on top of the table and looked down at my reflection. My eyes. It was to be expected, but it was still shocking and thrilling: my eyes, which I usually line very lightly with a medium brown pencil, were now lined in the black lines I had seen everywhere since we left the temple and flew through Time.

Although the reflection looked like the person I had lived with for my 50 years, I was totally transformed by makeup, skin tone, somebody else's hair and jewelry and even the air around me. This part of my breakdown or tumor was making me look like a woman from ancient Egypt. From the days of the Pharaohs.

Osiris entered the room. When he did, I realized I was alone. No Twin Me, no Bronze woman. My heart began to race, I grew very warm very suddenly, and my skin felt moist even in this desert.

He smiled at me. I smiled back.

I moved further down the huge table I was on, away from the mirror—onto an open part of the table. Osiris sat beside me. I turned to him and he was staring straight ahead smiling. I put my hand on one of his legs and he turned his head to me.

"Set tried to kill me."

"His jealousy is as poisonous as an asp," I said,

"He lost control, I am so thankful for Isis's relentless effort to save me." Osiris put out a beautiful bronze hand, took my hand and placed it on his heart. As he did this I had to stop myself from moving my other hand onto his body.

His face grew solemn. "My brother cut me into seven pieces. He threw each piece into one of the oceans."

"And Isis searched until she found them. She was blind with rage at him, but put that aside to find all of your parts."

"Set would have paid a heavy price if she had not saved me and stopped his plan. How did she reassemble me?"

"Bound your parts with linen. Clean white linen, then lay you down on this table and breathed life back into you."

"Is that when she and I were together again for the first time? Or did I need to recover?"

"You recovered as soon as Isis brought you back to life."

Osiris smiled as he reached for me: I had never seen anything like it. His eyes grew darker and brighter as if he had turned on a bulb inside his head. I could feel his desire for me, it was different than men or boys I had been with in my life. They were sweet but flickering candles of need; Osiris was a power station with the promise of an experience unlike any I had ever had. I was desperate to make love with him when Twin Me entered the room and Osiris and I sat up straight.

"Ah."

That was all Twin Me said. But she too had been transformed and was now, once again dressed identically to me. She was stunning with her eyes lined in black kohl. On her arm was the *faience* and gold bracelet she had bought for both of us. I wanted her to go. It was the first time since meeting her that she was not fascinating to me. Right now, all I wanted was Osiris. I had never known this kind of physical yearning. I could feel all the spring romances of the last thousands of years. All of the pleasure people had given each other over the centuries. Not mundane and functional pleasure; the kind of excited but tender stroking that binds peoples' souls to each other. I was already in love with him. I held Osiris's huge hand. I stared at Twin Me. She watched me and smiled. "Sorry. You'll have to wait for next time."

"Why?"

"Let's go, my dear." She gestured with her hand.

Osiris smiled at me and let go of my hand. "I'll be here when you come back." He got up and walked out of the room.

"Why did you do that?" I asked.

Twin Me was amused at this. That really irritated me.

"Treasure it," she said. "It cannot last. It never does."

"The story lasts. It's lasted 5,000 years. Something between them must have been special for their story to become mythic."

"Yes, that's right," she said. "And in order to become mythic you have to let this breathe. I will bring you back here. You will lie with Osiris. It will be everything you can imagine. But we have to allow the right amount of time."

I began to argue with her. I had waited my whole life to want somebody the way I wanted Osiris. And who was to say she could ever get me back here? Who was to say she wasn't a part of my disintegration into total madness? I had felt his thigh next to mine. Even inches apart, it had been more than I had ever felt for any part of any man's body. The desire for him made me woozy, I lay down on the table so I could close my eyes which were dry as dust.

Chapter Three
Positively Thompson Street

WHEN I OPENED MY EYES, I was alone in my apartment on Thompson Street. Outside, the deepest of sunsets glowed and covered my room, still sparsely furnished, in a series of beautiful colors from the reflected pinks and purples.

I got up and went into my kitchen. My little TV was on. I looked at my arms and the clothes I was in. It was me, just plain me. It was as if I had never touched the leg of the most mythic god in Egypt. It could be that it had all been a dream. I had no recollection of how it had happened.

I poured myself a glass of red wine and noticed that my husband was sitting in the living-room. I poured a second glass of wine and went to say hello. "Would you like a glass? It's a good red. Like you enjoy."

He reached up for the wine.

We stared at each other amiably.

"You're drinking wine now? I'm glad." He smiled.

I avoided his comment. "How did you get in here?"

"Do you mean into your apartment?"

"I meant how did you get back into the world."

"I've never left it. Just moved to a different place in Time."

"You look good," I said. "Your color has come back. The moment when you died was horrifying."

"I know. I'm sorry. But nobody was more surprised than I was. Heart attack? From where, from what? Nothing in my genetics."

"Well, it seems like you're all right. I mean, from here we never really know what the next jump in our lives will be."

"They certainly didn't teach me that in med school."

We both laughed and took big sips of our wine.

"What do you feel like?"

"They tell me I won't feel the full reality of my existence for a while. Right now I am adjusting to a non-corporeal self; although I have maintained an appetite for wine. And you've developed one."

"It used to make me uncomfortable, like the stuffing would fall out of the carefully constructed doll of myself."

He was silent as he took this in. That doll had been his wife, the mother of his child, and neither of us knew anything about her.

Finally, he spoke. "I saw your friend. Or sister. Or—who is she?"

"I was hoping you might know," I said. "Seeing as you are no longer living in the confinements of the moment."

"I wasn't being honest. Please forgive me. I guess I am a little jealous of you and Osiris. Of course, I know who your twin is. Or more accurately what she is."

"Is she the manifestation of a brain tumor?"

He laughed sweetly the way he did when we were in our home in Connecticut and I asked him something he found irrelevant.

"Please tell me." I said. "I am still trying to figure whether she's a figment of my imagination, a beacon of truth, or a malignant growth."

"You won't hear me if I tell you. That was very hard for me to learn. But it's true. You just have to figure this out."

We drank companionably and sat staring as the sunset turned darker and the light in the apartment faded. I got up and turned on every light available. I am not a fan of darkness or strangeness and the potential for both was extraordinary right now.

"I miss you," he said.

"You do?"

"Yes. I miss very little of physical form or substance. But I miss you."

"I changed my whole life when you died," I said.

"Do you miss me?"

"Yes."

"But you are free to find out some things you've been avoiding."

"Yes." I nodded and sipped.

"May I come back and visit when I'm in this frequency?"

"I would like that."

He finished his glass of wine and stood up. He was not as

big as Osiris. But he was handsome and held within himself years of memories of us together. This was valuable to me. I took his glass and we kissed goodbye, a sweet, simple kiss on the mouth. I almost couldn't feel his lips, and then he was gone.

I marveled to myself how much I had come to accept the unannounced comings and goings of Twin Me, my deceased husband. Even Osiris strode out of my reality without a backwards glance.

And then without warning, Time and Space reorganized themselves and took me with them.

I could not see the man I was with. I could only feel him. I had missed the foreplay, the initial strokes of our sexual get together. As I brought my body into focus, I was already in a state of ecstasy. It went on and on seemingly for hours. I could smell him, but still couldn't see him. I just felt the joy. It was a long time before my body quit shaking with pleasure.

When the time came to stop, we were both covered in sweat. I opened my eyes and saw his muscled, bronze thigh. It was pressed against my own leg that was also bronze. My vision cleared and I saw gold threads from the dress I had abandoned, and on the floor beneath us, I could see his loin cloth.

Osiris and I slowed down at the same time and eventually were quite still. He lay his head on the pillow, I put my head on his chest. We lay like that for a while before either of us wanted to speak. Finally, he turned to me and we looked at each other's faces.

"Is it like this with you and Isis," I asked.

"Yes."

"Is it okay that she is your sister?"

"Yes."

"Does your culture allow this?"

"We're a myth. Isis, Osiris, Set and Nephthys: All four of us siblings. You know the story."

"Your sister, Nephthys, is married to your brother, Set," I replied. "And you are married to your sister Isis."

"That's the cause for Set's terrible jealousy. Their marriage is just a marriage. Isis and I cannot live without each other."

"I have never had your kind of marriage."

"And it's what you yearn for every spring."

"How do you know that?" I was stunned.

Osiris did not answer me directly. "Human craving for 'forever after'. But it can't really be maintained. That's why we are a myth."

"People can feel that way for some amount of time?"

"Yes. Of course. Romantic love." He smiled at me.

"But it always ends."

"Have you read Romeo and Juliet?" He asked.

Twin Me entered the room.

Osiris and I covered ourselves with bed clothes.

She came and sat on the bed with us. "Did you enjoy this?" She smiled at me.

"Osiris just told me what all my spring yearnings are about."

Twin Me nodded at Osiris. "We don't need Set any more. We got to the heart of things without any need for playing out the story."

"Yes, I felt that." Osiris stood up.

Twin Me kissed him on his cheek.

He grabbed his loin cloth, ran a bronze finger affectionately down my arm, and left the room.

"Will I be with him again?" I asked.

"Sometimes," she said. "Nothing regular. You understand?"

"I do."

Twin Me began to help me dress and get myself back in presentable shape. She pulled a comb out of her pocket. It was lovely, ornate, like a museum piece.

"Is that from the Met?"

"Yes, I borrow something different whenever I make this trip." She smiled happily.

"You come here with other people?"

"You're not the only creature with an unmoored soul. I know you know that."

"Soul" was the last word I heard her say. I began to spin slowly on the bed, I felt my body rise up and fly gently. I could feel Her by my side. We flew together out of the ancient world, into the night sky and then simultaneously we dove directly down into an ocean that was light years from where we had been.

We swam with great intensity—in tandem—pushing

easily past huge fish and sea creatures. At the bottom of this ocean we came upon a trap door. Twin Me pulled it open and we both walked through it onto a flight of descending stairs. She pulled the trap shut behind us and I found myself on my bed in the Thompson Street apartment. I was completely dry, dressed in my standard New York black clothes and I immediately curled up into a little ball on my bed.

"Sleep. You've had a big day." Twin Me covered me with a small blanket from the foot of my bed. She turned off the lights in the room and quietly took a seat in a chair facing my window. "I'll watch over you for a while."

I stared at her for a few minutes. The sunset joined us in the room and made her look astral in shades of red and purple. It was the first time I realized that I had grown to love her, and I was beginning to understand the infinite scope of the journey she was taking me on.

Chapter Four
Come Hear the Music Play

THE CAFÉ WAS CROWDED and the jazz musicians on stage were loud. The interior was so filled with smoke that my friends and I chose an outdoor table. I was smoking a long, thin, pastel colored cigarillo in an ornate holder. My fingernails were black and as I looked at my reflection in the window of the café, I saw that my eyes were all blacked too. Not like in Egypt. This was a rebellious style of makeup. I looked around at my companions dressed in flamboyant reds and yellows. They too had on defiant smoky eye makeup, with bright red lipstick and lots of beaded necklaces over their glamorous dresses.

I was transfixed by a woman in pink plumage—pink feathers sewn to the top of her dress and flying out behind her head, created a huge collar. She wore a monocle, and I could tell something about her was different. I watched her moving and looked at her calves as she sashayed around the dance floor. Ah. She was a man. The legs were unshaven and the calves unmistakably male. I turned back to what was being discussed at my table.

The conversation was in German, but I understood every word. I spoke in an ancient Egyptian dialect when I was with Osiris. In Arles, all my years of French had served me so I could understand the conversation in the kitchen. Here in Germany, I became fluent in their mother tongue. This type of thing no longer shocked me.

My companions were pleasantly tanked-up, and so was I. We had been drinking everything in the café, from beer we had moved to mixed drinks. We ate no food and smoked one pastel cigarillo after another as we talked in loud voices with extreme enthusiasm for our subjects.

"Who cares about this silly man with the greasy hair and stubby mustache—why are people taking him seriously? A house painter for god's sake! Women like us are free! Not chained to a husband or children, we meet every night at the cafe to talk art, politics, sex. This freaky little man can't touch us."

The exchange was deep and intense, and I had never been so happy. Then the conversation grew louder. "He and his cronies call us Degenerates. Ironic, isn't it? Obviously, they're the degenerates—we're the way of the future!"

Twin Me was also at the table. For this part of our journey, we were dressed and made up so differently that if you didn't really look, you would not have seen that we were identical. I think she was giving me a taste of freedom. It allowed me to express my opinions about the paintings of Otto Dix and George Grosz without feeling like I had to avoid embarrassing her. These two painters transported me the way Van Gogh did when I stared too long at one of his paintings.

The discussion got louder and more frantic as we all got drunker. By now two of my companions, one woman in a bright yellow dress with a plunging neckline and covered in feathers, the other, in deep scarlet with some huge, red beads I envied—they looked like real rubies although that was impossible.

Anyway, these two came to verbal blows with one calling the other a "moronic revisionist with no understanding of history" and the other retorting with "wait, he will be chancellor and our freedoms will be the first casualty of his regime."

The first woman stood up, waving a cigarette drunkenly in a circle. By now she was crying and screaming. The wretched emotional outburst of a drunk telling the truth: "You'll see, we'll all be shoved back into the misery of the past. What the hell do you think they're selling with their constant shouts of 'Kinder, Kuche, Kitche?!' "

This was a phrase I couldn't translate so I looked at Twin Me. She was laughing, drunk—more relaxed than I had ever seen her. While the two women kept haranguing each other, I got up and moved to a seat next to her and whispered "What does that mean? Kinder, Kuche, Kitche?" She stared at me, her eyes trying to focus so she could cut through her drunken haze to answer me.

"You speak fluently. Translate for yourself!"

"I can't. My brain shuts down every time I try to remember

what the words mean. Please. Just tell me." I stared at her.

She picked up her cocktail glass which was half full, and in one gulp she emptied it.

"Children, Kitchen and Church. That's what it means."

She leaned back and I watched as she teared up.

"Do you want to go?" I asked her.

"Soon."

I could see a wave of something terrible come over her. I picked up a random cocktail that was left on the table. I took a sip, it was very strong and extremely sweet. I drank it all and then realized how much I needed to empty my bladder of my various alcohol intakes. I stood up. I was wobbly, but so was everybody else, so I stumbled my way through the tables and headed for where I had seen the bathrooms.

My bladder was an emergency so I ran in and almost fell into the first open stall, desperate to relieve myself.

When I opened the stall door the first thing to hit me was the silence. The musicians must be on a break. I washed my hands and looked in the mirror preparing to gussy up a little— re-apply some makeup. But the woman I saw in the mirror was devoid of the glossy red my lips had been showing off. My eyes were no longer smoky and enticing, I had on no eye makeup at all. My hair was not puffy and elaborate as it had been minutes ago. Instead, the hair was pulled back in a severe bun. My satin and velvet gown—the most perfect shade of Chambord—had been replaced by a drab grey suit jacket. I wore the matching drab grey skirt and looking down I saw that my shiny red pumps were gone. I wore Oxfords.

I ran out of the bathroom and stopped dead. The nightclub was gone. The music stands, the musicians, the instruments, the laughter, the joy of the dancers, the booze and cigarette smoke, all gone. The witty conversation and elaborate political debates were silenced. There was instead a butcher shop with a glass case that showed off an awful display of sausage, beef, pork chops. Not even chicken for those of us who don't like the taste of blood.

There were two butchers behind the case, and three women ordering from them. The women could have been nuns. Their clothes were colorless, their faces austere and without makeup.

I walked as unobtrusively as I could back to where the outside seats had been. I needed Twin Me—the woman who had brought me here. I spotted her outside the shop, and walked quickly to join her. She wore a severe black overcoat and all trace of her fantastic get up had disappeared.

"What's happened?" I asked her.

"You were gone, history moved forward."

"To what?" I looked around.

"Kinder, Kuche, Kitche."

She turned and began quickly walking away. As I followed her down the sidewalk, the world around us shifted and began to dissolve. I wondered where in Time and Space she would take me next.

Chapter Five
In Old New York

MY FINGERNAILS SHONE PINK. They were on my hands but not my grown woman hands. I looked in the window of the store Twin Me had brought me to and saw the reflection of an 11-year-old girl—clearly it was me. I looked up and asked Twin Me where we were.

"What does it remind you of?"

"The lower east side. When I was very young. I'm not sure. Maybe we're on one of the avenues that go way down past Canal."

"Remember when you worked here?" She smiled at me.

"I volunteered—at that hospital.

I pointed to a very large medical edifice that no longer exists.

"Do you want to go over there?" She offered.

"I would like to look at those shoes in the window."

"White patent leather. Very nice."

"I know the dresses I would wear them with."

"Pink and purple flowers. Gauzy fabric. Lots of crinolines underneath." She understood me so well.

"Yes. But I never got the shoes."

"Let's get them now." She took my hand.

We walked into a shoe store that hasn't been there for 30 years. The people were dressed from another time: the two sales women were in little shirtwaist dresses. They wore low heeled black pumps, and one wore a neckerchief that matched her dress. The saleswoman on her break was smoking a Camel and looking at a movie magazine. She looked up and realized nobody was waiting on us, so she approached.

At the other end of the store, a mother and daughter were arguing loudly. Staring at them distracted me. The saleswoman began to walk away. I watched a few more seconds and realized I could not hear the language they were speaking. But their fight had a universal feel to it. The daughter was trying to squeeze her somewhat chubby feet into a pair of the shoes I had admired. The white patent leather wasn't giving her much leeway for the fact that her feet were too wide to get them fully inside the shoe. I waited to see if the saleswoman or any other sales person would offer the girl a different size. But nobody did.

I turned to Twin Me to ask if I could try the shoes on myself and of course, she was gone. In her place was my father; he had been dead for 23 years. He looked well. He was wearing a suit, white shirt, and a very familiar tie. I went to him and he smelled like himself. Whatever aftershave he had worn in his lifetime was wafting off of him. He smiled as I approached.

"See anything you like?" He pointed to the display of shoes.

"Yes. I like those."

I pointed to where the white patent leather flats were placed next to their black and red sisters.

"Which color do you want to try on?" He asked.

"White. Please."

My father waved to the sales woman and told her I wanted to try on the shoes. She measured my feet on one of the old-fashioned metal planks all shoe stores used to have. She adjusted the lever until she had the length and then she did the same with the width. When she was done, she suggested we take a seat while she fetched the shoes. I sat down next to my father for the first time since his death. He was quiet, but friendly, I was excited about the present he would buy me.

He lit a Chesterfield cigarette with his flip top lighter and looked for an ashtray, found a tall standing one, and brought it over to where we were sitting. I looked up at him. He looked at me. We still did not speak.

The woman bustled out of the stock area with three shoe boxes and put them on the floor. "Try these first."

I took off the loafers I was wearing and realized the bulky socks I had on would not be right for the flats. The sales woman saw the problem. "Just take your socks off."

With my feet bare, I stuck a toe into the first of the white shoes. Then I slid my foot in—I might've been Cinderella—the shoe was a perfect fit!

My father smiled appreciatively and put out his cigarette as I put on the second shoe. "Take a spin around the store and make sure they're comfortable," he said.

"Okay." I walked past the mother and daughter who by now had broken into an extremely contentious fight. I spun around them and went to the mirror, but I kept staring at their reflection. I had only had one fight like that with my mother. I don't remember what it was about, but I do remember that my father told me angrily to lay off my mother—completely took her side. It was hard to accept from a man whose equilibrium was almost never shaken.

I looked back at my father now. He smiled and nodded his approval. All of this was lovely because in all of my real life with him, we had never shopped for anything together. He was always too busy although he was quick to offer me the cash to buy whatever I wanted. Here he was spending precious minutes with me in a shoe store. No one around to get between us. In a short time, we had bought the shoes, and were on our way out of the store.

On the sidewalk outside was Twin Me. She and my father exchanged pleasantries and then he walked off quickly without saying goodbye to me.

I was left holding the precious shoes in their box. I stared in the direction he had gone, trying to catch one more glimpse of him: his shoulders were broad—not like an athlete—just the perfect shoulders to stick into his lightweight, perfectly tailored jacket. He had a swagger to him that could have been arrogance but was not. He was a man who had enjoyed every minute of his life and seemed to be enjoying whatever comes next. I was sad to see him walking away, fading as he went. I wanted to hug him, to say goodbye, but, exactly as it had been when he actually died, my father felt no need to warn or acknowledge me as he disappeared into the ether.

"How do you know him?" I asked Twin Me.

"I know everyone in your family."

"Will I see all of them?" I looked at her.

"Show me the shoes. Do you love them?"

"Yes. They feel like springtime is coming."

"Good. Then you bought the right thing." She smiled.

When we arrived back at my Thompson Street apartment, I still had the box with the shoes, but I was once again myself. I had entirely missed the transition that happened to my body going from 11 years old to 50. I grabbed a couple of glasses and poured red wine for me and Me. Then I took the shoes out and put them on my chest of drawers. We stared at them as we drank.

"I will be gone for a few days. Maybe more," Twin Me said.

"Oh." I hoped I didn't sound too desperate.

"You have lots of work to do without me."

"Like what?" I asked.

"Like by the time I come back, please pick a name to call me."

"What is your name?"

"Have I ever answered a question like that?" she asked.

"No."

"Have I asked you any questions you did not want to answer?"

"I don't remember every question you've asked me." I said.

"Fine." Twin Me rose, finished off her glass of wine and headed for my door. Before she disappeared, she gave me instructions. "Nothing French or pretentious—nothing dull or repetitive. Think of a really good name for me."

"And what will you call me?"

"Good question. I'll think of something you'll like."

"Maybe you could think of a name that would give me some information about why you are here. In my life. Why you have chosen me, and what for?"

"Yes. What a smart idea." Twin Me smiled and touched my arm. I couldn't tell if she was being sarcastic. But I never could tell.

Having made her final statement, she opened my door, exited and closed it behind her. It would be weeks before I saw her again.

I was sick for the next three days. I couldn't figure it out because none of the symptoms were serious, but I felt like I shouldn't move or I might fall down.

I thought I might be missing the Journey I had been on with Twin Me. I thought I might just be missing her. I was probably right, but it came with a mild headache and terrible but intermittent bouts of stomach pain. I had no idea if I should eat something or drink some concoction. I lived just a short bit from a Natural Foods Store that had vitamins, minerals and lots of Natural Ways to Heal Yourself. It also had a knowledgeable staff of eager, healthy, young Natural Loving people.

Something inside me told me to just sit still. Lie still. Listen to the sounds outside my window. Through the maze of ambulances, sirens, neighbors screaming and tires screeching I could still hear as birds arrived and made their homes on the windowsills on my block. Most of them had window boxes with desperate little flowers trying to survive an on-again, off-again spring in Manhattan. I hadn't done any decorating yet so my window outside was naked.

I lifted the window screen up about a foot and began tearing pieces of bread and throwing breadcrumbs outside onto the sill. The bread was in my house to put something on my stomach before my now nightly glass of wine. When the birds got wind of my offering, they showed up. A lot of them; I counted 13. I didn't get a solid count of the snotty pigeons that feasted on much better food than this in our neighborhood eateries but who showed up to take an occasional peck and probably to stare at the array of unusual plumage on the visiting birds. I was very happy to see them all.

It was now past the bread portion of the evening, I was sipping my wine, staring out the window and hoping Twin Me would pop in. Instead, my windowsill population swelled with a startling array of multi-colored feathers. These were not city birds, not even American birds. I saw feathers of the most lavish shades of green, blue, pink, red, and purple. I walked to the window and quietly lifted the screen up higher to give more room to the birds. As I did this, the sheer mass of them were forced to fly into my apartment. Once inside, several made themselves comfortable on what little furniture I had. I put out a nice spread for them with the bread I had left and a couple of olives I assumed they wouldn't want, but I thought I should offer. The pigeons were now openly staring at the newcomers.

I lay down and watched as the whole room came alive with these fantastical flying creatures. They talked easily among themselves, chirping and nibbling. The olives were a great success. I hadn't given a dinner party since my husband and daughter and I lived in suburban Connecticut.

This made me think of my daughter and realize that in the weeks since I had met myself, I hadn't phoned her. I didn't know if she had tried to reach me because I hadn't listened to voice messages or read emails. I had been around the world, through centuries of time now gone. I had seen my husband and my father and never blinked at this contact with the deceased. And in all of this, my daughter had never entered my mind. It had always been like this for me. I had to force myself to remember her. Not because of anything unpleasant, not like the mother and daughter in the shoe store. My husband had been the real loving one, and his sudden death must still be terribly hard on my daughter. It was so recent.

Chapter Six
Someone to Watch Over

I PICKED UP MY PHONE and hit the button for my daughter's home number. She answered immediately.

"Hello sweetheart. It's me."

"Mother!"

"Yes. Sorry I've been so out of touch."

"Are you all right? I've left you a bunch of messages."

"Oh. My phone—anyway, that's not the point. I am sorry I haven't answered you."

"How's your new place?" she asked.

"I like it. It's totally empty, but I am glad to be in the city."

"I could help you fill it. I know a place with the stuff you like."

"Yes. Good. Let's do that." I said.

"Tomorrow is a good day for me," she offered. "Should I pick you up? We can get a lot done if we have my car?"

"Lovely. That's very nice. We'll do it."

"Where do you live?"

"You know my address don't you?" I was a little ashamed.

"You told me Thompson Street."

"Oh. Well, that's no good is it? The number is 2939. You won't want to park, but buzz me when you get here, and I'll come down."

"I should see the space so I know what we're shopping for."

"Yes. Right, there's usually daytime parking spots on my street. Come in and go upstairs. Apartment A. There is only A and B."

We agreed on a time for her arrival and hung up. I noticed that all the birds had flown back out my window and disappeared. I was totally lost in sadness.

I canceled the next day. I called early in the morning and left a message when I knew my daughter would be deeply involved perfecting Warrior One Two and Three, in her Yoga class.

I wanted caffeine. And sweets. Finally, I was well enough to eat something un-nourishing but pleasing. I threw on clothes,

sunglasses and shoes, grabbed my bag and went to MacDougal
Street.

The day was brilliant. Drink in hand, I walked uptown to
16th and East Broadway, went into ABC Home where I had
shopped forever and in 45 minutes I had bought everything I
needed for my duplex. This felt very satisfying for about an
hour.

Leaving the store, I walked to Fifth Avenue and kept going
north until I was standing outside the Metropolitan Museum. I
went inside and immediately dashed through the Egyptian
Exhibit and stood outside the entrance to the Temple of
Dendur. The exhibit was open, so I went inside.

I had not realized how small the exhibit is: one short tunnel
of Hieroglyphs then a turn into another short tunnel. Then a
dead end. I stared at the end of the tunnel wondering how I
could get to Osiris without Twin Me guiding me back to his
time in space. I knocked gently on the wall in front of me. As I
did this, the Museum Guard came into my vicinity.

"The exhibit is closing now, Ma'am," she said cheerlessly.

"Oh. Okay. I was just feeling the makeup of this wall. Is it
really the original?"

"Yes, Ma'am. It was brought here piece by piece. Are you
ready now?"

For a split second I thought she might be a messenger. "Are
you ready to see Osiris, Ma'am?" But as I looked at her, I saw a
tired woman ready to be off work.

"Sorry," I said. "Yes. Let's get me out of here."

I skipped in front of her and took myself quickly out of the
Temple. I stood in the large entryway to the exhibit deciding
what to do. I decided I would go back to the Van Gogh
painting and see if I could get into the house.

There was a small gathering of people in front of my
painting. One was obviously the teacher with her four or five
students. She was explaining something about Van Gogh, but
all I heard was a garbled "...maybe the ear was part of his
illness, hearing voices, feeling helpless."

"Was it true he cut it off in a fight with Gauguin?"

"Well, that's a difficult question, isn't it?"

I began having the same response I had had through high

school and college: a complete disdain for professors who were Less than Brilliant. She was officious and arty looking, this professor. I hoped nobody in her entourage would pay any attention to her. That had worked for me.

They stood there forever with their pedantic conversation and I was ready to leave when they finally moved on to another academically anemic destruction of somebody's beautiful work of art. I moved to the painting as soon as they were gone. I could swear I smelled onions sautéing and something else in the onions. But nobody else seemed to have sniffed when they had had their convocation at the painting. Oh god. Maybe this really was a breakdown of some kind. I just tried to pound through the wall at the Temple Exhibit. Maybe I should've said, "Open Says Me"— maybe this was one big delusional episode of a woman who lost her husband very suddenly and was bored with every single thing she had done with her life.

Go to the painting. Just do it, I told myself.

I was shocked and delighted when I lifted my foot off the museum floor and was able to get up into Van Gogh's bedroom in Arles! I went to the door that had, on my last visit, taken me into the kitchen. I opened it and went through. This much was allowed without my soulmate to guide me. Suddenly, alone in the ancient French kitchen, where a cast iron pan of delicious smelling onions was slowly sautéing on the stove top, I realized something important. My missing Twin was not my soul mate. We were not even Twins: we were One. The realization overwhelmed me and I was afraid I was losing consciousness as I grabbed an open bottle of something on Van Gogh's kitchen counter and drank half of it. I thought it was white wine; in fact, it was absinthe.

Quite drunk and totally spooked by the strength of the alcohol, I tried to exit the painting and nearly knocked over a couple who were approaching the painting just as I was climbing out. Luckily, as I began to emerge, they chose to look deeply into each other's eyes and as they did, I escaped back into the kitchen of the painting just as they got into a tiff about something.

And there he was. Wiping his paint dribbled hands on a rag

as he entered the kitchen from the garden that wasn't visible in the painting. He went to the pan and without a word to me he stirred the onions, tasted the spoon and grabbed the bottle of absinthe from where I had put it down on the wooden counter. He finished it off in one swallow and then stared accusingly at me.

"Avez vous plus?"

He pointed at the bottle.

"Non. Je n'ai rien."

He began to rant at me about the amount of absinthe in the bottle I had taken and the fact that I had brought nothing to replace it. I was embarrassed and extremely drunk.

I offered to go get another bottle without giving a thought to how it would be possible with no francs in my wallet and for that matter, no idea where to buy anything.

"Oui." He pointed out his back door. And as I should've guessed, a small, ancient store stood not 100 feet beyond his garden. I took off to the store passing through his amazing flowers. The absinthe was so pleasant I stopped a moment at each of the bigger flowers and had conversations with whatever insects were willing to talk to me.

Through the cottage window, I could see Van Gogh adding ingredients to his onions. He looked up to see how I was doing in my errand for absinthe. When he saw me stopped at a particularly stunning purple flower, he smiled knowingly, and although I was sure he would scream at me to hurry, he just nodded his head and kept adding garlic to his dinner.

I had to drag myself away from the oranges, the magentas, the blues of the petals. Finally, I got to the little store and it was empty of any goods except for endless bottles of absinthe. For a second I thought I had hallucinated the store, but as I stepped in, the owner approached me with a bottle in his hand and waved me back outside. This time I moved quickly through the flowers, looking forward to an evening of drunken conversation with the greatest painter ever. I brought him the bottle and saw that he had set his little dinner table for two.

He poured us each a massively large glass of absinthe. Then he filled my plate with vegetables, and a small piece of chicken. He did the same for himself. Then we each lifted our glasses and drank.

"Bon." He said, and then in perfect English "Tell me what you are doing here?"

"I have no idea."

"So much the better. A puzzle. A riddle. What is this stranger doing in my house? Do you know who I am by the way?"

"Everybody in the world knows who you are! You are the most revered painter, the most successful artist in history."

"That is a lie."

He was clearly annoyed at me. I felt awful about it. We both took giant swallows of absinthe. Then I began to talk, and once I started I could not shut myself up. The whole time Van Gogh stared at me as if I were from another planet. But as the absinthe built up in both of us, strangely, so did the trust. By the end of my diatribe about who he is in the present world, he was weeping. I thought it was joy, but in fact, he was horrified by the idea that his paintings sold for so much money, that every day people could not see his art because it hung in the mansions of the incredibly rich patrons who purchased it.

"Are you an artist?" he asked.

"No. I'm not."

"So you don't understand?"

"I think I do understand."

"Tell me," he demanded.

"You want your art to be there for everyone to see. Not cooped up in private houses."

"My paintings are my words, he said. "You tell me that I have been silenced."

"No, not at all. There are reproductions of your work in hundreds of books."

"Somebody paints and says it is me?"

I tried to explain the technology of art reproduction that hadn't existed in his time. I thought this would make him angrier, but in fact, he was somewhat relieved that his "words" had not been privatized completely.

"Why don't you paint?" he asked.

"I have no talent as a painter."

"Then what is your talent?"

"I don't know. Maybe I have none."

"Impossible. You're just too lazy to find it."

"Not everybody has talent." I felt a little defensive.

"Who told you that? It's a terrible lie. Get out of my house and come back when you know what your words are. How you convey them. Paint, dance, music, caring for animals. Find your spirit then come back and tell me what you have to say. And bring more of this when you come." He waved the now empty bottle of absinthe at me. Then he got up, put the plates in his sink and walked back to the garden to work.

I was still delightfully insane from the absinthe. I went to his kitchen sink and tore a small piece of chicken off my plate. It would be proof later tonight that this meal had actually happened.

It was a sensational early evening as I left the Metropolitan. I just kept walking down fifth avenue, staring into the park and arduously avoiding eye contact with the rigid stone buildings that house the rich, ostentatious people who live on Fifth Avenue. When I got to the Central Park Zoo, I knew exactly what to do after paying to enter:

I went to see the Snow Leopard. When I first approached their area, I didn't see any big cats at all. I did see a young domestic tabby who entered the Snow Leopard territory and began to play.

Within seconds, a spectacular spotted leopard sauntered into sight. She looked at the tabby and then at me. The rhythm of her step and her sly exchange of glances told me that all three of us were on the same frequency. I think the absinthe had something to do with this.

As the leopard walked toward me, the tabby ran between the big cat's huge paws trying to trip it up the way a two-year-old plays with its sibling. The leopard stopped for a split second. She stared at the tabby and I watched her mouth move, obviously saying words to the littler creature. I didn't hear anything, but the baby obediently got out of the way and with a final swat at the leopard's tail, the young tabby ran off happily to leave us alone.

The cat crawled up to as close as it was possible for us to be and sat up, front paws very straight.

"Are you drunk?" she asked me.

Before I answered she stared at me closely, then she stretched out luxuriously and stared at me some more.

"I just drank a lot of absinthe. But it feels like it was hundreds of years ago."

"You were drinking with Van Gogh, am I right?" she smirked.

"Yes, in Arles. How do you know?"

She licked her front paw. It's strange how hallucinogens like absinthe make things look different. I saw her licking herself as if to laugh at me because I had asked her my stupid question. Of course she knew who I was, where I had just come from, who I had been with. Obviously. She looked back at me and blinked her eyes. I blinked back: This much of feline ritual I understand.

"I got into a bit of a fight with him."

"He's difficult." She licked something off her paw.

"I know, but I think he was onto something and at the time I couldn't bear to admit it."

"Tell me."

"He says everybody has a talent, but some of us are too lazy to find it."

"Yes. That sounds like him." Again the smirk.

"Do you agree? That everybody has a talent?"

"Are you standing in a zoo having a perfectly lucid conversation with a Snow Leopard?" With that, she flicked her enormous tail, stood up and walked away from me. As she disappeared, the little tabby came running out of nowhere and stopped at my feet.

"Have you got something to add to that interaction? I asked.

"No, the tabby said. "I was hoping you might have a snack for me."

"I'm sorry. I have nothing edible on me. But I would love to chat."

The tabby began chuckling, as if she was the Cheshire Cat and had borrowed the hookah from the Caterpillar.

"If you want to chat, I need to eat. Sorry. Law of the Jungle."

I laughed and then remembered the small piece of my chicken dinner from Vincent's.

"Hold on," I told her.

She kept chuckling as she ran off until I had the chicken out of its napkin and in my hand. Law of the Jungle was right. The tabby smelled the meat and turned back toward me. What followed was a short, but engaging chat. When she had licked up the last of the chicken, she took off.

I stumbled home to my shelter on Thompson Street. When I opened the door, I smelled cigarette smoke. I walked into the next room and my father and husband were both smoking from my father's pack of Chesterfield's.

"My god."

"Would you like a cigarette?"

"No. I'd like to know how you two got here. Why you're here. What do you want?"

My father turned to my husband. "She's hungry. I could always tell because she would get snippy if her blood sugar dropped."

"Are you hungry? We brought take out from Carbone's for you." My husband stood up and went to my kitchen before I had a chance to answer.

"I am a little hungry. But mostly I'm confused. Am I dead? Is that why you are here together? Are you about to tell me this whole strange interlude of the past few weeks has been a preamble to me dying?"

My husband re-entered just as I asked my father this question. He had in one hand my cutting board filled with slices of French bread and cheese. In his other hand he had shrimp salad. He put the food down on one of my new side tables and put the whole thing right in front of me. "Do you feel dead?" my husband asked. "Would you like me to take your vital signs?"

"I'm at the end of a wonderful absinthe drunk. I don't feel dead, but I do feel disappointingly normal again.

My father laughed. This was uncharacteristic but seemed affectionate as opposed to the way the cats had chuckled at me derisively as I left the zoo a short while back. "Are either of you going to eat with me? Can you? Eat?" I looked at them.

"Yes," my father replied. "We do eat occasionally, for the flavors, we don't need the nutrients anymore."

"All right. Maybe the absinthe is still with me. I will definitely buy a bottle tomorrow."

I made myself a plate of various pieces of my husband's offerings. As I started to nibble, the two men began to talk about me as if I wasn't in the room.

"I prefer her given name don't you?" my father asked.

"I did. But part of what I think she's going through requires a new name to go with it."

"What new name?" I asked. "I haven't even thought about that yet? What new name?"

"Deborah," my husband answered. "Like the biblical judge."

"Why are you saying that? I haven't re-named myself at all."

"It's on the buzzer downstairs," my father said. "Deborah."

"Who is she?"

My father turned to my husband. "We didn't give her any religious training. And you and she didn't give any to your daughter either. It leaves a gap on a purely educational level."

"I know," my husband replied. "But my life was about science. And she—excuse me—Deborah had no interest in the Bible."

"I did not choose the name Deborah," I said. "I don't even know what it means. Biblically or metaphorically."

"Then take it off your buzzer, my father said. "You have a right to be called whatever you want."

The minute my father said this I knew what had happened. Twin Me had made a suggestion for me then left it in my mail slot. Deborah. I would read about her tomorrow when my head was cleared. For now, I realized how hungry I was, so I filled my plate and sat back comfortably with it on my lap. I had lots of questions for my two visitors, but of course, as is now obvious to anyone following this story, they were gone.

Chapter Seven
Just Call My Name

I RUSHED TO THE LOCAL LIQUOR STORE and replenished my absinthe immediately after my guests left. For one split second I wondered if I was drinking too much absinthe and should go back to wine. One split second, then I stepped onto the street, heading to the store for some absinthe. I looked at my mailbox that did in fact say, DEBORAH. I noticed that a corner of the little name tag was not entirely inside the frame of the name board. I gingerly opened it enough to see the secret words inside: JUDGES: Book 5. I replaced it quickly and jogged to the liquor store where I purchased my liquid hallucinogen and went back home. I immediately opened my computer intending to read about Deborah. But the information was scarce.

Deborah was a Biblical Queen. She was a warrior, a prophet and a judge—powerful, brilliant and on a definite journey to keep her people in a Just and Rational world. I felt we had nothing in common.

But Twin Me knew me very well, so I knew this Deborah message had to have some meaning as I lurched forward into the new life I needed.

Suddenly I wanted desperately to discuss this with Osiris. Yes of course I wanted to discuss it after sex. Reading about Deborah was mythic, and myths tend to make me feel at a depth that is not always available to me. It translated tonight into a desire for the pleasures I had shared with my Mythic lover. But beyond the sex, what would I ask Osiris? "Can you see me as a judge—a wise and powerful leader? A successful warrior?"

I stared out my window at the sky. It was dark now. Too late to even try to get to the museum let alone get inside the Temple. Anyway, it had closed hours ago.

I looked online and found that the Museum, and the Temple would not be open tomorrow, but the day after. I began to weep. I could not wait that long. I needed him, and my need was deeply unquenchable. I went and picked up the white patent leather shoes. My father had helped me pick them out. My father had just visited. Could I be content with this unusual and almost impossible reality? I took them with me for comfort, put them on my lap, as I returned to star gazing.

The stars were very bright tonight. I was transfixed, and by now I was hallucinating. The absinthe made the stars more yellow than usual. And it made me desperate to see Osiris. But how? My only hope was to find Twin Me. She could get me to ancient Egypt, she traveled Time and Space like a commuter rides the train from Connecticut to Grand Central Station.

She had put up the name Deborah for me. And she had asked me to name her as well. Clearly, she has had millions of names and faces over the millennia, but she wanted a name given to her by me. I watched as the stars began to shimmer, and slowly the constellations began to untangle from their original configuration and the stars were free for a split second to form something else. VITA. The brightest most yellow constellation I have ever seen came into existence for mere seconds, I caught its meaning, and as I blinked, the constellations were back in their formal configurations. Vita.

"I like it. I've been Lida more times than I can count—many, many, times Sita. But never Vita."

I should have been shocked to hear her voice, but I was not. She was standing in my kitchen drinking a glass of absinthe and finishing quickly the shrimp salad she had retrieved from my refrigerator.

"I like Deborah too. Thank you."

"Now we are named," Vita said.

"I need to see Osiris. Could you take me?"

"No. The museum is closed."

"You have no other way?"

"None I am ready to show you," she said. "Anyway, I'm off. I just came to say I like the name Vita."

"Could you come back day after tomorrow?"

"I will be out of the frequency. But I will unlatch the gate for you to go in yourself."

"How?" She smiled at my question.

"Have you got more absinthe? I just finished the bottle?"

"No. But maybe the store is still open."

"Don't bother," she said. "I'm off."

"How do I unlatch the gate? To see Osiris?"

"I love it when you ask me questions like this, Deborah."

"But?"

"Was Van Gogh a decent cook? I've never eaten with him."

"Yes, it was delicious and fresh. Everything tastes good around him."

"All right then. See you soon. I think I'll make it back earlier than I planned."

She put down her glass, checked herself in the new mirror that hung on my living room wall, grabbed her bag and walked to me. She kissed me on both cheeks; up this close she was more intoxicating than absinthe. But she also disappeared more quickly. Here I was on a lovely early spring night, and she was gone.

Days went by. I left the name tag Vita had chosen for me on my door. It made me feel close to her, though I still hadn't looked at JUDGES: Book 5. Instead, I was finally ready to try the Temple again.

I arrived at the museum and ran through the Egypt exhibit straight into the Temple entrance. This time it felt different. The light changed when I got into the second of the small tunnels and by the time I had turned the final corner I was thousands of years back in time.

As happened my first visit, the fast transition caused me to be a little woozy. I hoped the bronzed woman would bring me some special water, but she was nowhere in sight. As my breathing adjusted and my eyes stopped stinging with the dust on the Giza plateau, I did see a figure approaching me. My heart started pounding, it was a very large man, bronzed from top to bottom, black hair hanging loose this time. Osiris!! He has come to see me. I closed my eyes with delightful anticipation and when I opened them seconds later the man was much closer.

I saw that it was in fact not Osiris, but his brother, Set. This did not make me happy.

"You came to see Osiris?" he asked.

"Yes."

"They are away: somewhere on the Nile. Nobody has seen

them for days, so I assume they're on a sensual, sexual, celestial vacation. They do this when they need to re-vitalize their already perfect relationship."

"Oh."

"'Oh'?' Set seemed surprised. "That's your only response? Aren't you jealous?"

"No. Osiris is not my mate. I just wanted to ask him some things I thought he might have insights into. Things about me."

"Ask me."

"You don't know me. It doesn't make sense to bother you with questions."

"Shall we just have sex?"

"No thank you."

"Why not?"

"I didn't come to have sex."

"That's a lie." He hissed.

"All right. I came to have sex with Osiris. But I really did want to talk after."

"Fine. We'll have sex first and then you can talk to me. I'm mythic too you know."

"Yes."

"Take off your clothes."

"No."

"You know," Set crossed his arms. "I'm beginning to take this personally and that's a bad thing for both of us. As you know I have impulse control issues. You don't want me to cut my brother into pieces again because you annoy me. Do you?"

"You can't do that. The myth is set and there is no second attempt on his life."

"Ah. So now you're an expert in myth making. Sadly, your expertise is off. The myth is alive, not static. If I force myself on you sexually or rip my brother up a second time, it simply goes into Time and Space and some books will be written in the next hundred years about this having happened."

"Then I have no choice." I began to undress.

"You look angry. Are you completely disinterested in me as a man?"

Just at this moment Nephthys appeared in the distance. She was strikingly beautiful, and very big. She strode up to us in seconds. "Set?"

"Yes, my love."

"Get out of here. Leave her alone. Or I will make you very very sorry."

"But she came to me. This was not my idea. She came here and told me she had sampled Osiris and found it uncompelling. She wanted to try me."

"Is that true?" She addressed this to me directly.

"It is not." I told her the truth. I had to.

She turned back to her husband. She looked at him with millenia of rage in her eyes. Set began to back away. He was clearly frightened. So was I. As soon as Nephthys saw that she had him on the run, it inflamed her further. She began to scream as he turned to run from her. She followed after him, but I could hear her voice very clearly.

"I have warned you for the last time, you piece of frog shit. You will not lie to me. You will not harm anybody else. You will not blacken our name. You will act like a god, not a thug. Anything less from you, any more crap and I will tear you to shreds and nobody will come to tie you back together. You will be worm meat. I will not wrap you in linen, I will not put you in a pyramid, you will have to wait for Ma'at to take pity on you and re-connect the shards I will make of you."

By now she was out of sight as was Set. They had run a good distance from me, and then turned the corner of one of the huge pyramids and disappeared. I had no idea what to do now.

I sat on the dry Egyptian earth for a time before I saw Nephthys coming back towards me. She was striding with huge long strokes that brought us together in less than a minute.

"Deborah?"

"Yes."

"Accept my apologies. Set is a cautionary tale."

"Sorry?"

"The Jealous Sibling. The Cain and Abel disaster: every story written through time about the danger of family warfare. Set is the mark and copy. I think that's Shakespearean am I right?"

"Yes." I said, hoping I was right.

"He is especially jealous when he sees somebody special like you."

"I am not special Nephthys. I am as close to nothing special as you can be."

"That's not the opinion of your friend, Vita."

"Turning a sow's ear into a silk purse?"

"She sees something in you that can serve the world. She won't let that go unless you completely disappoint her."

"I'm a middle-aged former housewife. I had every opportunity to do something with my life and I didn't.

"Change." She said.

I admit I was slightly insulted, but also completely clear about what was going on: for some reason known only to the universe, I had been chosen to be changed, Vita was not Me as I had concluded in one of my simplistic assessments of what was going on. We are not One. She saw me as somebody whose potential could possibly be pulled out of them even after years of their own choosing to be nothing, mean nothing, feel very little.

"Can you point me in a direction?" I asked Nephthys.

"I hear you're doing fine."

"Set was about to force himself on me—I had no plan to stop him."

"Why?" Nepthys asked. "Because he is three times your size?"

"Yes. And because I come here representing somebody, I don't want to cause offense."

"So there's your first task."

"What is?"

"Your rage at injustice must be bigger than anything around you." She said.

"I'm not enraged."

"No?"

"Should I be?" This sounded stupid, even to me.

"Have you not seen anything that you want to change?"

"Like what?" Stupider.

"Go back. Take another look at where you've been."

"I've been to Van Gogh's kitchen."

"Is that all?" She was smiling at me now.

"No."

"Learn something you've missed." This time she was kind.

She turned her back suddenly. The discussion was over. In the distance I could see Set coming and Nephthys headed off to meet him. I could hear her start to scream at him. He started screaming back. I was clearly done here.

I had no idea how to get back home. So I lay down and closed my eyes and waited.

*

A loud clock was ticking as I lay on the sand. It ticked for what seemed like only a minute, but when it stopped, I opened my eyes and I was on the bathroom floor at the nightclub in Weimar. I was in my gorgeous Chambord dress, my red pumps were on my feet, and when I stood up and looked in the mirror, I was gussied up in true nightclub style: black smoky eyes, very red lips, hair all over the place, lots of beads. I was wearing the ruby colored beads I had admired on my first visit here.

As I stood staring at myself, I realized the music was back. I opened the bathroom door and the entire nightclub had been resurrected. I went back to my outside table and drank somebody's cocktail that was sitting there totally untouched.

The two-woman argument from before was now a full out screaming match with every woman at the table participating. It seemed right for me to join in.

"She's right. He will become Chancellor and you will lose all of this."

Everybody at the table turned to stare at me.

"Who are you? What are you doing here?"

"I've been here before. My name's Deborah."

The drunkest of the women turned to me. "That's a Jewish name! Are you here as a woman or a Jew?"

"I'm here as a person who knows what's coming your way. I would like to help you to stop it."

"Stop what?"

"The new Chancellor will embroil you in a ghastly, disastrous war. He will unleash levels of cruelty never seen in modern society. All of you will be forced into roles of abject submission to your husbands, fathers, ministers, even to the butcher who sells you your pork." I blurted all this out.

"Pork? This is about you being a Jew!"

"I am a WASP. From Connecticut."

"What?"

"I am American. An un-religious Protestant. I am not part of your history, I am just trying to describe the outcome."

"Ah. American. So of course you think you can affect the outcome by lecturing us!"

"I find the Americans unbearable. I have been to your country once. Truly a vast wilderness: no culture, no music of any depth, no intellectuals worth quoting."

"Where were you?"

"Pennsylvania. They call it Pennsylvania Dutch, but it is purely German. And it is filled with men in strange hats who don't drive cars or use electricity. Troglodytes. You really think you can help us?"

"You're right, I can't. I should never have tried." I stood up and began to leave but I was blocked by a very large man in a brown uniform.

"Where are you going? Where are your papers? What is this bilge you have been telling these women?"

Ah, the first test.

"You were on Lexington in your cab, fighting with another driver, many years from now. He called you a Nazi!"

Grabbing me by my shoulder, he tried to spin me around so my back was to him. Obviously he would then put his arm across my throat and snap my neck or just restrain me. It was not to be allowed. I turned back to him while his fingers dug into my skin. I looked at him closely, and then from nowhere I swung my fist at his throat and made a direct hit on his Adam's apple. He fell hard onto the ground and was choking. I was shocked at myself as I threw myself on him and pounded him with both fists. Pounded as he tried to catch his breath. A disgusting smell and a gurgling sound came from his mouth.

I looked at the women who had been my drinking companions on my first visit here. They were shocked and horrified by my behavior. They were also staring in awe at what I had done.

"Stop staring at me," I said. "Figure out how a woman my size could overpower this huge bully with nothing but my rage. Find your own rage before it is too late. You will not survive what is coming if you are complicit."

I tried to get up, but the monster in the brown shirt had miraculously regained his strength. He grabbed me by my ankle as I scrambled to get away. One of the women in the group reached her hand out to me and helped me stand up. As I did this, the Nazi in brown stood too. He grabbed me and wrapped his arm under my neck preparing to snap it. I had been Deborah for a very short time—my endurance was limited. I could feel myself weaken as he pressed his arm tightly across my throat.

Suddenly I felt somebody pressing something into my hand. I had no time to evaluate my odds of surviving my next move. I took what she had handed me in my fist and aimed at him as high up as I could reach. There was a strange feeling as the fork I had not seen jammed into his throat. His arm immediately released—he was bleeding profusely. All of the women scattered within seconds and I looked at him briefly before I began to run; the fork had struck an artery and he was back on the ground not looking like he would make it to the next meeting of the brown shirts. I began running amazingly fast considering I was in high heels.

I kept going until the street ended and standing in front of me with no structure around it, was a wall with a door in it. I walked quickly through the door and found myself on MacDougal Street in my normal clothes. The only way I could tell that I had not just dreamt this whole episode, was looking down at my knuckles that were bleeding and swollen. I ran to my apartment locked the door and all the windows. I washed my hands and could do nothing to salve them since I had no first aid kit yet in my home. But I didn't need it.

Vita was sitting on my couch and I knew she would take care of me. "Good start Deborah," she said.

"I have no idea how I lived through that."

"Yes, you do."

"I've never even slapped anybody."

"I gave you the name because I know who is living inside of you. Beneath all the dull, bourgeois affect, your contract here is very clear to me."

"Contract?"

"You must have agreed to this. They don't just force people to become heroic. That doesn't work." Vita shook her head.

"Did the man die?"

"Die from what?" she asked.

"Look at my hands. I didn't get bloodied up crawling along on my knuckles."

I waved my hands at her to prove my point. As I should have expected, my hands had not a mark or cut on them.

"So it wasn't real?" I said.

"It was very real and he was very dead at the end of it. But it was decades ago. You don't believe that cuts on your knuckles would have lasted since 1934."

"I had them when I first got here."

"Yes, you did. But that has to do with the depth of the memory."

"Was I back in Weimar or not?"

"You were. And a neophyte Nazi engaged in physical combat with you. You won. There's no need to know more than that—the information comes in when it should."

"What now?" I asked her.

"I would do some thinking. Why did I choose Deborah for you? She is in the Book of Judges. Briefly. Not much explanation about her, which is one reason she's perfect. Sculpt your own vision of this woman."

Chapter Eight
I Like New York in June

IT WAS FULL-BLOWN SPRING NOW. The city was constantly moist with urban humidity: frequently wet from rain, warm during the day and breezy at night. It was on one of these perfect Spring nights that I walked east towards the Strand bookstore on Broadway to find whatever I could on Deborah and the Book of Judges.

I had read the online stuff about her, which was extremely limited, and I had read Chapters 4 and 5 of Judges in the Bible. Much more limited. But I knew I could find something about her if I searched the material at a bookstore or library. I pulled open the door to the Strand and approached a sales person who looked to be about eleven years old but who was probably a PhD candidate at NYU.

"I'm looking for material on Deborah from the Bible. Can you point me towards that please?"

"Ummm. Let me get somebody over here, I'm very new and the Bible stuff is all over the place. We need somebody who knows more."

"I can show you."

The voice was deep, and when I turned I almost fell over the huge piles of books that were everywhere. A dramatically handsome man of 40ish was smiling at me. He had dark hair and eyes, and there was something endlessly sexy about him. I didn't dare look too much, but I had a sense that his body moved like a dancer, and that he was well developed in the ass and legs.

"Oh. Thank you."

I was so incredulous that he was standing there smiling flirtatiously with me that I became tongue tied. The baby sales girl walked off to help somebody else, with her Total of No Information and the man turned his full body to me, stretched out a hand to shake mine.

"Tim Carbone. Timothy. Criss cross Irish and Italian. I know my Bible women very well. It helps that it's my teaching area as well."

"You teach?" *Come on! Say something vaguely intelligent!* I scolded myself. *"You teach?"* He just said he teaches. "I mean—Irish and Italian. Yes a natural mix. What do you teach?"

"History. But I'm on sabbatical. Let me show you the books you might like."

He put his hand under my elbow to guide me. I had the same shimmering electric current go through me as I had the first time I sat next to Osiris.

"So what's your interest in Deborah? You becoming a rabbi?"

His smile was a captivating combination of a tease and genuine interest in me. I was immediately suspicious. Tim was 40 something. I am 50. I am happy as I have said before, with my appearance but not ignorant of the proclivity of men to seek younger women.

"No, not a rabbi. I'm not Jewish. I'm not anything religiously. I'm reading up on Deborah because a very smart friend told me about her and she sounds exceptional. I wonder why there is so little about her in the Bible or anywhere else."

"She had no children."

"Making her unimportant? Not a woman to be bothered with?"

"Yes. If you're talking about the inventors of the Bible. They are the progenitors of the worst misogyny on earth."

"Definitely. Not that things have changed much since the first draft of the Bible."

"Here. 'Women/Heroines'. Let's browse the shelf."

Tim put down a leather bag he was carrying and began to study the books on the shelf. I continued for a minute to study his hind quarters, but then I joined him.

"This one mentions her in one chapter. It's about three lines, Prophetess, Judge, Warrior. Same as always." He flipped through some pages. "Wait. Here's the story of her and Sisera, the Canaanite who got a tent peg driven through his head."

"Deborah did that, or was it somebody she trained?" I had read this story with many variations and it made me feel smart to have something to say.

"There are several versions. In one, yes, Yael entices Sisera into her tent during the battle with the Canaanites and feeds him a laced cup of tea. When he is out cold, she sticks a tent peg through his temples. In this version, she is a mentee of Deborah's who does this to one of the last Canaanite leaders."

"I've read both of those versions. Wikipedia. Not deep, but very broad." *Please. Can you sound any dumber?*

"I've got a couple of books at my office that are more of what you need." He was clearly making me an offer.

"That's great. Could I meet you there and borrow one or two?"

"It's right around the corner. Let's go pick the books up and then we can have a glass of something. You want to do that?"

"Weren't you looking for something here for yourself?"

"Yes. And I found you. Much better than a dusty book jacket on a book I don't really need to read for the third time."

I hesitated. This was New York City and walking off with a strange man, no matter how enticing he is, is Step One of What You Never Do in New York if you want to stay alive.

"If you're sure you don't mind taking the time, I would be grateful for the books."

"Let's go."

We both slid through the check-out gates at the front and reunited outside the entry door.

"What's your name? I've told you mine. And please don't call me Timothy. It makes me feel like I have to confess something to you."

He laughed.

I didn't know what name to tell him. I didn't remember what I was called for 50 years. Maybe now I really was going through the doorway to dementia.

"How about you just call me Deborah?"

"You doing research for a part? Are you an actress?"

"No. I'm a widow."

This time we both laughed.

"It sounds strange, but my husband died very suddenly, and I've been a bit lost since then. I've been seeing a therapist who deals with grief and she suggested I call myself a new name so I could adapt to my new reality."

Tim knew I was lying. I could see it in his eyes and his smile.

"I can call you anything you want. Deborah. What happened

to your husband?"

"He was an oncologist."

"And?"

"And he was bending over a very sick woman giving her what was actually very hopeful news about her cancer. In the middle of giving her this prognosis, he fell forward, slid onto the floor and by the time the emergency team got to him, he was gone. Unrevivable."

"Wow."

"I know. We've laughed about it. A cancer doctor keeling over from a heart attack."

"When?"

"Oh. I meant we talked about how strange that would be. Obviously before it happened."

"Obviously."

Again the intensely savvy smile. As if he knew damn well that I had seen my husband by now twice since his death.

"Where is your office?" I tried to get off my slip up.

"I forgot. The building has a scaffolding up until tomorrow. I can bring the books to you. Where do you live?"

"Thompson off Bleecker."

"You know Carbone's?"

"Yes. I go there a lot. You related?"

"No. Just a good place. We could meet there tomorrow at five. Have a nice glass of something red. Look through the books. Sound good?"

"I would love that."

"All right then. I will see you tomorrow, Deborah."

He kissed me very lightly on my cheek and I thought my body would spontaneously combust. So I turned quickly away from him and headed home. I could feel him staring at my departing self; it made me walk with slightly more swing of the hips than is my usual tread on a New York City street.

The walk home was magical the way things are when you know something is bubbling up in your future. I almost skipped up the steps to my apartment, slipped the key in the lock, and smelled something cooking.

Vita was making appetizers—there was Greek pita on the counter, what might have been hummus and something else sat on the stove.

"Hello! How nice to see you. What's cooking?"

"I am making my version of flaming saganaki. It's a special goat cheese. You pour ouzo or, in this case, brandy, which is all I could find, over it and when it's melty, you set it on fire and it gets a delicious crust. I think it's ready."

She pulled the lighter out of my kitchen drawer and lit the stuff in the pan on fire. When she was satisfied with its crispness, she took a lemon, cut it, and squeezed it on the hot cheese until the flames went out. Then she dumped the whole piece of cheese onto a cutting board.

By then I had taken out two wine glasses and opened a bottle of some wine she had brought. I poured us each a snifter full and together we walked with our goods into my living room. Once settled in, having tasted her cheese masterpiece and a sip of wine, we stared at each other.

"Yes? You waiting to tell me something? Am I drinking too much wine as part of being an avoidacholic?"

"Not at all," Vita said. "You seem more available to yourself."

"But you think something isn't fine?"

"Be careful now, Deborah. Many people will be attracted to you for all the wrong reasons."

"Like what?" I was a little scared.

"Like to prove me wrong. Like to stop your development. Like to make sure that darkness prevails on earth."

"You don't mean Osiris? Or Van Gogh?"

"Definitely not," Vita said. "They're with me. With us. Part of the Team."

"Then we're fine because I dream of being with Osiris again. And I yearn to have another talk with Vincent. He asked me to call him that. Anyway. I have enough on my plate without newcomers."

"It's a mistake to lie to me." Vita looked over her glass at me.

"What are you talking about?!"

"Timothy is a very well-made creature. He has to be. But don't be fooled by his smile and his charms. He does not want you to be great."

"How do you know?"

"I know that you realize how stupid that question is. I know Timothy Carbone. I know he has latched on to you. I simply want you forewarned."

"Is he a serial killer? Rapist? Member of the Klan?"

"How do you like the saganaki?"

"Okay. Conversation over. I appreciate the warning. If I get confused I will ask for your help."

"I cannot help you with Timothy."

"Then why bring him up?"

"So you will be sensitive to the clues you will find as you get to know him."

With that, Vita downed her glass of wine, stood up, and left my apartment. I wished she was not so abrupt and enigmatic, but strangely her words of warning had only made me hungrier for this guy's very real and available body.

I got up the next day with nothing on my mind about Deborah the Biblical Queen. I was very taken up with me and Tim, the Irish-Italian man. I examined myself closely in the mirror. My skin was slightly tan from all the walking I had been doing in the sunny days we'd had dribbles of. I was firm and slender, I was usually firm and slender, but my husband's death could have thrown me off. Luckily, eating was not solace for me, so I hadn't gotten to be a dumpy widow. Just a lonely one.

For the first time since my husband had died, I wanted to do some form of disciplined exercise. I had a yoga DVD which I slid into my machine. I dressed in loose pants and no bra, and for the next 45 minutes I was a Warrior, numbers one and two, I was Buddha, breathing in to a count of ten and out to a count of 20. I felt fantastic bending, stretching, and the whole time the memory of my amazing sex with Osiris was running through my brain.

The DVD finished, and I went to bed. I woke up early and had a light breakfast and wondered how I would fill the time before my assignation at five. I knew I should be on the computer reading anything more I could find about Deborah, but for some reason that didn't interest me.

Instead, I threw on street clothing, applied some eyeliner and went clothes shopping for tonight's study session at Carbone's.

I am not a shopper. I had to provide clothing for my daughter and keep up my husband's array of appropriate doctor clothes. I also shopped for dinner for many years. Now, I couldn't stand the idea of a clothing store or any other kind of store, and I do every bit of consuming I have to online.

But not today. Today was Timothy day. I liked the combination of Irish and Italian. Some of my first boyfriends had come from Our Lady of Pompeii, a Catholic high school on the opposite side of Bleecker street on sixth avenue. The first boy to touch one of my nipples had been Irish and more scared than I was. I thought that was sweet. We continued getting to know my nipples together, as I got on a first name basis with his penis.

Next had been a couple of very charming Italian teenage boys. One of them was the son of a family that owned a great fish restaurant on fourth street near Sheridan Square. I had spent many a happy hour in the office above the restaurant with Sal. We had almost "done it" once or twice. Maybe we had actually completed the act. I couldn't quite remember who Mr. The First One was. But Sal's family had taken a liking to me, and I really enjoyed hanging around with a family of restauranteurs. My family was great. But Sal's family was redolent with smells of cologne, garlic, and smart people whose intellect was large, but unimportant to them.

Was that my attraction to Tim Carbone? Vita was very clear that he was not to be trusted. These teenage boys had been very trustworthy. We liked each other, we liked sex, we didn't go all the way (I think) and I often got some delicious food after a visit with Sal.

I walked up sixth avenue as I was having these flashbacks. I came across a number of stores that I went in and tried on a dress, a sweater, a skirt. Nothing grabbed me.

Finally, I turned west on Eighth Street and ran into a brand new store. The stuff in the window was fantastic. For a young woman. But I was undeterred. I went in, bought a black dress, some black toned tights, a bra that pushed my breasts up almost too high.

After that I found delicate black sandals and a black sweater perfect for carrying in case I needed it. Which I knew I would not.

Back home, I tried on everything with an enthusiasm I had not had since I was 14. That thought stopped me cold. I was just becoming menstrual back then. I was now at the end of that part of my life. I felt for a split second like a foolish old woman trying to regain her sexiest memories of being a teenager. But then I caught sight of myself in the mirror. I didn't exactly look 14—I could have been any age. There was something about the black dress, so typical of my city, and the way I had applied makeup, as if I spent all my time practicing this, which I did not. In the back corner of the mirror, I could see New York. In my brownstone there were many windows and most of them gave me a view of the small village I lived in. In front of this image of the village, there stood a lovely, ageless woman who looked available for a special time in bed without a scintilla of guilt.

Tim. Not Timothy. He had nothing to confess to me

That evening at exactly five, Tim was sitting at a table with his back to me which allowed me time to gasp at the breadth of his shoulders and the way his hair sat just at the collar of his shirt. I could've stood there longer, but a waiter came up to greet me.

"Ciao Bella, how good to see you. I believe you have a seat with this gentleman."

He led me to the table and Tim did not turn around until I was within feet of him. When he turned towards me, I had to fake a cough so I could cover my face with my hands. What the hell was going on with me and this man? Yes he had huge brown eyes, and a mouth that looked like it traveled well around the human body. But I was practically gasping for breadth with my desire for him. He smiled at me.

"You look stunning. Here. I took the liberty of ordering you a pinot noir and some bread."

He stood and helped me into my chair. He smelled of smoky wood. That made me want to jump on him right on the white table-cloth.

"Thank you. I'm ready to drink. And talk."

I needed bread as I always did to give the wine a nice landing pad in my stomach. But I got shy and didn't want to eat in front of this man. I sat down, put my bag on the floor and took a very small piece of bread. He was uncannily aware of my every move and what was behind it. That made me relax for some reason. He had seen people eat bread before and still felt like being with them.

I finished the small piece and began to drink my wine.

"I decided not to bring the books. I spent some time reading what I have on Deborah and it'll be more fun just to talk about her with you."

"Great."

It was happening again. I was tongue tied, I was afraid I had bread stuck in my teeth, the wine tasted like nectar of the gods, although I saw the label and it was just a good bottle of Italian red. I willed myself into being with Tim without inhibitions. This was not adolescence. This was part of my new life. Deborah's life. And a warrior, judge and prophetess has to get over worrying about herself and just know that she is unique, and sexually perfect for the market she is in.

"You want to tell me some stuff about her? You're a teacher, you want to teach me?" I sounded like a 14-year-old girl.

"I do. But first, let's drink and flirt for a while. Sound good?"

"Yes. It does."

We finished two bottles of the red wine and ate two baskets of bread. I was very drunk, and Tim seemed to be touching me more and more often. Pouring the wine into my glass with his other hand on my leg, wiping a couple of crumbs off of my face and finding a way to run his forefinger across my lips as he did this. I was done for now with Deborah. And so was he.

"Is your place right down Thompson?"

"Halfway. Not far, and then one flight up."

I was now a moronic teen on her first sexual date. But I didn't care. Tim nodded to the waiter and the bill disappeared. We got up, grabbed our stuff and moved onto my street. It was just turning from day to night in the warm spring air, I took his hand. Part of me felt like I was grabbing on to my daddy like I always tried to do when we were on outings as a family. Part of me wanted to stuff his hand down my dress before we had even gotten inside my apartment.

But first, we needed to kiss. Every road starts somewhere, and the road to bed with Tim needed to start with a kiss. Tim's mastery of human pleasure began with his mouth. We stopped and looked at each other and I let him press his lips against mine: a cloud of sweet air enclosed us. An airy place we would play in where all body parts have a good time. The kiss was not sloppy or tongue down my throat. It was the delicate, pressure of four lips signing on for prolonged enjoyment. A contract we began to fulfill immediately.

It was a dreamy three days and nights. Isn't that a Biblical time frame for something? How long Moses took running from Pharoah? No. Three days of Plagues? No.

My incoherent wondering about any Biblical connotation to our three days of Splendor in My Bed was probably guilt. We had jumped into sexual union as my front door lock clicked into place. We kissed again and then he moved behind me and began to kiss the back of my neck as he pulled up my dress. All that wine and I didn't have to pee. I just had to let him keep pulling my dress over my head as I reached back for his belt and zipper.

From here we did a clumsy but fantastic dance of getting off my tights, his shirt, and so it went. Finally, naked enough in the areas that mattered, we took our first sexual tour of each other on the floor at my front door. That lasted a long time. We finally crawled to my bed where we did things I had never done in my life. With no shyness. I was proud of my body in a way that was different than I had ever felt before. Something about this man, knowing how many women he had been with, and seeing his enthusiasm for being with me took away all childishness and left me flexible, lubricated, enthralled.

On the second day it had begun to rain. A fine excuse to just stay in bed. When it turned to thundering, it was like our bodies were meteorologists: the louder the thunder overhead, the stronger our sexual rhythms became. When the thunder subsided we took a short break and ate something I don't remember and shared drinking directly from the mouth of the wine bottle.

In between trying to invent sexual positions new to the human species, we ordered in food and wine and ate and drank. It was purely the necessity of keeping enough calories inside ourselves to be able to keep up the mating.

At early evening on the third complete day of this, I went to my bathroom and looked in the mirror. I was disarranged but glowing. My body was still on fire and I could not understand it. I hadn't ever spent three days of this kind of constant sexual back and forth before.

We had talked very little. The name Deborah was never mentioned, except he did call out to me using that name once when he wanted me to bring the bottle of wine from the kitchen to the bedroom.

Day four the sun broke through. When I saw the sunlight I

saw Vita's face. She looked neutral, certainly not angry, but she was looking at something in the distance behind me and I felt absolutely no connection to her. It worried me momentarily.

But as I stared at where her image was, Tim tenderly grabbed my breasts and within a millisecond Vita was gone and so was I.

Chapter Nine
The City That Doesn't Sleep

NOTHING LASTS FOREVER. I can't say exactly how many moons came and went with me locked into Timothy Carbone as the only reality. Eventually, we were both ready for a break. It came as easily as the mating had been. This should have been a clue to me. But I just thought we were an extraordinary pair of lovers and in time we would meet for many long Nothing But Sex days together. Osiris and Isis on the cruise on the Nile flashed through my head. Set had described it to me derisively, but clearly it was just jealousy on his part.

Tim left my place and we kissed goodbye and agreed to see each other very soon.

I did not want a specific time or date. I think he might have wanted that, but I was so clear about my enchantment with the ease of our relationship, and Tim was so smart about how to keep somebody hooked into him, that we just said "bye" and I closed my door.

I was surprised at how I felt. I was lost again. I had no interest in reading or chasing up to the museum to talk to Vincent. It was as if my mind had been vacuum cleaned and had nothing left inside. I had been drinking steadily and the idea of absinthe was not appealing to me. I picked through my kitchen and put together left overs from food I had eaten with Tim. Then I went to sleep.

Vita floated through my mind as I was sleeping. She was totally non-verbal. She just moved through my unconscious mind seeming to be cleaning up a room that was in disarray. She picked up chairs, set lamps back on the tables they had fallen from. There were scattered books and papers on the floor everywhere. She gathered them in a dreamy waltz she was dancing, bending and reaching out to put things away with the beauty of one of the 1940s movie queen dancers I had loved watching.

In fact, her whole appearance in my dream was like a scene from a movie. She was dressed in a glamorous gown of the most beautiful lilac silk, it accentuated her grace as she moved. A spotlight followed her through the room she was re-setting even though there was ample lighting everywhere. The spotlight made her look like Cyd Charisse.

The dream seemed to go on and on but in fact only lasted about one minute. When Vita finally sat down on one of the chairs in the room, she had created a perfect place to sit and study. Big beautiful chairs and a huge comfortable couch. Lots of side tables, lamps, and stacks of books lined up against the back wall where an empty book case reminded me that I needed to pay attention to thinking again.

I woke up after this dream-filled sleep. I put on a shirt and pants, grabbed my wallet and went for caffeine. It was a beautiful day, but I was driven to get what I needed and return home. To that room Vita had made for me.

My apartment was not the same as the room, but it had enough elements of it: books, lamps, comfortable places to sit and read.

I drank two huge lattes and ate a pastry I had picked up. Sugar and caffeine. Soon they took effect and I picked up a book I had found on Women of the Bible. I turned to Deborah, and I was back.

I had no trouble becoming enchanted again with the ways I could change myself and find my talent.

A few hours into my reading I got up to stretch out. Vita opened my door and stepped inside.

"Are you back for good?" I asked.

"Yes. I'm back from this trip."

"I have pastry. Are you hungry?"

"No. Thanks."

She looked around my apartment. "You got back to work?"

"Yes."

"Good. Shall we sit here and each do what we need to?"

"All right," I said. "What will you be doing?"

"Turning many thoughts into a few conclusions.."

I smiled at Vita, but she did not return the favor.

"He'll come back Deborah."

"Is that so bad?"

"We'll see."

Vita sat on my couch and began to stare inside herself. I had nothing to say as a comeback to her warning. I liked Tim, but I felt like I had recovered nicely from my wasted days of bliss with him. Why was that such a problem?

I picked up the book and sat in an armchair. I opened it to the foreward and was instantly bored. I flipped through to the first chapter. Also, instantly bored. So I looked in the contents for Deborah, found her pages and was certain this would hold my attention. I was wrong. When I looked up, Vita was staring at me.

"He's still with you. You can't concentrate. That's his specialty."

"This man just goes around trying to distract women from their work? Is that what you're saying?"

"I would have said distract women from their Destiny."

At this moment the phone rang. I knew it was my daughter calling and I couldn't make myself answer.

"Do you want me to tell her you'll be back later?" Vita asked.

"No. I'll talk to her now. I guess."

I dreaded picking up the phone. I knew my daughter had something "special" to say, I could tell by how the phone rang, what it sounded like as it announced who was calling.

"Hello sweetheart."

"I have the most incredible news!"

"Wonderful! Tell me please."

"I am pregnant. You're going to be a grandmother!"

I looked at Vita. I was trying not to put the phone down and later tell my daughter that I had lost her call. But I stayed on.

"That's so exciting! I'm delighted for you."

"I'm the same age you were when you got pregnant with me."

"Yes."

"Mother?"

"Sorry I am having trouble hearing you. Let me go to another room."

I clicked the phone off.

Vita looked at me. "It's her, not you," she said. "This should be relatively easy."

"Grandmother? Easy? That's the first stupid thing you've ever said to me."

"Okay."

"I never wanted to be "mommy" I just did it to prove I deserved a place at the human dinner table. A woman with no child damn well better be Madame Curie or at least Martha Graham."

"Okay."

"Are you going to go beyond saying that?"

"You are on a path. This is not going to deter you. You'll buy some presents, do some billing and cooing, give the child some love. I understand you don't want this, but it will not be as oppressive as having your daughter was."

"How do you know? What if the child is sick or somehow desperately in need of my time? I'll lose any hope of becoming something different." I sounded pouty to myself.

"You don't have to tell Mr. Carbone you know."

"What does that mean?"

"This is a splintery part of your life. Your past life. Your future life is what's really important. Maybe this will give you some sense of separation from the past. That could be helpful."

This was the first time I felt that Vita was not a perfect mirror. Her assessment of my impending grandmother-ness was ignorant of the pressure I had felt to be a mother. An unspoken pressure that was not imposed on me by my parents, it was part of the air I breathed: "When are you and your husband going to have kids?" or "He's a doctor, you'll be a perfect family!" and "How lucky for you, a big home, some kids, you have a whole new life."

Nobody, not one friend had asked me if I had planned the pregnancy. I had not. Nobody asked me how I liked Connecticut instead of my base in the West Village. These were givens: of course as one aged—I was 25 when I got pregnant—one should want more than a life in New York as a single woman who wasn't quite sure what she was.

But I wasn't ready. I wasn't ready to move to Connecticut but did it because of my husband's tremendous growing reputation as an oncologist and a researcher. He was given a whole hospital full of admirers, and endless research facilities. I decorated the house.

What was worse, my husband would have fully supported me if I had known who I wanted to be. Graduate school, a stint as a writer, teaching At-risk kids. The sky was the limit. Except none of it was me.

So, to return to the question posed to me by Vincent Van Gogh—"what is my talent?"

I appeared thus far to be ignoring my inner self and doing what was appropriate. But this is such a cliché. There was no messaging coming from my inner self, and not much feeling for anything.

These were the thoughts going through my head when my daughter called again. This time I could not answer the phone. Vita had gone, and I was afraid of sinking any deeper into self-pity over nothing. The voice message came on and my daughter was crying.

"Please pick up. Are you there? Mother? Please!"

I ran to the phone.

"What's wrong?"

"Can you come up here? Please. To my place. I really need to see you."

"All right. I'll hop in a cab. Hang on sweetheart, I'll be there in 15 minutes."

I grabbed a cab on Sixth Avenue, directed him to my daughter's Upper East Side address, then I leaned back in my seat and worried. We made it to her apartment building and I quickly disembarked and began to run into her lobby towards the elevator. I stopped momentarily. She lived in a swanky but totally ugly building. Typical of the hated Upper East Side: parquet floors, low ceilings, small rooms, thin walls, and nothing to distinguish one apartment from another.

My daughter had no artwork on her walls, although her husband, was pulling in a lot of money. The walls were covered with textures my daughter had seen as classy in a magazine. One room had very expensive curved French wood tile covering the walls, in another room each wall painted a different color of blue: I had seen an image just like this walking past a Madison Avenue décor shop. The furniture was reaching for chic, and accomplishing only a mass of plush cushions over a mammoth sofa covered in varying shades of beige. The coffee table was slate with metal legs, and there was one lonely magazine, never touched, on top of one catalogue from the Metropolitan's Impressionist collection. Her whole life could be reduced to other peoples' taste. Even the rug over the parquet floor looked like a painter's drop cloth had not been removed. Though there were no drips of color on it. Just a different type of beige.

She opened the door and was still sobbing. We hugged and went into her living room where we sat on a couch and she put her head in my lap. Like a little kid.

"What's happened? Please, Sweetheart, tell me?"

"I don't want this baby."

Maybe acting was my talent. I put on a very generous display of being terribly sanguine about a newly pregnant woman's inevitable moments of uncertainly. I assured her that she would settle into the pregnancy and create a fantastic family as ours had been.

"Shall we have a glass of wine?"

"I don't have any wine in the house. After I got the news I was pregnant, I knew I couldn't drink for a while."

"Of course. Very smart." I hid my disappointment well.

"Would you like some juice? Or a banana-protein shake?"

"No thanks. Maybe we could go onto Third Avenue and get me a little wine to celebrate your new baby?"

"Or could we just stay in? I was thinking we could look through some photo albums. I miss daddy."

"Yes, so do I."

For the next two hours I continued to comfort her. It was easy, a role I was used to. Because, as I've said, I love my daughter. I did not share with her that I had felt the same way about pregnancy the whole time I carried her. And for her entire lifetime. Hopefully she would take to this role better than I had. Although no living being that I was aware of knew about my mothering ambivalence. Except for Vita.

We looked at pictures for a while. My husband looked strange to me now that I had seen him post mortem. The pictures looked like something I had never been part of. Although I was in most of them. Smiling. For at least an hour I went as far as I could towards showing her the real love I feel for her.

When we ran out of photos to laugh at, to weep at, to reminisce about, we moved on to her favorite thing: shopping online. I bought her a bunch of bed things and made mildly ribald jokes about the fun she and her husband would have "hooking up" while she was pregnant. A wonderful new duvet on soft new sheets. I added puffy towels so she could dry her newly pregnant body in great comfort.

By then it was time for her to prepare dinner. I lovingly declined her offer to stay and eat with them. All right, I lied and told her I had a dinner date with a close friend and then a plan to go on to a movie. There was no such plan. But seeing that she was distracted by her wifey chores allowed me to slip out the door feeling like I wasn't leaving her alone and miserable.

I had the downtown cab drop me on the corner of Sixth and Bleecker so I could walk a few blocks in the beautiful air. As I stepped out of the cab, a hand reached for my hand. It was Tim. Timothy. I was ecstatic. We kissed on both cheeks, then linked arms and headed to Carbone's.

When we got there, I saw Vita at another table. At least I think it was Vita. She was facing me but made no eye contact. Also, she was different looking. I noticed that she sat with a woman who had her back to me, but I could tell that Vita was dressed identically to her. Her hair was done like the woman she was sitting with. I was jealous. Surprised. I suggested to Tim that we sneak out with an appetizer and a bottle of wine, and we headed with our goods to my apartment.

This time, in spite of his artful hands on me, I couldn't stop thinking about Vita.

"You're not really here with me are you?"

"I am. Yes. Of course. There's nowhere else I want to be."

"Except back at the restaurant. Spying on the creature you call Vita."

"I was surprised that's all. I know I'm not her only—what should I call it—friend, I guess. Student really. I know she helps many people. But why come to Carbone's?"

I thought Tim would continue to push for some sexual union. I wasn't quite there, but I assumed he was. Hoped he could get me distracted from the hollow feeling I had about

Vita. Instead, he surprised me as usual.

"Let's grab a cab and head to the zoo."

"It's closed."

"Not for us it isn't."

"Okay, I like one of the Snow Leopards a lot."

"I know. Let's go."

In minutes we had cabbed to the zoo, and without any effort I could see Tim walked us past the closures and we were inside. He said he would join me and took off towards a different part of the zoo. I went to the Snow Leopard enclosure.

It was empty, totally dark, the sun was down, and there didn't seem to be any nightlights for the cat. Why would there be?

After I stood there a couple of minutes, I saw a big figure emerge from somewhere in the enclosure and walk toward me. Her walk was unmistakable. When she reached where we could be close enough to speak, she sat down, licked her tail a few times then turned to me.

"Nice evening."

"Have you already had dinner?" Oh wow. Back to the time when I couldn't say anything intelligent to this community of creatures, people and other species who I had been introduced to since that first day at Bloomingdale's.

"What are you and he doing here? Is Timothy going to come say hello?"

"You know him?"

"For thousands of years."

At this curious statement, I heard footsteps behind me and smelled Tim's unmistakable scent of burnt wood. Then he was beside me. He nodded to the cat. Her fur was so glossy that the spots almost looked painted there. But of course, she was a leopard. The spots were hers. They went beautifully with the very white base coat of fur, and her traffic light green eyes.

"You look spectacular, as usual." Tim entered the group.

"Have you been working out? You look particularly broad in the shoulders and delicious around your ass. A feline male with an ass like that would have his choice of some very sexy big girl cats."

"I know." He smiled, trying to look modest, but that didn't work.

The leopard nodded in my direction.

"And I like your friend. She's stylish the only way I can stand: it's natural to her to look good. Haircut, makeup, clothing. Subtle and sexy. If I didn't have this incredible pelt on me, I'd consider wearing some of her clothes."

"I agree, she's easy to look at."

"So why aren't you back at her place?"

"Deborah needed a little reinforcement. She saw her friend, the one she calls Vita, with somebody else."

"Deborah?"

The cat stared at me like a cat stares at a bug it is enthralled with. And might like to chew on.

"Yes?"

"If Vita doesn't do her work she feels like crap. You do know that about her?"

"I guess."

"So take Timothy home and enjoy yourself. Walk from here, by the time you're downtown, you'll be ready."

"Always a good advisor my sweet spotted friend."

"You usually bring snacks. Anything for me tonight?"

Tim surprised me once again by pulling a packet out of his pants pocket. He opened it up and I saw some of the delicious cheese we always order at Carbone's. He put the packet where the cat could get to it. She sniffed it, then took her paw and delicately moved the Buffalo Mozzarella onto the ground where she picked it up in one large piece and ate it.

"Lovely. Thank you. I almost ate a rat today. For no good

reason. Just a little bored with pre-killed red meat. But the rat is nursing her babies. It would've been wrong. I took her into my living space and they are enjoying themselves now. Mother Rat has an endless amount of patience, and the babies laugh all the time."

"Where's the little Tabby from my last visit?"

"Somewhere in the complex here. She has lots of friends."

"Well, good to see you. Keep your tail clean, Kitty my sweet."

"Not much fun in that! Not with the new lion they just brought in, directly across that path."

The cat and Tim chuckled together, we all signaled goodbye, then Tim took my hand and took me home. By the time we were there, I was ready to rock and roll.

Tim only stayed overnight. In the morning he was gone. He left a very sweet note about a meeting that I knew he did not have and said we would meet up soon. I felt the need to get back on my journey to wherever I was heading.

This time, after my debauchery of an evening, I was anxious to read about Deborah.

There was little to nothing written between the lines of the constantly repeated descriptions of her: "Deborah was one of only 5 women prominently featured in the Old Testament. She was a Warrior, a Judge, and a Prophet."

I began to feel itchy. Something in this lack of description of the one woman ever made a Judge in the bible? I had never read the bible. But I was shocked that this woman was of no consequence. And it made me realize how important Vita's gift to me is: to find my own importance.

I was in my bedroom working on my studies of Deborah, when the doorbell rang and Tim entered. I know the door was locked. I had the strange sensation that he had walked right through it. But that seemed silly. I didn't care. Anyway, I was glad to see him and he carried an armload full of books.

"I found some stuff for you. I knew I had it."

"About Deborah?"

"Yes. And about why there is so little written about her."

I gave him a welcoming hug, a moving-towards-passionate kiss, and then I tried to take one of his books.

"No. Not here. Let's go someplace special. You know Penne y Pesci down Bleecker across Seventh?"

"I do. But I've never been in there. Not since I moved back. Is it great?"

"I know the owners, they'll set you up so you can read and drink some wine and their food is exceptional."

"And Vita won't be there."

"No. Vita doesn't frequent this place."

"I'm not avoiding her. It's just hard to see her in a different role."

"Come on. Penne y Pesci and I'll give you the 411 on Deborah, Mother of the Israelites."

"She never had her own children."

"That's why she could be Mother of the Israelites. Come on. Listen and learn."

We walked in the beautiful sundown lighting across to the west side of Bleecker Street to a small storefront restaurant with a sign that had a bowl of pasta and a fish painted on it.

Inside there were no customers, and the back table was filled with Mama, Papa, and the son who obviously worked there. They were all smoking cigarettes and drinking red wine. When we entered, they scrambled to put out the smokes, as it is illegal inside a public place. Tim waved to them and when they saw it was him, they re-lit their cigarettes and resumed drinking and talking to each other animatedly. It was in Italian, but from what I understood, a very hostile customer had come in for lunch. She was a heavyset woman who had eaten one dish after another, but at the last minute, complained bitterly about the branzino she had eaten every speck of.

She had demanded they remove the charge for it from her

bill since it had been sub par. They were rolling around
laughing. Clearly she not only loved it, but she had suggested
they bring her a new branzino to replace the completely
desiccated skeleton of the one she had finished. They had
obliged. In the end, she had paid her bill, left no tip and walked
out. They were comparing this behavior to the woman's last
visit when she had pulled the exact same routine about their
alfredo sauce.

I was very relaxed, and the son had, between loud guffaws
about this fish-eating woman, brought us both big glasses of
red wine; I was lubed and relaxed. Tim had left me for a
minute and gone to speak with the family. He spoke fluent
Italian—I tried listening in but only got some of what was
being said. As I waited, I peeked at one of the books he had
brought.

"The Myth of Woman as Warrior." I flipped to the index
and found a long string of pages devoted to Deborah. I
opened to the first of these pages.

"As with so much of fictionalized mythology, the myth of
Deborah in the Old Testament is rife with inaccuracies and
false statements. The war she is credited with winning, the war
against the Canaanites, never happened. She was not capable
of warfare and instead spent her time under a Palm tree giving
out Judgements that were mostly advice on various marital and
domestic issues."

I read on—the book was directly contradicting not only the
words, but the spirit of everything I read so far about this
Warrior, Prophetess and Judge. This was strange. Was Tim just
grabbing every book he had in which Deborah was mentioned? Or
was his opinion the same as the author of the first book I looked at: no
woman could excel in combat. No woman could give out judgement
of any greater depth than—"let the baby cry, you can't go to him every
time or he will take advantage of you."

I picked up a different book, but before I could get a good

look, Tim was at my side.

"Hey wait. I want to give you a little background before you dive in."

"Sorry. Can you wait until I pee? Do they have a bathroom here?"

He laughed, picked up the books and took my hand.

"Follow me. You can use the bathroom, and they just offered us their downstairs office to sit and do some studying in. There's a bottle of wine down there too."

I grabbed my bag, jumped up and followed him to the way back of the restaurant. It was the real deal, the floors sagged with age, the original floor tile looked like it had been in Rome while it burned before being transplanted to Bleecker street. There were incredible smells emanating from the kitchen, and we found a flight of steep stairs that we walked down to the next level. Tim pointed:

"The bathroom is down one more flight. I'll be right here in the office."

I started to follow him to the office so I could drop my bag, but he stopped me.

"Take it with you. I don't want to be responsible for it if we have to change spaces."

Having no idea why that might happen, I obliged and took my stuff with me down another flight of steps. I looked right and left but saw no bathroom. Just another flight going further down into the guts of this old building. Down here it was badly lit, and the lovely smells from the dining room turned to the kind of stench that comes from a garbage dumpster. And still no bathroom.

Should I just go back up to Tim? That seemed a little embarrassing: *Uh, I couldn't find a bathroom.*

No. It must be down one more flight. I walked down. One more flight brought me to a nightmare. There was a door that said LADIES, but when I pushed it open the toilets were all off their centers and broken. It looked like the room had been bombed or had been here since the Dutch had built New Amsterdam. I tried to find the cleanest, most solid toilet. In the end, I pee'd into what felt like a sewer drain. I was horrified and there was no toilet paper. All in all, I just wanted to get out of this hole as soon as I washed my hands. I should've known there would be no sink, no paper towels, this was a bathroom from bygone years. Luckily, I had some hand wash in my bag, so I cleaned myself up and left the bathroom.

The space had changed completely. It was now like a lounge or living room in a very antique whore house. There were chairs and sofas, but you wouldn't want to sit on any of them. A thin veneer of dust and something sticky covered every inch.

Time to go back upstairs. I spun around assuming I had become disoriented, but in fact, the staircase was gone.

I yelled as calmly as I could:

"Tim?"

No answer.

"Hey Timothy?"

Nothing.

"Where are you? I'm way down in the bowels of this old place."

I heard a sound. I thought it might be somebody a floor above me coming to show me where the stairs were. I was wrong.

"Timothy Carbone? Can you hear me? I am stuck. Lost. Please come get me."

This time I heard a very faint answer. But not from Tim.

"Deborah? Where are you?"

"Vita? Is that you?"

"Where are you?"

"In hell. Way downstairs in a restaurant. Penne y Pesci. Can you help me?"

There was a pronounced pause as if Vita was negotiating

something with somebody.

"I am sorry. He says no."

"Who? Who says no?"

"I will come to you when you are safely out of there. For now, you are going through something I cannot stop."

"Just tell me where the stairs are. I can get myself back to the street."

"Not right now. You cannot leave where you are."

"For how long?"

Vita's voice was gone. In her place I could just hear wind. Inside the ugly space I was in the wind was picking up to gale levels. It threw the accumulated dust and crud and stench into the air where it formed a small tornado in the space. I watched this and realized Tim had sent me someplace that was not meant to help me with my transition to Deborah. Tim had sent me to somebody's Underworld.

Clutching my bag to my chest, I tried exploring, but the floor tiles were either crumbled to nothing you could step on, or so broken that parts of a tile stuck up and could have impaled me if I had made the wrong move. Way in one corner I saw what I thought was another person.

"Hello?"

The body in the corner moved a little, and then resettled. As it did this, dust blew out of it. This was not a living being.

"Anybody down here who can help me?"

I heard rustling but couldn't see anybody.

"Hello?"

"Glad to see me this time?"

It was Set. He was dressed in jeans and a T shirt. Very West Village. Except for his extraordinary size and the bronze skin.

"Set?"

"Do you know where you are Deborah?"

He walked towards me and kicked up dust with every footstep. He was too big and powerful for the cruddy delicacy of this room.

"Is this your Underworld?"

"My Underworld?"

"Excuse me. Is this the Underworld? An Underworld? Where am I?"

"I asked if you're glad to see me."

"Yes."

"Well, you should be. You're temporarily dead."

"Shut up Set."

The voice was unmistakably Nephthys, but she was nowhere in sight.

"Nephthys?"

"Yes, it's me. But I'm quite far away."

"You're on your own, sweet little thingy. Tiny Female. Nobody here can protect you."

"Set!! Let her get through this by herself. Get out of there."

"But I like it here. And you can't get here in time to save her."

"Save her from what? You can't do anything to her and you know it."

"I was thinking more of my dear friend Timothy. That's what little Missy calls him."

"That's not his name? Nephthys? That's not his name?"

She didn't answer me. Set chuckled unpleasantly.

"Is your name Deborah? Are you a warrior, judge, prophetess? Or did the one you call Vita set you up for all this?"

"You're a liar!!!"

From nowhere near me, and without moving a muscle, Set flung me to the ground.

"I don't like being called a liar."

His voice was a snarl. He began walking towards me. I tried to stand, but I was stuck in the cracked tile. My hands were cut from the fall to the ground, and my whole body ached and felt weak.

"I am sorry I called you that."

"I'm sure you are."

My body was lifted by unseen hands, Set was still a good distance from me. The hands pinched at me and poked me with something sharp.

"Stop that please."

Set laughed out loud, delighted to mimic me.

"Stop that please."

He was a pretty awful mimic, but his point was clear. He was going to make me pay for rejecting him. He was going to try to hurt me. And worst of all, he claimed a friendship with Tim which meant that Tim had known exactly where he was sending me when I went to find the bathroom.

The hands holding me up dropped me very suddenly to the hard, broken floor. This time the wind was knocked out of me and I gasped for breath.

"Tim? Your girl is in distress. Aren't you going to come to her rescue?"

Set seemed to hear a response from Tim that I was not able to hear.

"He says 'let the warrior fight this out for herself.'"

I tried to stand, but my chest was still in great pain and my breath was not flowing in and out.

"You heard him didn't you? Fight this out for yourself!"

In spite of the pain, I noticed as if I was somebody outside myself, that I was not frightened. I was angry.

"I heard him. And I am happy to fight for myself."

"Excellent!"

This time as Set snarled and laughed the lights went out and all I could see were his eyes, which were a terrifying bright red in the darkness of the room.

I stared at his ugliness through the darkness.

"What did you mean I am temporarily dead?"

"You're on a Time Out."

"From what?"

"From what? From Life. You are currently not being recorded on the Spacetime Continuum."

"Why?"

"Ask Vita."

"Why?"

"I'm not here to answer your questions. Figure this out. And do it fast."

"Is this a dream?"

Suddenly and from nobody I could see in front of me, a hand slapped my face very hard."

"Does that answer your question?"

"No. Because you've been having unseen creatures throw me around since you started to attack me."

This time the thing that hit my face was a fist. It knocked me back to the ground in the total dark and as my body hit the shards of tile, I could taste blood in my mouth from the punch.

"All right. Please stop. Not a dream. Very real. But why?"

"Vita wants you to be a heroic figure. All of us have to face Death."

"Are you including yourself?"

Set began to move towards me and within seconds, I could feel his huge hands on me.

"I am mythic. You will at best become an improved mortal being."

He smelled of dust and of thousands of years of Egyptian desert.

"What am I supposed to do? Prove I can face this dip into hell and become a more worthwhile being on the other end?"

"Kiss me. Like you kissed Osiris."

"What will that prove?"

This time Set picked me up like I was a small child, he wrapped my legs around his waist. I could feel his huge phallus pressing against my underwear.

"We're going to have sex," he said. "For as long as I want. And if you can make me feel like it's better than any sex you've ever had, I might ask Tim to let you go back upstairs."

Before I had time to speak a word, he had ripped away all my underwear and jammed his penis inside of me. It was strange. It didn't hurt, although he had done nothing to prepare me for this invasion. But it was icy cold, and he moved me up and down on his penis like I was a little toy, lifting me up and slamming me back down on his sex very fast. Still, I felt little but coldness. And my heart breaking.

"You like this?"

"Yes."

"Not very convincing."

So he continued his freezing rape of my body, now freeing one hand so he could maul my nipples, twisting them painfully and still bobbing me up and down on his penis. It was beginning to hurt, and I became filled with an unfamiliar rage.

"Stop this Set!"

The voice was Nephthys' from far away.

"Stop it this minute."

Set lifted me off of him and threw me to the floor. I was in shock and felt practically none of the tile shards that tore into me as I landed.

"Or what?"

"Or I'll make you sorry when we both get back to our frequency."

Set clapped his hands and the dim lighting in the room came back on. About 20 feet in front of me, there was an enormous, ornate bed. On it lay Hades and his bride Persephone. I knew the myth well: He was a fifty-million-year-old virgin raping his kidnapped niece with all the brutality and clumsiness of anybody who doesn't know what sex is.

The young girl was clawing at him and screaming, but he kept forcing her back onto the bed and kept trying to be her lover, husband, anything but the uncle who had stolen her from her family and dragged her to his home in the Underworld.

Even knowing the myth, I couldn't bear actually seeing it carried out. I crawled painfully across the broken floor to the mammoth bed, dragged myself onto it, and punched the ugly old man with all of my strength directly in his back. His skin was dry and desiccated and he smelled of Death and shit. My punch to his back caused the old tyrant real pain and he rolled off of his young victim to care for himself.

I grabbed Persephone by one arm and helped her off the bed. Together we crawled as far from the bed as we could before we were exhausted and sat down on the cruel floor.

She was crying. I reached out my hand to wipe away her tears. Her face was starting to freeze. A thin veneer of ice formed everywhere a tear had dropped. I tried to wipe her face with part of my blouse, but the ice was forming too fast and before one more tear had fallen, she was no longer a lovely young woman. She had become an icy figure of despair and rage.

"Get out of here Deborah," Persephone hissed. "Tell Vita what you've seen. She will find my mother."

"How? How can I get out?"

Persephone turned to the old man on the bad. "Hades! Let this woman go back to the land of the living. If you do, I will forgive you."

Set intervened from a distance.

"She's lying, Hades. She will never forgive you. She wants Deborah to find her mother and have you destroyed."

Hades was still nursing his back. He was a big, ugly, old baby and I had landed a blow like only a warrior could.

"I'm letting this woman go. She's trouble, Set. She's protected by forces we can't overcome. Anyway, Persephone wants her to be set free. To live again. Isn't that right my dear?"

The old god stared at Persephone, who was frozen by my side, but who could, miraculously move freely and speak through the ice that was her face. "I already told you, Uncle Hades. Let her go and I will forgive you."

Set was outnumbered. He knew what he would face back in Egypt with Nephthys, and now he was besieged by Hades, the great mythic victim of the House of Olympus, to let me go. He was too big a coward to take on two mythologies and a raging wife.

"Get out of here Deborah," he said. "You have ten seconds."

I tried to thank Persephone, but she was gone. She had gone back to the bed Hades was on and had begun punching him relentlessly in his groin. The old man was wailing in agony, and his young niece was laughing like any school girl having a great time playing with her friends.

"Five seconds Deborah," Hades whimpered.

I turned away from the bed and saw, within a few feet of where I was, a stairway. I stood shakily, aware that blood and dirt and deadly viruses were covering my legs. I didn't try to swipe at this mess all over me, I knew it would go when I had left the Underworld. I made it to the first step and as I began my ascent, the nightmare room disappeared and I was once again walking up a typical New York stairway in a 1930s high-rise building.

I went up a first, then a second and a third flight. The walls around me became increasingly solid, and by the third landing I reached, I could see inside the office Tim had said he would be in. I could see Tim himself talking on a phone, smoking a cigarette and drinking from the bottle of red wine. I went into the office, and he turned to smile at me. This time, I saw through his handsome features that he was more reptile than human. His eyes were a very pale green, and his face was no longer attractive to me. Maybe because I knew who he was now. "You're back!"

"Am I allowed out on the street? Am I really alive again?"

"Go out and see for yourself."

"Goodbye Timothy."

"Tim."

"No. Not anymore."

"Well, no loss. You were a little old for me anyway."

"You're not 40. You're much older than that if you hang with Set and his family."

"You got it finally. I am not 40. I am not 60, I am as old as this planet."

"That's not the truth either. You are incapable of telling truth, aren't you?"

"I am one of the Lost. Prototypes developed as the earth was being shaped."

"What the hell does that mean?"

"Get out. You're boring me now. You made it through the test. I have no further interest in you."

I started up the stairs and heard him go back to his phone conversation. His voice sounded different. Not so suave and sexy—more gravelly and hoarse. He was laughing and telling somebody the story of what he had just done to me. I ran up the stairs and was back in the restaurant.

Every table was now full. I could not tell why the people in the seats looked strange to me. Maybe they were tourists. I heard a babel of languages, none of which was English. I looked at the table where the family had been, the proprietors of this weird restaurant. They were not there. I found each of them serving food, pouring wine, taking dinner orders. As I walked out the door, I had the sense that they each looked at me and smiled derisively.

Chapter Ten
What Becomes of the Broken-Hearted

IT WAS DARK OUT, but the lights of the street lamps, and the many open restaurants and stores made Bleecker street look like the most beautiful painting I had ever seen. Briefly I thought of Vincent. His painting of a café in Paris at night. I wanted to go visit him, but I was disgusting and filthy and I needed to go home.

I was walking slowly because of all the tossing around I had been through. I knew I was a bloody mess, but this was the Village, and nobody gave me a second look. Two people asked me for a cigarette, but I just shook my head "no" and kept walking.

The steps up to my apartment felt very steep. Then the climb inside the building to my second-floor unit allowed all of my fatigue and confusion to hit me like a wall.

Inside I locked the door and lay down on my bed. I had hoped Vita might show up, but my apartment was empty. I worried momentarily about how Tim had gotten in before our trip to hell, but I was pretty sure that he wouldn't come near me again. He had tried his best to do exactly what Vita warned me about, and he had failed.

I turned on the TV news. It was a shock to see the date on the screen: I had been gone for three whole days and nights. Never mind the cliché that it had seemed like no time at all, it had seemed like Forever. But if you had asked me, I would've estimated that it was only about 14 hours since I had left with my former lover, Timothy.

The TV screen was mesmerizing, and I hoped it would lull me to sleep. At a commercial break, Vita appeared on screen.

"Are you all right Deborah?"

I had no idea if I was hallucinating. I no longer thought I was entering dementia, but maybe I was wrong. So I answered the screen image.

"Yes. Embarrassed but home safely."

"You have nothing to be embarrassed about," Vita said. "You passed the toughest test there is. You died and resurrected yourself. You should be very pleased. You can now become a real Prophet, a shaman, Deborah, and definitely a Warrior."

"Tim?"

"He's among the best. And you overcame him. He's very angry at me about it! The pathetic truth is, he actually likes you. Make him miss you, Deborah. That's part of being a warrior. Never underestimate the power of your opponent."

Vita laughed happily on the TV screen. Then the commercial break was over, and the News cast personality reappeared in Vita's place. I turned the TV off and as I did, I heard my door open and close. For a split second I was scared. It could be Tim, or Set even. But instead, Vita, back to her "Me" appearance, and Nephthys, who had to duck to get through my front door, both came into my bedroom.

"You are amazing," Nephthys said. "Set is completely humiliated. Nobody has dismissed his penis for many centuries. Except, of course, me."

"I have no idea how that happened. He is well stocked and very rough. But I practically couldn't feel him."

Vita and Nephthys both laughed. Vita spoke while Nephthys continued to chuckle at her husband's expense. "You learned an extremely important lesson with Set: if you are not afraid, your opponent is limited and ultimately defeated."

"I stopped feeling him thousands of years ago," Nephthys said. "It drives him insane. And me too once in a while. Before he tried to destroy Osiris, Set and I had a good thing between us."

"Why did he ruin it?" I asked.

"I don't know," Nepthys said. "For years I thought it was sibling rivalry with Osiris. Just enraged him so much he self-destructed. But now I think it's the other side of the moon."

"Sorry?"I was confused by this.

"I know Tim as you called him, mentioned the Lost to you. Vita is part of that, but me, Set, Osiris and Isis are man-made mythology. All of us share certain things, like immortality, but we mythological forms are prone to human frailty. We were made by human minds. So Set is not that different from any human being who ruins everything good that is given to him. The Lost are workers, they have personas obviously, but they have a job to do." Nephthys finished her explanation.

"What is it? The Lost?" I looked to Vita.

"In the years that the planets took to cool off, to become inhabitable, the force of the Boson Particle made up some experiments," Vita said. "Among the biggest failure was that Human-like forms were created as prototypes of what primordial single cell creatures would evolve into. It was done mostly out of impatience, so it wasn't well thought out."

"How many of you are there?" I asked. "Are you all in human form?"

"No. Not all, but mostly. Your friend the leopard was among the most successful prototypes. The one hundred of us that were created to help build pithicanthropis erectus were corrupted. We divided into the Lost who look for progress, and Timothy and his side of the equation."

"Is he any worse than any other arrogant, powerful man who has no respect for women?" I asked.

"That's the problem, isn't it? He is no worse, but he did represent from Day One the struggle the rest of us would face. Have been facing. Continue to face." Vita stared into my eyes.

"Is there any hope that he will change? Become more of a force for our side?" I sounded whiny and desperate to myself.

"Yes, of course there is always hope, always change, but there is no guarantee which side will ultimately dominate, or what each individual from the original Lost will become."

"I will fight to win him to our side." I thrust my fist into the air like I was in the sixties at a rally.

Vita laughed.

Nephthys stood up.

"Good to have you with us Deborah. I'll be heading out now. It's a long trip home and a big fight with Set to look forward to."

"Sorry. I didn't make it easier did I?" I touched her huge arm.

"Not to hurt your feelings, but you are irrelevant to our situation. Set is an angry, dissatisfied spirit. If anybody is to blame for that, it is the people who created the myth. Not you. Look at Cain and Abel. The originators of the early stories could not envision a world where there could be harmony among all the differing people and other creatures. They didn't even think it was desirable. And then the food chain, it was impossible not to smell the blood in the air, hear the shrieks of one creature ripping open another. The dye was cast."

Nephtys put her huge arms around me and gave me a warm hug, then she kissed Vita on both cheeks, and she was gone.

Vita and I sat down in my bedroom, she on a chair, me on the bed. My body ached and my mind was in a state of disarray.

"You saw me at Carbone's?"

"Yes. I knew it was you."

"I left when I figured out what Timothy was up to." Vita said.

"I needed it to happen. I needed to be tested."

"Now you have a lot more power. A lot more responsibility. You have done what all shamen or gods must do. Now move on to the completion of Deborah. You don't need to concentrate so much on her warrior status. You have killed a

Nazi and defeated one of the most charming emissaries from the Other Side. You took a lot of kicks and insults from Set and ultimately he's at home crying like a baby, and you are fine. Take some time if you're given that option, and recoup."

"Are you leaving now?"

"Yes, I have to go back to the woman at Carbone's. I froze her in time. I have to go back to work. You and I will be seeing each other a lot more now that you are no longer my student."

We looked at each other for a long time. I saw her back at Bloomingdale's, I had no idea what she saw in me right now. I looked down. I was filthy, covered with blood, and dirt and terrible memories. I needed a bath.

"Take a nice glass of wine into the bath with you."

With that, Vita left and I went to run my bath. As it turned out, taking some time was not an option. As I stepped somewhat more carefully than usual into my claw foot tub, glass of wine balancing tenuously in my hand, the phone rang. As always, I could tell the call was from my daughter. I slid gently down into the water, put my wine on the table by tub-side, and picked up my cell phone.

"Hello sweetheart."

"Mother? Can you help me? Can you please come up here?"

"Of course. But I am bathing—I had a bit of a fall I need to clean out my bruises."

"Please. Just come. I have a bath tub, I will help you with your cuts."

"What is it? What's happened?"

"He has a girlfriend!"

"What?"

"All those nights at work, closing important deals. That was a lie. She works at the law firm. He's been seeing her for months. I'm getting an abortion!"

"I thought you want this baby."

"Yes, but so does he. He wants me to forgive his affair. He

says he will end it. He wants to be a family. I will abort his baby and he will know what he's made me feel like!"

I unplugged the bathtub, grabbed a towel, and oblivious to my own pain, I dressed quickly and went to be with my daughter. When I got there, she had run a warm tub for me, and sweetly, she had put a glass of wine on the rim of the tub. She watched as I undressed and she gasped at the bruises and cuts that were up, down and all around my body. Some of the cuts were deep. She wanted to get Neosporin, but I told her that soap and water was all I needed. I sunk into her grand, extra large tub, she turned on the jets of water that sent soothing warm water all over me, and then she began to cry.

I let the warm water take care of my body. She offered me soap, but I knew it would be too harsh for some of my cuts. I also knew, that having died and returned, I was now pretty safe from minor cuts and abrasions. I could feel the sting, but they couldn't get infected. Why? I had no idea of the science of post mortem infection, I wished my husband was here to explain it, but I was alone with my daughter. Anyway, I knew I was still mortal. That was the big issue: I hadn't become one of the Lost. I was however a survivor of The Big Deal called Death, and knowing what real death is like, I had some complex understandings that would've really helped me when I was young.

I bathed, she told me the details of her husband's infidelity. I had heard the same story over my lifetime thousands of times, from boyfriends and girlfriends who cheated on each other in middle school, high school, college, and then the ultimate: marriage. The stories were all sadly similar: some involved boredom, some misunderstandings, some were just about couples who had no more time left in their relationship and an affair was the way to end things.

She continued to sob as I got out of the tub. She wrapped me in one of the luscious bathrobes I had ordered for her online during our last "shopping trip" on her computer. All the items I had bought her to make her pregnancy "soft" and "comfy" were now there for me.

I grabbed my wine and with my daughter's help, we waddled together into her living room and she put me down gently on one of her pricy pieces of today's type of couch. I looked on the wall above the couch—there was a new painting. A palm tree. This seemed astral, important, strange. How did my daughter know that Deborah, as a judge, was generally pictured giving her advice and opinions sitting under a palm tree?

I sat and listened and nodded my head and once in a while, between sips of wine, I made a sound with my mouth to agree with something she had said. This went on a long time. Then, very suddenly, my daughter's posture grew rigid, she stopped crying, and she listened as her husband opened the front door and was standing in the room with us.

"Get out! I told you to stay with your girlfriend until I have decided when to abort this child."

He and I had never been close. In fact I didn't think he was the right man for my daughter. But he had always been very kind to my husband and to me, very respectful of my husband's prominence. Now it was just me. I wondered how he would be.

"I am so sorry. (He directed this at me) I will do anything to make this right."

"Mother? Tell me what to do. Like daddy would have. I need to hear somebody's judgement that isn't my own."

I was now in full Deborah mode. Sitting under a palm with two people looking to me for judgement. This test seemed harder than Set's frozen penis. These were people I cared about. Being forced to pretend to like Set's sexual ugliness had meant nothing to me.

"I can't make a judgement. But I can try to listen. To both of you. Then maybe I can tell you what I think."

My daughter turned to her husband and began to cry slightly.

"Tell her. Tell my mother that you've been bending your law partner over the books in the law library for six months. Tell her about the wild sex in an empty office while your wife is home making Hollandaise sauce for your f*cking asparagus!"

He looked down at his hands. Clearly he had never heard my daughter this angry. I'm not sure any of us had ever heard her say "f*cking" anything, let alone asparagus. I saw his embarrassment.

"You don't have to tell me if you aren't able. You two can find a therapist, and work this out."

"I DON'T WANT A F*CKING THERAPIST!! You are my mother. I want some sound judgement from you!"

"She doesn't want to go to therapy," he said. "I've asked her many times."

"I'm not that knowledgable, but I can to give you my feedback."

"Judgement!" she shouted. "I want your f*cking judgement! I have never asked that of you. Now you tell me whether to carry this man's child to term when he has been spilling his sperm into a plastic bag with another woman the whole time the fetus has been growing inside of me! I want to hear what you think I should do."

I wished I felt like Solomon the Wise. I wish I felt like the guy who played Adam Schiff on Law and Order. These men never skipped a beat in assessing a situation, and the solution to the problem. I had always given opinions tentatively. Mostly because this kind of issue had always bored me. I never got cheated on, and when I cheated, it was to end a relationship. I had no experience in forgiveness, moving forward through the hurt feelings, or any of the other clichés that are the building blocks of monogamy.

I remembered Vita telling me to go slowly and infrequently

with my passion for Osiris. She had given me a quick but solid lesson in the impossibility of smooth sailing forever in any given relationship. She had not however, given me info on when to end, and when to mend. Forgive me for that. It sounds like needlepoint on a very dowdy pillow.

"Why did you start seeing this woman?" I asked him.

"She was a partner," he said. "She liked me. I figured it would help me make partner if I acceded to her constant flirtation."

"F*ck you! You are a f*cking liar!"

"Are you sure he's not telling you the sad but genuine truth? He wouldn't be the first person to use sex to climb the corporate ladder."

"I found pictures of them. At company parties. All smarmy leering smiles, hands brushing against each other. Sipping out of one champagne glass. He's a f*cking liar. He wanted this. And I don't want to have a baby with a f*cking liar! What if the baby is just like him? Boring, without culture, conversant in nothing but case law. What should I do, discuss the Molineaux decision with the little baby as he sucks on my nipple and drags my breasts to the ground?"

"I didn't know anything about methotrexate—your father and I had to find other ways to communicate."

"But daddy adored you. I saw him follow you with his eyes whenever you left the table."

"I made him a lot of Hollandaise sauce for his asparagus. It didn't make us a perfect or an imperfect pair."

"You got lucky. He died before the real tedium set in."

"Sweetheart!"

"I'm sorry, but you have been different since he died. Do you think I can't see you blossoming in ways that the marriage didn't allow?"

"That doesn't mean it was his fault," her husband said. "It doesn't mean your mother wanted your father to die, for

Christ's sake."

"YOU SHUT UP!!! If you want to make a f*cking argument, get your yellow legal pad and write it down. I can't stand the sound of your voice."

It didn't take Solomon to get that my daughter's rage had something inside it besides this infidelity.

"Sweetheart? Have you never ever been with another man since you got married?"

Her husband looked directly at her, and so did I.

"You're supposed to be on my side mother. I asked for Judgement, not Judgementalism."

"Please answer your mother's question."

"Yes! All right. Yes!!! The reason I was so thrilled to be pregnant was that it gave me an excuse to break off some silly liaison I was having."

"With whom?" I asked.

"With her yoga instructor. Tell your mother. Tell her please how you became so incredibly flexible after practicing underneath him."

My daughter looked totally stunned.

"You knew?"

"From the first time you were with him."

"Why didn't you say something?"

"I got mad. I got hurt. I felt like dying. Then this woman at the office began to play games with me and I felt like it wouldn't mean anything and maybe revenge would actually help us heal our marriage."

"So you f*cking her is my fault?"

"I didn't hear him say that sweetheart. I heard him say he needed to feel alive and vital after he found out about you and—what is his name?" I asked.

"She calls him Bodhi. Like short for Bodhisatva. If that isn't bullshit what is?"

"His name is Bill. He's a white guy from New Hampshire. I

was embarrassed, so I made up a Buddhist name for him."

"All right. I think I have enough information to make some suggestions." I was trying not to chuckle. "Bodhisatva?"

"No. Now I don't want to hear anything. You're not a judge. You always avoided being a judge. What if you make a really lousy judgement?"

"Please. Let her give us her feelings. You owe that to me and to your mother."

"I owe nothing to anybody. But okay mother, go ahead."

"I suggest you start by deciding if you want to use your baby as a bludgeon. If you really don't want a child, then I am all for you to make that choice. But you seem to have weaponized the pregnancy, and that is a terrible mistake."

"I agree with your mother. The baby is important to both of us. It can make us a family. I will learn to make Hollandaise sauce for you. I will take on half of everything I can to help. I want this child. I have no doubts."

"You also have no swollen ankles or sore back. I do!"

"Please. We both strayed for no good reason. We like each other. I love you. I watch you when you go into the kitchen just like you described your father watching your mother. Please. Let me love you and our child."

"I will think about it and discuss it more with my mother when you are not around. I'll let you know by next week."

With that, my daughter stood up, kissed me on the cheek, and walked into her bedroom. I stood up too, and her husband rose to walk me to the door.

"You'll help us, won't you?" He grabbed my sleeve.

"I'll try. Let her have some time. Once she decides about the baby, we'll talk. I will do everything I can to help her with that decision."

"Thank you. You know she is still in mourning for her father, I think your presence is incredibly helpful to her. Do you want me to get you a cab?"

"No thanks. I'm going to walk a few blocks in the nice air. I will talk to you soon."

We kissed goodbye, and I left my daughter and her husband to their lives. I took a cab home, and finally got the chance to climb into my bed and sleep.

Chapter Eleven
Moment of Truth

WHEN I WOKE UP, I was only mildly surprised to find myself with Vincent in his kitchen in Arles. By this time, the specifics of how I got there meant nothing. He was part of Time and Space; I am too.

We sat with our glasses of absinthe and I told him about the trip to the Underworld and he seemed totally unsurprised.

"The greatest people who have ever lived have to pass through this test. What did you learn?"

"I learned I am not to be ignored. But I'm not sure that qualifies as my "talent" as you call it."

"*Oui, bien sur.* Of course, it is your talent. To speak your thoughts, to stand for a Just world. To kill the people who kill the human spirit."

"I'm not Joan of Arc."

"Just as well. Nineteen years old and charred like that beef I just overcooked."

"You knew her?"

"I know her. She visits when she is in my frequency. She is stranger than you. But she has her own brilliance."

"What do you talk about?"

For the first time since I had met Vincent Van Gogh, he seemed unable to tell me something. He took a huge swallow of absinthe, looked at his hands and finally spoke.

"I need to get my paintings back."

"What?"

"That is what we talked about. It is impossible that I leave this planet with my work scattered throughout the Bourgeois homes of meaningless people."

"Are you leaving this planet Vincent?"

"There will be an accident. Can't you see it? You are now supposed to practice prophecy along with judgement and being a warrior."

I heard him through the absinthe. I froze for a second, but then I had a vision: Vincent was in the woods painting. Two teenaged boys approached him. They were admiring his work, he was sharing his absinthe. One of the boys had a gun. Vincent asked to look at it more closely, as the boy handed it to him, the gun went off and a bullet struck Van Gogh in his gut. I closed my eyes to end the vision. I felt his hand on my arm demanding that I tell him what I had seen.

"I am not a prophet yet Vincent. My visions cannot be trusted."

"What did you see? I have a right to decide for myself the truth of your vision."

I told him. And I watched his face as the words sunk in. Then he refilled my glass.

"I know these boys well. They come on Sundays when they are free of their families. They want to be painters. One of them shows talent, the other is too shy to show me anything."

"Is there a gun?"

"Yes the shy boy brought it to show me once. It was his grandfather's during the Revolution. He is proud of it."

"Then what I just saw?"

"Will come to pass. I must paint as much as I can before this happens."

"What can I do to help you?"

"You have correctly seen my end. I have been told this story by others with vision who have come by to visit. I will make sure it appears to be a suicide. I will not let anything happen to these boys. They do not shoot me on purpose."

"I am so sorry."

"No! Please waste no time on sorrow. I will have completed hundreds of canvasses and said what is in my heart. And because I have spoken, though I am often in the depths of misery, there is still calmness, pure harmony and music inside me. My death will be acceptable to me."

"I see what I can do for you Vincent."

"What are you talking about?"

"I will retrieve your paintings from the houses where they are not seen by the public. I will get my mythic friends and we will find a way. I swear on my soul, I will free your canvasses and return them to museums where you can be heard."

"The paintings will just be sent back to the 'owners.' You told me these people paid fantastic sums for my work. They will get them back."

I stood up unsteadily, put down my drink and took him by both hands. We looked deeply at each other.

"They will not be given back. And nothing will be able to undo this once I have found a way to get hold of them. I promise you this."

I looked at him and he was smiling more deeply than I had ever seen him smile.

"Thank you, Deborah. I believe you will do what you promised. "

We kissed on both cheeks, agreed to meet again soon, and I was, in seconds, back in the gallery of the Metropolitan Museum where his paintings hung.

I began to exit the museum but an eerie feeling overtook me. I was uncertain of myself, but I went straight to the Temple of Dendur. I slipped around the roped off blockade and went inside, by now I was scared of the scope of what I planned to set in motion. I turned the corner onto the Giza Plateau. In spite of my self doubt, I was determined to honor my promise to Vincent before I lost him. I had unconsciously come up with a plan and was now anxious to carry it out.

I sat down to allow the Time and Space Lag to leave me, and I saw a familiar, huge figure of a man coming towards me.

For once I was disappointed to see Osiris, I needed the skullduggery of the outlaw, Set.

Osiris sat down and handed me a glass of liquid. I drank it immediately. We sat quietly, it was not a time for sexual intimacy, it was a time for righting a wrong. I had wanted to ask Set to help me, because he is thrilled by bad behavior, but I would ask him later.

Osiris sat quietly until we could both see Isis in the near distance. She was heading for us quickly and arrived within seconds. I stood to embrace her. Then we all sat in silence together.

Isis was the first to speak.

"Will we need Set and Nephthys?"

"We will."

"But not yet?"

"No. I have to see what you think of my idea, then we can bring on the others if we are going ahead with it."

Osiris spoke for the first time.

"We know why you've come to us. Vita was just here briefly."

I hadn't told Vita any of this. The exchange of information in the Spacetime frequency was still a little surprising, but I had no time to figure it out. I asked my two friends for their take on my idea, realizing there was no need to explain it to them.

"Do you think what I want to do is possible?"

"Yes." Isis nodded her head vigorously. "We're accomplished at re-acquiring stolen objects."

"Isis can do anything. She saved my life when nobody else could, and you are a real warrior now Deborah. The worse the odds against you, the more I know you will be victorious."

"I'll go and think, when I have a strategy, I'll come back."

I stood up.

Isis said as a farewell: "I think you should plan a party."

"But how many paintings will that retrieve?"

"A series of parties on one night. A blitzkrieg of parties that keep the very wealthy and powerful divided into their circles of influence. It will also assure that they are drunk. That will make the whole thing easier for us."

"Isis is right. We can move from home to home, from country to country in the blink of an eye. Within hours we could retrieve most of his work."

"Then people will notice."

"Yes. Isn't that the point? People should notice."

Osiris looked concerned at this statement his wife had made.

"We'll get Set and Nephthys and confer. He has a very good head for criminal enterprise, and Nephthys knows about keeping him from getting caught."

"Should we call on them now?"

"They are on a trip. Down the Nile. We should wait for them to get back."

"Please tell me when it's a good time for us all to meet. I will get Vita to come too."

"It will be within a few days. Have a safe trip home."

The two giant figures stood, took hands and walked off together. I looked down at my glass and when I looked up again, they were miles in the distance. It was time for me to go back downtown.

Once again as I entered my apartment, I smelled cigarette smoke. I walked into the kitchen and found my father, Chesterfield dangling from the corner of his mouth as he held my white patent leather shoes in his hands. I wondered briefly why he seemed so physically complete. My husband, on our last visit, felt like he was evaporating—but I had been told that once the process of losing this lifetime's shape was complete, he could have it back. So here was my *bon vivant* father as he had been in the years I had lived at home. He still smelled of his old cologne, mixed with Chesterfields. It was beyond lovely to see him.

"They're such perfect shoes. I'm sorry we never got them for you when you would've worn them."

"You bought me plenty of pretty things.

My father held both shoes in one hand as he took the cigarette and put it out in the sink.

"We bought what we needed you to have. I've been thinking lately that we never really asked what you wanted to have. Or who you wanted to be."

"Want a glass of wine, dad?"

"Absolutely. I see you have a nice red. I am finally able to drink again. I went through a longer than usual period of transition where cells were changing and alcohol was of no use."

I poured us each a glass, grabbed some crackers in their box, and we went and sat in my living-room. My father kept the shoes with him like they meant something to him that I couldn't fathom.

"Dad? Why are you holding those?"

"When you were eight or nine you wanted a pair of tap shoes. At the time your mother was taking you to ballet class twice a week and the idea of adding anything else to your schedule did not make sense to us. We didn't notice that your attitude towards ballet class was perfunctory. But your eyes lit up whenever you saw musicals with us. Especially the ones that included tap dancing."

"Every parent misses clues. Anyway, I never would've been a good tap dancer."

"Maybe. But you cried when we took you to those musicals. And we never asked you why."

"You were a wonderful dad, Dad. You have nothing to feel bad about."

"We never asked you who you wanted to be. We loved you very much but had no idea who you were. Then you got married, got pregnant, and finally I noticed what the hell was going on, and I still said nothing."

"Noticed what?"

"You got depressed when you got pregnant. The same way your mother did when she was carrying you. But your mother and I worked together building our organization; that meant we gave each other great support and companionship."

"I had a good life. I loved my husband. I wasn't forced to have my daughter."

"Is that the truth?"

I poured us more wine. And I borrowed a cigarette and lit it. I hadn't tasted nicotine for decades. Doctors' wives don't generally smoke. At least not out in the open.

"It's close enough to the truth."

My father put down the white shoes.

"No. It's not."

"The whole truth and nothing, but the truth is clearer to me now. I have had experiences like sitting with you and others who live on other Time Frequencies. I wouldn't trade that for a Phd in something. I wouldn't trade this last few months— with everything I have been allowed to see—things most people never see until they're dead."

"Are you changed because of it?"

"Yes, of course. Can't you tell?"

"I looked at the writings on Deborah. I see your admiration of her. Is it more than admiration?"

"I have killed a Nazi, withstood a serious attempt on my life, fought off the sexual assault of a mythological figure three times my strength. And gotten to see my connection with life. I am happiest when I try to fulfill it. I got that from looking into Deborah."

"I guess you did just fine without those tap shoes. Our benign neglect was the best we could do. You are an exceptional person. Your mother and I were not."

"You were nice, you were smart. You did great support

work for human rights. You raised money, you lived fairly."

"And we raised somebody who would go on to become a heroine."

There was a strange smile on his face. As if a knot in his stomach had been untied. He stared at me, lit a cigarette, and left. There was no need to kiss goodbye, clearly we would see each other from time to time. And clearly both of us had figured out that sometimes if you leave a person alone and don't cause them any harm, they will do better than you could ever imagine.

I finished the bottle of wine after he left. I started to take a shower, but I heard a rattling against the living room window. I went to see what it was. Maybe rowdy pigeons who hadn't enjoyed their offerings of food tonight.

I saw two green eyes staring at me. It was the Tabby from the zoo. She was scraping with her paws against the glass of the window. I went and opened it, she hopped inside.

"Do you mind if I bunk here with you for a little while?"

"Have you been evicted from the zoo?"

"You know that rat the leopard told you about? The nursing mother?"

"Yes."

"She took offense at something about me being too close to her babies. She got nasty and bit me."

"And?"

"And I broke all the rules I've learned and killed her."

"Uh oh."

"So I am safest away from the zoo until I can figure out a way to make up for this terrible thing I did."

"You're welcome here. Come and go as you like. I will leave this window open a few inches for you."

"I have a friend on the street, Ricky, the Deli Cat. He's a bit of a celebrity on Bleecker. He and I will pal around together until I figure things out. My name is Louise, by the way."

Louise The Tabby jumped back to the window sill and somehow got down the building, maybe digging claws into the mortar between the bricks the building was made of. I realized as she disappeared that I should have been clear that birds on my window sill were invited guests, not to be eaten. But I understood as I began to worry, that Louise knew she was not welcome to eat anything else that was alive and minding its own business. I would make sure to get extras when I ate and bring them home for her. I was glad to have her company, my parents had traveled too much to allow me a pet.

Chapter Twelve
Let's Plan a Robbery

I SPENT DAYS JUST LIVING MY LIFE. Walking in the autumn air and thinking. I spoke to my daughter several times. She had decided against the abortion but had asked her husband to move out. I had so much money from my husband's practice, I decided to give her another very large chunk so she was able to raise her child in comfort if she truly stayed away from her marriage.

I did wonder why he was so disgusting to her when she had been cheating on him at the same time? Monogamy. Somebody always has to say they're sorry. At a deeper level, I wondered if my daughter's love affair with the Buddhist from New Hampshire was an expression of her dissatisfaction with her life. I hoped she was dissatisfied and could find her way before she was my age. There is nothing duller than the role she was playing. I should know.

I sat down at an Italian restaurant diagonally across from Our Lady of Pompei. I had my two lattes and a pastry. As I was licking the pastry off my fingers, I realized what I needed to do to keep my promise to Vincent.

Paying my bill by throwing cash down on the table, I ran home, high on caffeine and sugar. I needed to talk to my mother but had no idea how to find her. Maybe Vita could help. But I hadn't seen her in days. On an instinct I went to Carbone's and found Vita Not Like Me sitting with an identical looking woman to her. I realized I could not interrupt, but I needed to talk to her. I smiled at her, and headed to the Lady's Room. Within a minute she was in there with me.

"What? You look like you've set yourself on fire!"

"I need to see my mother."

"You've told me often that you aren't ready to see her?"

"I have had some time with my father. Time just for me and him."

"That wasn't allowed by your mother?"

"It wasn't even an issue. She did the mothering, he was her partner. Very deeply in love with her."

"Have you been reading Freud?" Vita laughed as she said this.

"I know all about his theories. In my case, he was right. I loved my daddy in a way that was somehow threatening to both of them."

"All right. So you want to see your mother why?"

"I am going to plan how to get back Vincent's life's work."

"Your mother knows how to do what you want to do?"

"Nobody in New York gave a fundraiser like her."

"Ah."

"Can you see my plan?"

"No. But I can see your enthusiasm. And I know you can do whatever you want to these days."

"How do I find my mother, Vita?"

"I have no idea where she is or what she's been doing in her current Frequency. I will ask a few questions and get back to you."

"Hurry. I don't know how long Vincent has before the boys shoot him."

"I need to get back to my new—friend. But I'll find your mother in the next week at the most," she said as she stood.

"Thank you."

We air kissed on both cheeks. I smelled a trace of an unusual perfume which I assumed was what her new "friend" wore. I thought it was slightly cheesy as opposed to smelling opulent. Jealousy is a hard master to serve.

I stopped at a market, picked up some cat food, paper plates, bread and cheese. I moved on to my liquor store and bought two bottles of absinthe and three good red wines. Finally, I went into Carbone's and got some pasta to go. I felt the planning stage of my Way to Get Vincent's Paintings back, would require a lot of reflection and I wanted to be in my home to do it.

The sun was perfect, the leaves were turning, and Timothy Carbone was sitting on the stoop to my brownstone.

"Why didn't you just break in like you usually do?"

"I don't break in. I walk in. And only if you're there."

"A well-mannered version of you. How confusing."

"I'm hoping to have sex with you again when you're done hating me."

"I don't hate you. I just wish you were —"

Before I could finish, Tim jumped in. "I spent a few days with your mother. I understand you're looking for her?"

"Bullshit. What do you and my mother have in common?"

He smiled at me and I realized that he had been having sex with her.

"Why?!!!" I screamed. "How much more revenge do you need on me, Timothy."

"It's okay. I am confessing to you so you should use my confessional name."

"Why did you seduce my mother?"

"First of all, don't assume that's how it went. Your mother and I were in the same place at the same time. If anything, she came on to me."

"No."

"No? Because why? I'm not attractive enough?"

"Because." I said trying to sound nasty.

"Ah."

"Because she is too sophisticated to fall for your line, whatever it was."

"I said I was a friend of yours."

"And she seduced you?"

"Yup. Right down to the ass grabbing while she pulled down my zipper."

"Lying sack of crap. She's dead, she doesn't need sex."

"Will it inflame you further if I tell you what you just said is a huge pile of uninformed bullshit? Everybody is different. Your mother still feels her sexuality."

I decided I was getting too upset, as usual, while dealing with Mr. Carbone. So I started up the steps to my apartment. Tim followed me inside.

"She's very attractive. Looks a lot like you." Smirking.

"Shut up."

The Tabby was asleep on my bed, but as we entered, she woke up, I headed into the kitchen. Tim greeted her.

"Hello Louise! I'm glad you escaped the zoo. They're looking for you, you know."

"Just the reptiles?" The tabby asked him.

"No. A couple of human guards too."

I opened a can of cat food and put it on a plate in front of the cat.

"Thanks, but I'm not hungry."

I picked it up and put in on the kitchen counter.

"Eat it when you want it."

I left the cat and Tim to discuss the seriousness of her exile. Eventually she would be allowed back but not for a while. Tim offered her his place, but she said it was too dusty and she preferred to stay with me. I smiled when I overheard this from my bedroom where I had marched off to. Jealousy does have its rewards.

"Okay if I come into the Inner Sanctum?"

"What do you want from me? Another dinner at Penne y Pesce?"

"You should be grateful it was me who got that

assignment. I went easy on you. And clearly you came out on top."

"Did you enjoy your time in bed with my mother?"

"Yes." He smiled sweetly, annoying me a lot.

"Good." I shot back.

"And?"

"And nothing." Of course this was not true on my part.

"Now who's bullshitting?" Tim looked slightly serious.

"Fine. Do you like her better than you liked me?"

"I like her as a person better, she has no ambition but to enjoy learning about her new way of existing. But your desperation to figure out what's going on inside of you, makes you a nice edgy piece of ass."

Louise walked in.

"I'm going to see Ricky at the Deli. He swiped a big chunk of corned beef for us. I'll see you both later."

I was about to go open the front door for her to save her the long downhill climb, but she was already out my window and on her descent. I turned back to Tim.

"This is awkward."

"Why?" He looked pleased.

"I need a favor from you."

"I can put you in touch with your mother. She'd love to see you."

"What's the tariff? The charge? The quid pro quo?"

He smiled the sexy smile that had originally drawn me to him. He began to unbutton his shirt. Miraculously, he did not disgust me as he had at the end of my Trial by Fire in the Underworld at Penne y Pesce. In fact, he looked good.

"Why would I ever want to have sex with you after you betrayed me and then bedded my mother?"

"Because we do well together. And I'm no longer a threat to you."

By now, he was down to his jeans and opening his belt

buckle and unzipping his pants.

"Ask Vita if you don't believe me. I did my best to set you off your path, but I failed. I'm too big an opportunist to let that cost me a great fuck." Tim laughed, he liked being witty.

"You think that's a compliment? 'Deborah, Prophet, Warrior, Judge, Great fuck.'"

"It adds some dimension." He was right.

Tim was now on my bed and a strange desire for him came over me. I checked in my mind to see if Vita would come to me. She did not. The sun was going down, and there was a cork in a bottle of red wine by my bed that I knew would still be good. Without saying anything, I climbed into my bed.

Sadly, the sex was better than usual. I say "sadly" because I had shame about trusting him again. Shame about wanting to outdo my mother at an activity that really shouldn't be a contest. But Tim was a clever guy. This time I led the way, we did things exactly at my tempo, in my choice of postures. He knew enough not to try to play games, but just let me enjoy his body.

When we were done, Louise was on the large chair in my room and with her was the jauntiest little orange cat I had ever seen.

"Deborah, this is Ricky. I told you about him."

"Hello Ricky, I assume you know Tim."

"Old old friends. How are you Tim?"

"Working hard Ricky. Always working hard."

After this exchange the two cats went to sleep wrapped around each other and Tim and I got dressed. My anger had disappeared, so I offered him food.

"You want some of my take out?"

"No, I'm meeting somebody for dinner. You eat it."

"Can you get in touch with my mother?" Hard to ask him.

"Sure. What do you want me to tell her?"

"I have a plan that involves a marathon of parties in one

night. I need to pick her brain about this." The truth.

"I'll help." Tim was really trying.

"Okay. Go. Get my mother to contact me by whatever means she chooses. Please. The sooner the better."

"Not sure where she is right now, but I'll find her as fast as I can."

He kissed me on the forehead, grabbed a piece of bread I had laid out and left.

I had wanted to meet my mother at Carbone's. But in the end, her need to see my new place seemed reasonable to me, so here we were, sitting at my living-room table. My mother's physicality, like my father's was completely back to what I had known all my life. She was a handsome woman, a little taller than I am, slender, elegant. It was interesting to me in this new juxtaposition to realize that I had been very proud of her as a child. We didn't relate much, but she was the social engine for my father's organization, and she was smarter than most people I've known. Why hadn't I missed her?

"You didn't miss me because you never felt that I loved you."

"Please don't read my mind, mother. It makes me uneasy."

"Sorry dear."

"Daddy said you didn't want to have me. You got depressed."

"Yes. I did what you did with your own child, I was always there for you for the Mother things: sewing your costumes even if we had five events I was putting on that week. I made up in sweat equity what I had lacked in maternal instincts. And I did grow to love you very much."

"As much as you loved your life with dad? The feeling you shared with him of doing important work for the world while holding the hand of your debonair husband?"

"No."

"Did you cheat on him? Did he cheat on you?"

"No. And that took up a lot of my energy."

"You mean keeping tabs on him?"

"I mean keeping the marriage more alive than most. Even after many decades, your father was still my favorite human being on the earth. I still got a little thrill when he came home. I loved how he smelled."

"Me too." I was looking straight at my mother.

"You had normal feelings for your dad. Meaning you wanted to take him away from me. Unconsciously of course. You wanted to look pretty for him."

"And it was unrequited. He really did only have eyes for you."

"I suppose it doesn't matter now, but he had his own Freudian dilemma with you as you grew into a sexual being. He made his share of derisive comments about your boyfriends from the Catholic school."

This was thrilling information to me. "You knew about those boys?"

"Yes, Sweetie."

"You made no effort to stop me." I was curious about this.

"That was part of how we kept our marriage vital. We both loved you, but we didn't suffer your behavior like many parents do."

"That's how I treated my daughter. Build her a princess dress, take her to any place she needed a ride. Pay very little attention to what path she traveled or how it made her feel."

"But now it's different. Now you are a judge and you are helping her with complex decisions. I never really got there with you." My mother looked sad.

"Well, please get there now. I need your help."

"This Festival of Art Thievery you want to pull off?"

"Yes."

"I have to admit, it sounds like fun. But I have strategic questions for you that we will need to answer to do this right."

"Good. I was hoping you would put your brain to this. You have the best strategic brain of us all. Do you want a laptop or anything to write on?"

"I don't keep lists anymore."

"This will involve several households, all of them wealthy enough to have security of some kind. And we have to coordinate them each giving a party on the same night." I told her the obvious.

"Yes?" She was getting interested.

"First, we need to decide whether to replace the Van Gogh originals with brilliant copies or not. And if yes, how do we get those?" She was decisive in her response. Good.

"Of course, we have to replace every painting. Also, every frame although they don't need to be real gold and I have friends I can call on to do the framing for us. The issue is, who will do the copies of Van Gogh's masterpieces?"

"I have some ideas."

"Shoot them at me sweetheart."

"I think Matisse, Monet, and Otto Dix."

"Why not Gauguin? They're cousins." she said.

"Gauguin has been very angry at Van Gogh for judging him after he left his wife and moved to Tahiti. Van Gogh insulted his integrity, wounded his ego. I don't think we can count on him."

"Ah."

"And although Otto Dix is not their contemporary, he is the most amazing painter and he lived through Hitler. I think he will be with us in the spirit of democratizing the art."

"Yes. That sounds right. And you've met him?" she asked.

"Not formally, but I have danced at the club he was in. I got a strong sense of who he is. And his paintings are among the only depictions of women and men dancing on equal footing. In Weimar days."

"Matisse, Monet, and Dix. How many paintings do we need

to retrieve?"

"I want the major works back. Anything that is not in a museum but once was, or should have been. Everything from Arles that is not in public view." My plan was getting clearer.

"Talk to him. Don't be too specific about our plan yet. I don't want him disappointed if we run into a wall. Drink some absinthe and let him talk. Then we'll make our choices, and find who owns them, and where they are hanging. Most of these people have multiple homes, we have to figure out the logistics of which homes hold which paintings. We will need your Egyptian friends for some carrying in and out too."

"We both have planning to do before we meet again mother."

"Yes, my darling. You talk to Van Gogh, get Isis and her family involved, and eventually you should approach the painters. You will need to use flattery of course."

"Of course. I learned from the best." That was who she was.

"I will put together the names of paintings," she said. "Their owners and where they are currently hanging. I will talk to my framers and make sure they know how to duplicate the frames properly. When we are further along, we must plan times, dates and specific ins and outs of who to rob first."

"Thank you, mother."

"My pleasure. I've missed the parties your father and I threw to raise money. This will be a new adventure! You and I will of course dress to the teeth in outfits we can put together as we go along."

"I love you, mother."

"I love you, too. And let's not forget that Clinique has a Gift with Purchase going on right now. Even those of us who live in many time frequencies can use a good lipstick."

This was, for no understandable reason, the most loving thing my mother had ever said to me. And because I could not cry on her lap, I began to laugh. She began to laugh and soon we were both laughing so hard that the Tabby came in to see what was going on. We explained our plan to her. She seemed annoyed.

"You feel no need at all for my help?" Louise asked.

"Yes, of course. We can barely pull this off without you."

"I can crawl up twenty stories and climb into an apartment to make sure everything is as we need it to be. Can Isis and Osiris do that?" She swished her striped tail.

"Absolutely not. You are an invaluable member of the team." I would've patted her on the head, but she didn't like that.

"Do you have any chicken? Ricky missed his chance to grab us a bite at the deli and I am famished."

Happily, I had decided to put food in my kitchen on the off chance that my mother and I would want to nibble as we drank. There was a lovely array of Tabby friendly foods laid out on my kitchen counter. I led Louise to them. She jumped up, sniffed around and went off to get Ricky from the Deli to share her bounty.

I went in to say goodbye to my mother, and instead, I found her note.

"My sweetest child, I am so proud to be your mother. You are truly an amazement to me. Talk tomorrow."

She and my father had perfected the unspoken goodbye. I was not insulted by it any more. I don't remember ever having felt as excited and surrounded by love as I did in this moment.

Chapter Thirteen
The Leaves Dwindled Down

IT WAS AUTUMN IN ARLES. The flowers I had fondled on one of my first visits here were gone. Instead, there were brightly colored orange, red, yellow leaves on the ground, on some tree branches, on the path outside of Vincent's where I was standing as he prepared lunch for us.

"Bon. Je suis pret. Allez."

"Here I come. Oh my, that smells fantastic. Onion soup?"

"Oui. I was a little low on francs for a few days. I've been gorging on this soup with some bread a friend baked. The cheese was donated by a friend with a cow."

"Are you out of absinthe? I can go get a bottle."

He smiled at me. It was a friendly if ironic smile. Without another word, he ladled out the cheesy, brilliant onion soup for us. Laid out big spoons. Then bent underneath the cabinet and brought out a full bottle of absinthe. He poured us each a tumbler full and we sat down to eat. And talk.

"I am putting together a team of people to retrieve your paintings from private homes."

"What will you do about the police coming after you?"

"We plan to hang replacements—copies—in frames that look identical to those we steal."

"These people will not notice?" He seemed surprised.

This time it was my turn for a friendly if ironic smile. "The people who can afford your paintings know nothing, but the price tag and the prestige of a painting. And we are not having the copies done carelessly. We will enlist painters who worship and understand your art."

"The paints themselves? The way to make yellow was one of the biggest catastrophes of my life. You know 'was there mango in the pigment along with certain kinds of animal urine?' and on and on. I don't know what you can do about this and remain authentic, even to the most unschooled eye."

"We are doing expert recreations. The same materials as you used."

"I don't know what to say." He looked like a little boy.

"You need to give me a detailed list of every variation of everything you painted. We have to track down the ones that don't hang on public walls. We have to know who bought each one and which of their mansions the painting is in."

"Why?"

"Why are we doing this?"

"Yes."

"You've said your paintings are your words. They symbolize the statements you want to make about life as you have seen it. One of my discoveries since my descent into hell, is about symbols. They become stories. And stories are what people learn from and re-enact. Ferreting out the good from the corrupted stories is vital.

"You have taken on a Biblical name."

"I have. And surely the stories in the *Bible* have caused some of our greatest misunderstandings as a species. We cannot reclaim those, but we can use the parts that help. Others have taken on the persona of Eve. I feel so sorry for them. I am Deborah. And I am trying to become stronger, fairer, more loving. And a better fighter."

"Do you compare my paintings to the written word?"

"When I first looked at the Arles bedroom as a child, I would get scared. And I would have to walk away from it so nobody would see me crying."

"Why?"

"The story was so clear. The man in the simple home who could paint images that came from another universe. A universe I wanted to enter."

"That was my story?" he asked.

"That was the possibility your paintings created. For millions of people. A vision of the universe that was different. That presumes there is hope."

Vincent jumped up and cleared the table. He brought a piece of paper and covered the table with it. He had a crayon in his hand. He began to list his works. He created categories first: ARLES, SUNFLOWERS, PARIS, NIGHT SKY, and on through his works. He drank absinthe straight from the bottle and as he got more blissful, he would doodle a little example from every painting he listed. It was magnificent.

When he was done, he gently rolled up the piece of paper and gave it to me. "Thank you, Deborah. I am deeply honored."

By this time he was so absinthe'd that he handed me the roll of paper and stumbled back out to his garden to stare in stony wonderment at the stars. I stepped out of the painting, back through the museum, and walked in the gorgeous autumn air all the way home.

I halfway expected to see Tim, or my mother or Vita in my apartment. Instead, Set and Nephthys were sprawled on my bed watching my TV.

"You're back!" I was so glad to see them.

"Yes, we got back two hours ago. Isis immediately filled us in on this nefarious plan and we were here fifteen minutes later!"

"Are you hungry? Would you like absinthe or wine?"

"No. We're here for a very short time. We both yearn for the dry air of our home. But we want to get involved in this caper so we're here to do that." Nephthys gave Set an affectionate poke.

"Shall I lay out the general scheme and let you ask questions?"

"We know the general plan. We are ready to weigh in with ideas for how to carry it out." Set jumped in.

"And maybe a glass of wine would be pleasant." Nephthys added.

I ran to the kitchen got three glasses, a semi full bottle and a big piece of chocolate pastry. I wasn't sure if their diet included chocolate, but we would know soon enough. I returned to my bedroom to find the two mammoth figures crouched over my desktop computer. They were researching art heists that had never been solved.

I spread out the glasses, wine and chocolate, and joined in the research.

We argued about which articles to read. There are a lot of art heists in history. I had never really thought about this, but Nephthys and Set were pretty much geniuses both in terms of specifics of thefts, and more interestingly, in their assessment of why art would be so attractive to steal.

Of course we can all talk about how much money a slightly slippery person could get selling paintings to the ultra-rich collectors. But the fascinating stuff was their description of art and its connection to the very essence of life. Set, who is in many ways a coarse thuggish mythological creature, had a very moving way of talking about art.

"Life is empty," he said. "The lucky human fills their life with things, either material or ethereal to escape mortality, boredom, bad sex, etcetera. But art, fills people up. Even the dumbest mortal may be moved by paintings."

"Why do you think that is?" I asked him.

"It's a vision of something real enough for the painter to create on canvas, but it doesn't actually exist." He was a little frustrated with my ignorance.

"And?" Here Nephthys nudged Set to go on..

"And it blunts some of the sorrow of mortality. Something can exist and not exist. Like life. Although that's wrong. Once you have lived, you are forever on the Spacetime Tape. "

"Yes, but the average living thing can't just go there like we can." Nephthys pointed out to Set.

"I am so lucky, looking at Vincent's paintings in Arles, always gave me a yearning to go live there. To never leave."

"You leave every time you visit him." Nephthys said.

"I have to. I can't stay in another century indefinitely. Maybe that's the sadness I feel."

"And you have this charming place here," Set said. "So reminiscent of you in another time in your life."

I was surprised that Set had realized that my return to the West Village was an attempt to return to my very early childhood home. Before my parents had bought a huge brown stone mere steps from Riverside Park, the highway and the Hudson River.

Nephthys interrupted my thought. "You never belonged uptown."

"I know."

"And Connecticut?" Set sounded slightly sick to his stomach.

"I was doing the expected thing."

"You left that life within hours of your husband's death." Nephthys took Set's side for once.

"Not within hours. It took two weeks. My daughter had moved to the city with her husband. I didn't have to stay there one more minute than it took to empty out that life."

"Look!" Set had gotten bored with my short chat with Nephthys and he had found research material on a particular art heist. "I have read ten stories of ten big heists," he said. "There are several that were never solved. The thieves never captured, the paintings never returned. These are our models."

We bent over the article he had pulled up on the computer. He scrolled back to the top of it and the three of us read it through together.

"The largest number of paintings stolen in one night was 13." Nephthys read.

"And they got away with it!" I was drunk and enthusiastic.

"They didn't have four mythic Egyptian royals, two standard house cats, several extremely clever humans, and two Losts with them. We should be able to pull off twice that number." Set saw the larger possibilities.

We printed out several of the articles and sat for a few hours drinking and underlining the specifics of what was stolen, what was retrieved, who the painters were, etc. After this study session Set and Nephthys clearly wanted a break.

"Would you two like to be alone for a bit? I can work in the dining room, and I have a bunch of calls to make."

After my horrible encounters with Set, it was lovely to see him staring at his partner with a tenderness I didn't think he was capable of. And as much as Nephthys had insulted Set in different ways, her look at him right now was mythic. Forever. The love of a woman for a perpetual "bad boy."

They got up and stretched, I picked up what I needed to work in the other room. As I took myself out of my bedroom, I saw them already launched on my bed into some primitive, thousands of years old, love sex that I had to force myself not to stare at. A sweet smell came off their bodies in a thin film I could actually see. Were these pheromones? They were paying no attention to me, so I allowed myself one more glance. The thin film was now a golden screen of the wispiest fabric I had ever seen. It created an enclosure in which they could enjoy each other. And they seemed to be doing that with great gusto as I left the room.

My mother was sitting in my kitchen. I was so happy to see her. Our relationship was incredible now that the rules were gone: She is not living on the earth, I still am. And that seemed like the least of the changes: she had acknowledged her ambivalence about me as a child and that had freed us up. It had relieved a lot of the loneliness I had felt when I was around my parents, who only had eyes for each other. It also made me understand my relationship to my own child, which was now quite deep. My love for my one offspring had grown exponentially to my understanding of the universe.

I had planned to call my daughter for a quick catch-up while my bedroom was in use, but instead I caught my mother up on our research about art heists. She in turn filled me in on the number of painters she had already signed up to make the fake frames, which would be fake only in terms of the amount of gold on the frame. They just wouldn't be as gold as the originals, although it would be very hard to tell. She explained it to me and then went off to do more work on her task.

My daughter called. These days I was happy when I heard the robo voice announce her name.

"Hello sweetheart. How are you?"

"I'm doing well, mother. Thanks again for all that money."

"Of course. My pleasure."

"I've invited Bodhi to move in."

For a minute I couldn't understand—Bodhi? Ah yes the New England Yogi.

"That's interesting. Does he like children?"

"He loves them. He's just never wanted to father a child."

"Ah." I hoped she didn't hear the irony in my voice.

"I mean literally. He has a little thing about his sperm. That he doesn't talk about much, but I think it's connected to his Yoga practice."

"Ah."

"Does this sound stupid to you?" She sounded scared.

"Not at all. If he likes children how he gets them is unimportant."

"Exactly."

"Are you getting a divorce?"

"No. I'm just getting a financial arrangement whereby he can't have any of the money you gave me. And I won't ask him for child support."

"Ah."

"He feels that he won't be able to stand seeing his child raised by Bodhi instead of him."

"What will be his relationship to the child?"

"I haven't decided yet. I'm going to a retreat this weekend to do a Vision thing."

"Sorry?" I had no idea what she was talking about.

"A Vision Quest. You sit alone for 24 hours, with food and water, but no human contact. You ask for your internal voices to give you their vision of what you need."

"Yes, okay."

"It's no stranger than what you've been doing. Is it?"

"Not strange at all. Any path to understanding what life is, is a path I'm glad to see you on."

"Bodhi suggested it."

"Wonderful. I'm glad you have him."

"Thank you, mother. That means everything to me."

"We should visit soon. Right now I'm in the middle of a big project that I will tell you all about when I see you."

"I'll be gone from tomorrow for six days. It's a full two-day drive each way."

"Where are you going?" I wondered where two days would take them.

"It's not clear yet." She sounded embarrassed.

"But you plan on a two-day voyage each way?"

"I have to go mother. The roots are boiling over and I need them for my plant medicines."

Oh my. Roots to go with her plant medicines. Well, I knew this could be totally legitimate in the hands of a real healer—I doubted that Bill or Bodhi was that, but I kept my judgement to myself.

"I love you my sweet. Have a charmed—Vision Thing."

"It will be wonderful. Bodhi makes me so happy. Even just counting backwards from 100 is fun with him."

"Call when you get home!"

We hung up. My mother looked up from her work.

. "Vision Thing?"

"Yes, mother. Just like the Native Americans. And many other indigenous peoples."

My mother smiled at me. It was like the first time I had lied to Tim. She knew exactly how dumb I thought the idea was of having a man move in with her. A man who had issues about sperm. But she also knew that you can't tell anybody what to do, and at least my daughter would have somebody in the house if the baby ever needed another set of hands. Yes, I was embarrassed.

I received a text after my mother left. On it was an address to a warehouse off of the West Side Highway—far downtown. It simply said the address. I got dressed, grabbed a jacket for the autumn weather, and ran out my door. On the street outside was Ricky, the Deli Cat. "You heading over to the warehouse?" he asked.

"Yes. What's going on there?"

"Painting. Painters," Ricky said. "It smells rancid from the way they've authentically mixed their colors. But I understand your mother had food sent in so if you don't mind, I'll drop by with you, grab a couple of things and head back here to share with Louise."

"Walk or taxi?"

"Taxi. I'm hungry and I have to walk back."

I waved down a cab, slipped Ricky into my tote bag, gave the address and soon we arrived. The cat jumped down to the ground and led the way. It was one of the only warehouse buildings left in this part of town. The air smelled of the river, and there was a mild breeze blowing. The cat stopped at a bright red door.

"Here?" I asked him.

"Open it, please."

I opened the door and we entered a world that encompassed several centuries of the finest painters on this planet. I spotted Matisse, Otto Dix, and Monet, but there were many others I did not immediately recognize. They were all either intently bent over a painting or scarfing down what Ricky had correctly predicted would be the elaborate spread my mother had ordered.

"See you home later Deb," Ricky said. "Is it okay if I call you Deb?"

"I prefer Deborah. Sorry to be snooty, but it sounds more like who I want to become."

"No flies on me, Deborah. Later!"

Ricky headed to the enormous table of food. At a loss without opposable thumbs, the cat showed an incredible ingenuity for filling a paper plate with more than it could hold. Then he brought over another paper plate with his teeth, plopped it on top of everything and walked over to Matisse. He put a gentle claw in the painter's leg, which startled him, but he looked down kindly at Ricky. Ricky explained (in French of course!) that he needed to borrow Matisse's thumbs for a few seconds. The cat and the painter put the two plates together with the food stuffed in between. Then, Matisse had the idea to take a piece of string he had in his pocket and close the whole thing up. Finally, he took a beautiful scarf he was wearing and made a backpack that he tied onto Ricky firmly and opened the red door for the cat's exit.

I felt this gave me an opening, so I approached Matisse. I introduced myself, thanked him with all my heart for his help and was about to get into a conversation about his rather stunning copy of a Parisian café when Otto Dix joined us.

"You look familiar?" He addressed this to me.

"We met in Weimar, Café Metropole. You were dancing, I was drinking."

"Yes! You're the one who killed the stinking brown shirt!"

"I am."

"You know they used that as an excuse to close down the Metropole."

"I'm sorry."

"It was a good thing. We had all been lulled into thinking the Nazi's were just clownish jackals, not to be feared. Your encounter with the thug opened our eyes. Saved my life. They didn't like men in dresses. Probably too close to home for them."

"You think the Nazis were gay?"

"Grim not gay. But do I think many favored sex with each other. Look at their uncontrollable fear of women. Their disdain for people making choices about who to love? Yes, certainly some of them were in tight, ugly closets that made them tight and ugly."

Matisse had grown restless while I talked to Dix. "She was speaking with me when you inserted yourself into the conversation, Otto."

Otto Dix bowed to me, gave Matisse the finger, and walked back to his painting.

"So this is all because of you—your transition?" he asked.

"It came from a conversation I had with Vincent. He was horrified that his work had become displays of wealth for people for whom he has no regard."

"I understand. My work does not get the attention of Vincent's, but still, many of my paintings have landed in second bedrooms in beach mansions. It is very depressing."

"I'm sorry."

"Or worse, greeting cards, wrapping paper, sheets. Taking my designs and colors and sticking them on sheets?!! Where people spill their bodily fluids during moments of ecstasy if I'm lucky, and from incontinence if I'm not."

"You are considered a great master painter. Does that help at all?"

"No."

Matisse turned to walk away in a snit. Then he pivoted back to me.

"Accept my apologies Deborah. What you are doing elevates us all. I can be petty. Especially around Otto Dix!"

With no explanation for his antipathy towards Dix, who I found quite kind and charming, Henri Matisse headed back to his copy of one of Vincent's paintings.

I strolled around the warehouse in total wonderment. There were ten or more long tables and on each one there were at least two canvasses being copied by incomparably talented men and women. Yes. There were women master painters and I did not know their names. A shame came over me.

"Excuse me. I am Deborah, I think your paintings are wonderful."

"Yes."

"You are Elizabeth Shippen Green?"

She turned to stare at me. She stared in an angry amazement that quickly turned to a huge, broad smile. "How do you know my name?"

I had to lie. "I am a great admirer of your work. And I cannot thank you enough for taking the time to help with this project."

"I'm dead. My time is my own. Anyway, I'm sorry I snapped at you. I didn't get much recognition in my lifetime. At least not as much as I would've liked."

"To be honest. I know who you are because your name came into my head when I saw you. I probably have stared at your paintings in a museum."

"Not bloody likely."

"Ah."

"It's all right. I keep on working. Vincent has his sorrows, I have mine, no artist ever really gets past their pain."

I pledged at that moment to look up women artists and

educate myself. I thought the Strand would certainly have illustrated books, and maybe even the mercurial Mr. Carbone would weigh in. He is a sexist, but an admitted one. So much cleaner than the liars.

I wandered away after a few more pleasantries with Ms Green. I found myself standing next to Claude Monet. I thought for a minute I would faint. It was like Van Gogh, even though I've never wanted to live on a water lily the way I wanted to live in the wooden house in Arles.

"Hello *.monsieur.*"

"Deborah?"

"Yes."

"This is a marvelous idea of yours. I am thoroughly revived after years wandering around to see how my paintings are holding up under museum lighting."

"Beautifully. They are fantastic works."

"Yes. I made my contribution and I was well paid for it. If you discuss me with Vincent he will call me a talented opportunist. But I needed the money, Van Gogh seemed to live on very little. Although miraculously his wallet always contained sufficient francs for a bottle of absinthe."

"If Vincent does have any criticism of you it would only be because he is so saddened by his paintings becoming status symbols to people he cares nothing about."

"I understand. I have my share of paintings that were purchased by the useless among us."

"But you are also hanging in any museum in the world that has any Impressionist collection."

"I founded that movement. I brought us together in Paris. I arranged for gallery exhibits. I deserve recognition."

Clearly he was not shy about his success.

"Do you like her work?" I pointed to Elizabeth Shippen Green who was back to complete absorption in her painting.

"Of course. She learned a lot from me. But her talent is

prodigious and she never got the success she deserved. The lot of a woman artist is dog shit."

"Hypocrite!!!" The voice that yelled at Monet was from a large woman, dressed like a 19th century painter, which is what she is. Or was.

"You will make it better," the large woman said. "This wild-eyed art thievery on behalf of Vincent will come off smoothly and you will be ready for the next rectification. You could call attention to the brilliant women whose names nobody knows. I am one of them." She extended her paint dripping hand to me, "Berthe Morisot."

"Yes, yes. How exciting. You standing right here and working on this project."

"You have no idea who I am do you my dear?"

Otto Dix walked by just at this moment with a huge turkey leg he was working on. He had a cloth napkin wrapped around it to keep the grease off of his work.

"Nobody knows my name either. Everything isn't about your sex."

He strolled away before either of us could respond.

"Well, everything is about his sex! Brilliant man, totally destroyed by the Nazis for his little cross-dressing tendencies."

"Is that true?"

"How the hell should I know? We lived decades apart. But I do know he fancied himself in a nice frock during Weimar. And I know the Nazis ended up calling him a degenerate. Put it together for yourself."

"Yes. I will," I said.

"I need to paint," Berthe said. "I left some stars that need completion."

"Wait! Do you think being a woman was an impediment to getting the acknowledgement you deserved?"

Morisot looked at me like I was a badly learning disabled chimpanzee. "Yes."

She turned and walked off. I wanted to ask her more, but I realized how stupid the questions were. I looked up her paintings on my phone and even in one inch squares I could tell they were magnificent. On a par with Monet, Renoir, any of the Impressionists. I watched as she returned to her painting station. She did not look in any way disturbed, although it's hard to tell with the 19th century garb and the totally different feel than a modern woman would have. But still. She was steady, self assured, and once she was bent over her painting, any hint of injustice or lack of recognition had been replaced with her sheer mastery. I was relieved.

I walked over to the food area to see if my mother had ordered any wine.

Of course the table looked like a vineyard, but there were myriad choices ranging from chilled champagne in buckets of ice, to vodka, absinthe, and even some hoity toity beer. The foods on display were beyond even this.

I was reminded of the fundraising parties my mother gave so adeptly to keep my father's organization afloat. For tonight, she had kept the food low on the animal chain: no red meat, a lot of turkey, vegetables in sauces that made me weak, breads, pastries, and desserts she had clearly gotten from Vienna. I grabbed a piece of smoked tuna and moved on.

I had put together a small plate for myself, and of course a large glass of absinthe. By now, I was in Wonderland—every table was covered with Vincent's masterpieces: the variants of yellow and blue mixed with the hallucinogens in the liquor had sent me to a world I had never visited before. I halfway expected the Red Queen or at least the Mad Hatter to hop in.

Instead, the red door swung open to a whooshing sound that I assumed was wind. But I was wrong. The sound came from the entry of Isis, Osiris, Set and Nephthys who had created the wind as they flew through the centuries to get here.

I put down the food, kept the glass of absinthe and

approached them. "You're all here!"

"Yes, we got Vita's message."

"Oh. Well, could you fill me in?"

Isis was very kind, although I felt strangely out of the loop not knowing what was going on.

"Vita and your mother called us to a strategy session. The paintings are coming along well, and it's time to begin the specific plan for the heist."

"Heist?"

Set was ridiculing his sister.

"Remember my darling, how you stomped your way into that pyramid after Giovanni Belzoni had pushed the door open? You stole everything you could stuff in your bag. That is a heist."

"I know that. I was just making conversation." Set chuckled.

Isis, Nephthys and Osiris nodded sympathetically at his desperate need to be part of everything.

"So where and when exactly is the strategy session?" I felt foolish asking, but I pretended to mere curiosity.

"Here. Now. In the back."

Isis hung back with me while the other three went to get food and drink. She laughed watching Set.

"If you're surprised to see Set here helping, I will let you in on a secret: Nepthys caught him in another of his insulting rape dramas. This time with a woman who had died young and had come to Ma'at for his judgement on her future. Set whisked her out of this incredibly important meeting with our spiritual Judge, and was having his way with her when Nepthys came upon them. She came very close to chopping him to pieces with a nearby scythe, but instead, she told him he could redeem his dismal misbehavior by participating in this art plan. He had no choice but to come along. And he will, in fact, do a good job because Nepthys was angrier than I have seen her in two thousand years."

Isis joined her family at the table as they perused my
mother's food and drink offering. They each grabbed a bottle
of champagne and not much else. They headed to the very
back of the large warehouse where a black door I had not
noticed was slightly ajar. I followed along.

Inside, to my great surprise, were Vita, and my mother.

"Hello!"

I tried to sound like I belonged. Nobody much cared. In the
good sense. Of course I was welcome.

"Everybody seems to have picked out a drink, please have a
seat, Vita and I have put together an agenda."

All of us were seated.

"My daughter has been meeting with Vincent Van Gogh, as
you all know. The purpose of this endeavour, is in part, to give
him back his rights to the work he did by taking his paintings
out of the hands of his billionaire patrons. The principles of
this are clear to me. But we still have a big question to answer."

"Yes. It has taken a bit of brain work to come up with
something that could serve the dual purpose of putting Van
Gogh's soul at rest before he is shot, and also finding a place
for the original paintings we will take back from where they
currently hang, and show them on walls where they can change
lives.." Vita sounded very serious.

Isis spoke up.

"Have you decided how we can distribute these magnificent
pieces?"

"Yes." Mother answered her.

"My family is very sensitive to the wholesale filching of art
objects that happened to so many pyramids. Granted that
those objects did not belong buried in a pyramid, they usually
were stolen and sold purely for their financial worth. We are
saddened to see works made by hand 5,000 years ago sitting on
desks next to the computers of hedge fund owners, cyber
billionaires, and in one case, I believe a *faince* and gold statue of

Osiris, my brother and husband, is being used as a door stop in a grotesquely tasteless home somewhere in Russia."

There was a respectful moment of silence as we tried to figure out which Oligarch had a statue of Osiris in his home. My mother continued the conversation.

"What we have decided to do, is to distribute these paintings where the people who will see it, will get their first look at the wonderment on the canvas."

"Although not their first look at this kind of art." Vita chimed in.

"Our plan is to go to museums that already have one or two Van Gogh's hanging, and add a new one to the collection."

"If I may," this was Osiris speaking, "there are places in Egypt and all of Africa, where the paintings would go unnoticed by anybody capable of returning them to their purchasers. There are cities nobody has heard of, where the population believes in traditions of pantheism, and where Vincent's imagination would fit perfectly with their believe in spirits living in the natural world."

It was my mother who answered.

"We talked a lot about that: bring the paintings to countries where no Van Gogh canvas has ever been hung. But it felt a little imperialistic, you know? These cultures have their own traditions to worship through art. Van Gogh is part of the development of Western Capitalism. There's no gain from denying that."

"So suddenly these masterpieces arrive at the Louvre, or L'Hermitage, or the Metropolitan?" Set sounded skeptical.

"Yes." My mother sounded very comfortable.

"Then the billionaires who have purchased them will know they were robbed?" More skeptical.

"These wealthocrats have had no problem buying art that the Nazis stole and never were punished for."

"Well, some of them were punished, posthumously." Set

interjected. Osiris jumped on him.

"If you mean that lots of Nazi descendants are now mere workers, driving cabs in New York or building Volkswagens somewhere, then too bad."

"But won't the owners think they were sold forgeries." Nepthys was always practical.

"I hope so. Because there's not much they can do about it." Osiris chuckled at his own cleverness.

"They can go back to the seller and demand their money back."

"The sellers were huge auction houses. They will demand authentication and then the fun begins." Mother.

"Why fun?" Isis was also pragmatic and curious.

"Because. The way they have re-created the paints, is identical to everything that Vincent himself did. There is no way to tell which is a fraud and which the original." I was surprised Osiris knew this.

"But…."

"It explodes the idea that anybody can be certain that they own an original piece of work from a dead artist. This will bring the value down low enough that small museums throughout the world will be able to afford them." Again, a pragmatism Osiris was not known for.

"Is that going to satisfy Vincent?" Isis asked him.

I took on this question.

"Yes. Vincent's poems as he calls them, were made to speak to the public. They contain his deepest thoughts about religion. It allows millions more people to see life and death through his eyes. That's why he paints."

"To share his own religion?"

"No, Isis. To share the sorrows and beauty of mortality."

"And all the litigation that might happen?" Set was right about this possibility, and looked ghoulishly thrilled to bring it up.

"Brings the issue to the front lines: who should own art?" I answered.

"It's big business. You're messing with something huge." Set was by no means opposed to this, but he did enjoy throwing a monkey wrench in.

"Isn't that a good thing?" This from my mother.

The discussion was going on among everybody at the meeting. It was fast and full throated arguing about where art belongs on this planet. I came to understand that in other solar systems, art was the highest form of commodity and was not for sale. But these were solar systems that contained carbon based life forms who lived vastly differently than our little earth: no animal ate another. No person had more than any other. Nobody suffered from want. Our planet clearly had nothing in common with these others.

Based on that conclusion, that earth is essentially filled with myriad injustices and terrible inequities, the group tilted towards letting the owners of the filched masterworks know that they had either been fooled or robbed. And it didn't really matter to us because either way, the attention it would bring to the subject would allow more people to be involved in art, and less involved in their other, more mundane distractions from mortality.

My mother and I shared a good laugh about giving up going to department stores each season to scarf up a Gift with Purchase. It was one of our meaningless leftover pleasures and we agreed to keep doing it. There was still a thrill to the picking which tone of makeup you wanted your gift to have. Which little bag it would be packaged in. So incredibly meaningless. We agreed that we each needed some worthless something once in a while.

Mother was learning how to transition from her life on earth, to her life in Time and Space. I was trying to become a heroine, using as a model a lesser known Biblical woman. We deserved some extra mascara we would never use.

The meeting went on to discuss how to get the canvasses, some of them very large, in and out of homes. A list was brought forward of the most important paintings and where they were currently hanging. We left it to our four mythic Egyptians to get into each of these homes and figure out how to get the painting out during the course of a party in another part of the house.

We considered stealing paintings while their owners were on vacation somewhere else. There was nobody on earth with enough money to buy one of Vincent's paintings who didn't have other houses, and many places to go for pleasure.

If it wasn't for the obnoxiously rich, polluting the planet in every way from physical to spiritual, where would be?

It seemed smartest after quite a bit of thinking, to check the schedules of the super-rich painting owners, and create one irresistible event that all of them would want to attend.

The four Egyptians were approximately eight feet tall. They were actually bronzed in real bronze so clearly they looked less like a huge person, and more like a god or goddess. This had its advantages. For those canvases that would be removed during our party, the huge, gorgeously dressed mythics could fly from home to home in seconds finding each painting. But who did that leave with the strength to move the paintings?

As we were chewing on this detail, Tim Carbone entered the meeting. This was apparently what he had been working on. He carried a large roll of paper that reminded me of the roll Vincent himself had given me that listed his paintings. Tim placed the roll in the center of all of us on the floor, we all sat on the ground and began to examine his map.

Many of the paintings were in New York. Some in Moscow. There had been a flurry of Japanese billionaires buying up Van Gogh's. In fact, it seemed this next piece of research, begun by Tim, would take some time.

We agreed to meet again in ten days. At the warehouse. By then we would be bringing in the framers to add their magic to the canvases which would hopefully be dry. At the same time, we would each bring our research findings: where each canvas was, where the owner would be for the next two months. This intelligence on schedules would allow us to plan a huge gala that most or all of them would be able to attend.

It was clear this could not be rushed, but at the same time, the "changing" of the originals for the forgeries needed to happen in one fell swoop or we could get stopped by security measures that we hadn't anticipated.

Everybody filed out of the meeting room and went back to the food table. Some of us fanned out to admire the work of the painters. I went to look at the women forgers. My mother came with me.

"I never knew any of these women existed. And you took me to so many museums."

"You thought Camille Pisarro was a woman. Remember?"

"Yes, mother."

"I'm sorry I didn't think to introduce you to more women artists."

"You read lots of books by women."

"I did. Thank you. That makes me feel better."

"Mother? Shall we go on a little trip together?"

"You mean looking at the paintings of women that hang in museums?"

"Exactly."

"As soon as this job is done. Let's make it a plan."

"Right. Of course. First, we accomplish this."

My mother and I had poured ourselves big glasses, she took the champagne, I chose absinthe. Then I filled a plate with some food, and we went to sit together and chat.

Tim had gone. The Egyptians were gone. And now I noticed Vita too, had slipped out. I sat with the woman with whom I had spent my first 20 years, not really knowing her at all.

Chapter Fourteen
Moscow Nights

FROM THE ENORMOUS picture window, I stared out at Moscow. It was night time and the lights made Red Square look like a set for an expensive movie: three-dimensional and totally fantastical.

I needed to stop staring at St. Basil's Cathedral and return to my hosts at the dinner party they were giving for me. Tim had made this meeting along with an identity for me—I was a major New York art dealer. Here I was in the home of a Russian whose billions were less impressive than his capacity for vodka. And blinis. This man was part of a large black market in art that I had never discovered in my research for the private Van Gogh's that had not been put in museums.

The trip had begun the night before when Tim found me at home studying the official roster of who had bought which Van Gogh and for how much. He had taken the pages out of my hands and torn them up. I was about to get angry when I looked at his face and saw the smile that meant he was about to bring me deep inside something I would otherwise never experience

"I found a dealer in Moscow," he said. "I need to get into his house and find exactly where he keeps his Van Gogh."

Tim pulled two airplane tickets out of his leather bag and handed them to me. They were dated for midday the following day and they were for first class passage from JFK to Sheremetyevo Airport servicing Moscow.

"How did you know?" I asked.

"You know how I knew."

"Did I tell you? While we were embroiled in a little sexual come-as-you-are party?"

"No."

"Okay. I see. It's Timothy the Silent is it?"

"No. It's Timothy the If You Want to go to Moscow then I better have a good dinner and some real fun tonight."

"These tickets are for tomorrow!"

"I know. So we don't have much time for sex." He laughed. Then he began to undress.

"Wait! I have to find my passport and pack and let a few people know."

"I have a passport for you, in the name you'll want to use. We'll arrive with time to go to Gum's and get you a perfect outfit. Our dinner invitation is for 9. The Russians eat late. Takes time to prepare their stomachs. So we will arrive around 8:45 and you should already be sauced, because they will be."

"Why would they want to meet with me?"

"Look at the name on your passport."

He handed it to me. I opened it to find a better-than- usual passport picture of me. The name on the front page was Anastasia Romanov.

"You don't think they'll notice?"

"The guards at customs? No. They won't notice."

"But isn't she dead? And wouldn't she be two hundred by now?"

"Wanna do it with our clothes on?"

"Okay. I'll take your word for it. First class to Moscow. Then we're greeted by an emissary of the people we will dine with. I'm supposed to be the granddaughter is that it?"

"Yes. Are you so sure she didn't live and have a family?"

"You've made it clear to them that I may Not Be Who I Say I Am?"

"They're Russian. Lying is compulsory. Especially when dealing in high volumes of rubles. You deal in black market art and they are bored with their Van Gogh. They want a new painting."

"By whom?"

"We'll find out tomorrow night. Then we'll have one of your merry forgers make it for them."

"Berthe Morisot. That's who I want."

"Sisterhood is Powerful."

"Shut up and take your pants off. I'm not a cartoon character of second-wave feminism."

He began to undress and so did I. We were moving as we did this toward the bedroom, but we usually didn't make it to the bed and tonight was no different. When we were both done, I realized I hadn't eaten all day.

"Want dinner?"

"I want to know how you do that twisty thing you do."

"Buy me dinner, I'll tell you where I learned that."

"I know where you learned it. From one of the lucky lads at Our Lady of Pompeii, I want to know how you pull it off so perfectly."

"Okay, I'll explain and then you tell me about the Romanovs over dinner. I should know enough to get through the caviar course tomorrow night."

"Da."

We were in Carbone's at a nice quiet table towards the back, drinking and eating bread as the lesson began. Tim had known the Romanovs of course. I believe he and the Czarina may have practiced her version of the twisty thing. But I wasn't sure. Anyway, Tim's knowledge of the transition from Russian Dynasty to Soviet Russia to Russian Oligarchic ruthlessness was extensive. I was transfixed.

How many stories include a mad monk—or was he really mad? A family in desperate need of a male heir because their only male heir had hemophilia? And the truthful or totally bullshit story of how the terrible Bolsheviks had killed them all? It was like Gothic, operatic in scope, the 1917 Revolution. And Tim included spicy stuff about Vladimir Lenin and his hatred for Joe Stalin.

As we consumed the wine, Tim began to embellish the story with a Russian accent and side tidbits of information about the Russian philia for France. The Faberge eggs. The truth about Katherine the Great and her horse. (According to Tim, the horse was no better endowed than he.) When I laughed at that he was offended. But please, I was a young horseback rider in childhood, riding at the stable off of Central Park. I had seen a horse with a hard on. With all due respect, Tim was a better lover, but not because his penis was bigger than Call Me Johnny, the horse I rode as a kid.

Back at my place, Ricky and Louise were in the kitchen.

"You guys bring anything home from dinner?"

"Here."

Tim tried to intercept my toss of the bag to Ricky.

"That's my steak. Give them your chicken."

Louise and Ricky looked like one of them was going to spray Tim with urine. He saw it too.

"Fine. Enjoy the steak. Watch the pieces of garlic in the sauce."

The cats were ripping open the bag when Tim and I walked out of the kitchen.

"You staying?"

"For a minute. I want to play something for you."

He reached into his bag, took out a CD and a little CD player. In seconds the music came on. It was hauntingly beautiful and sung by an all male chorus.

"Soviet Army Chorus?"

"Used to be. Now it's just the Russian Men's Chorus. This is their national anthem."

I was shocked to find myself crying.

"Good. Now you understand. These people are the World's Greatest Contradiction. Nobody can drink as much, write so much scorchingly sad music, dance like they were born in toe shoes, or create books like Dostoevsky."

"And?"

"And they have become a society divided between the real Russians, and the rich Russians who have all the sensitivity and artistry of Hitler painting an apartment."

"How did this happen?"

"Let's lie down and I'll explain it to you."

We left for the airport late the next morning. I was ready to fly to Moscow and build an outfit at Gum's, their very finest department store. I looked stunning by the time we arrived at our host's mansion. And so, here I was, standing staring at the crayon colored onion domes of St. Basil's Cathedral, in the center of Red Square. No longer a Connecticut housewife, I was now an art thief. I was feeling very pleased with myself.

Dinner started at nine as promised. It was now well past midnight. We had been drinking and eating the whole three hours. In that period of time, my host, a chubby little man with florid face and a jolly smile, had schooled me on the world of painting as it exists today.

First of all, nobody knew if they owned an original because the black market was the very spine of Russia. And for that matter, of all of the art world. And, like our forgeries, the forgers who made up the black market for painting, knew how to mix paints that would not show signs of being created in this or the previous century.

We were not the first to think of swapping out originals for fantastic copies. Our reason for doing it was more noble, but I wondered if Vincent would mind what was happening: this mass market in flawless forgeries meant that his paintings were not only in museums but also in many more homes than the 15 or so listed in our documentation. Still, the ownership was privatized and the beauty of his images and his message were confined to private houses owned by hedge fund billionaires, drug lords, and other leaders of the free world.

I actually liked my host. He insisted that I call him Mischa, I insisted that he call me Anastassy, a nickname I came up with after way too much vodka.

Tim had done a good job of giving me an introduction to the Romanov Dynasty, and on the long plane ride to Moscow, I had read feverishly about the October Revolution, the kidnapping of the family, and the murder of all of them except (maybe) Anastasia. It was complex: on one hand, they were a dynasty eating off of gold plates as the vast majority of Russians were freezing and starving to death.

On the other hand, the alternative was the Bolsheviks who had high ideals that unfortunately were unattainable at that time—" Everybody should work for the state, and each person would be cared for by the state from cradle to grave. From each according to his ability, to each according to his need." A pipe dream to be sure. We are clearly a species that is barely out of the primordial ooze, asking people to share equally when not everybody contributed equally was an idea whose time had not yet come.

The Bolsheviks under Lenin tried to convert an agrarian society into the most advanced and egalitarian society ever imagined on earth. They failed.

If Lenin had not died so young, and Stalin had not taken over, the story might have ended differently. But because of many factors, including the loss of a whole generation of young men to the fight against the Nazi invaders, Russia, no longer the Union of Soviet Socialist Republics, was as big a pile of corruption, greed, brutality and fantastic food as any place on earth.

Before finishing dinner with Mischa and his wife, Galina, I asked what kind of painting he wanted. It turned out he wanted to keep their Van Gogh because the colors matched their green marble bathroom, one of seven bathrooms in their huge apartment. I slipped out of the conversation and snuck off toward the green marble room and almost tripped on my way: standing as a door stop was an incredible *faince* and gold statue of Osiris. I thought to take it in my bag but decided that would be unwise.

As I said, Mischa and his wife liked their Van Gogh, but also wanted something special for their new mansion somewhere in the mountains.

Mischa, eyes red with too much of everything, turned to me. "Stassy, would you do us the honor of helping us choose a painting for our dacha?"

His wife spit out a little vodka laughing at him.

"Our little dacha? Oh my Mischinka, what a charming liar you are." Then turning to me. "Lady, whoever you are, it is not a little building, it is massive. And we lost our decorator to a purge by Putin last year."

"She doesn't need to know this Galina! She needs to know how much we would appreciate her coming to visit the castle which now stands empty. She is a sophisticated New Yorker, she knows about paintings, she can give us tips."

"We need a decorator Mischa! A Russian decorator who is here when we need him."

"Or a her." Mischa smirked.

"We will not work with a woman my dear, fat husband. You have a bad track record and I will not discuss this further."

He actually seemed frightened of his wife. I thought that was hilarious. Although, he was built like a Beluga whale and she worked out everyday. So possibly she had knocked him over a few times.

"I could look at pictures you send," I said. "Of this lovely new place, then I could make some suggestions of paintings that might suite up well with it."

Tim, by now as drunk as everybody else choked a little on this. But joined in anyway. "Yes, Anastassy must help you decorate. After all, she's of royal descent."

The conversation made me slightly sick. But on the plane going home, I realized that his honesty about his complete ignorance of anything about art was no more disgusting than the privatization of the work by pompous bourgeois who believed they did know something about paintings when in fact they had no souls with which to take in the images. If Mischa wanted some nice bright colors for his new living room, I would get somebody to forge something perfect for him.

It took me a day to recover from the vodka, the jet lag, and the new information. I called a meeting with my mother and Vita and explained that I thought our plan required re-tooling. All of wealthy Europe and Asia were buying forgeries alongside of originals with the same gusto. This made Van Gogh's pain a little more complex. I needed to talk to him as soon as possible.

After all, if the point was to let the world see his work, did it matter if an unimpeachable copy was hanging where his original should be? Mischa had assured me that L'Hermitage, the Metropolitan and the Louvre were as filled with copies as they were with originals. Same thing for the Van Gogh museum in Amsterdam and other museums in Holland and Scandinavia that specialized in his works.

It would be virtually impossible to take apart this cat's cradle of black market art. Nobody but Van Gogh himself or any of the other Old Masters could absolutely say what was real and what was not, and they could not travel forward in time to see their paintings.

I planned to go to Vincent the next day and get his input. In the meantime, Tim was gone, and the three of us had a wildly hilarious talk about the Romanovs. Vita told me with great certainty that Anastasia had not made it out alive, that she had died along with the rest of her family. I started to ask her how she knew, but realized the answer myself: the Romanovs were mortal, in spite of their wealth and power, their deaths followed the same pattern as my mother and father and husband: die, disintegrate temporarily, learn what you need to learn to go on, and then get back into a shape that could move through Time and Space.

Before we said good night, my mother went into the kitchen and Vita put her hand on my shoulder. "This is the last time you will see Vincent in Arles."

"Why?"

"It is his time."

"Are you saying he will commit suicide? I have never seen him so alive!

He'd never commit suicide. That is a myth."

"Meaning?" I had forgotten my vision of the teenager with the gun.

"Van Gogh will die at the hands of a drunk teenaged boy. It will be an accident, but a fatal one."

"You are talking about the new study on him? I can be there. I can prevent it!"

"No, Deborah. You cannot intervene in another person's destiny."

"He dies from the accident! Can I at least help with that? Get him to a hospital?"

"He will be taken to a hospital. But the injury is fatal. There is nothing you can do and nothing you should try to do. This is the world you live in, at least you know how it operates."

"But he is my friend."

"And I am your friend. So, listen to me carefully: do not intercede, do not try to change anything. You will find Van Gogh after his transition, I promise you."

I started to argue with her just as my mother re-entered the room from the kitchen. I realized there was no point in saying anything else. I kissed them both good night and went to bed with a bottle in my hand.

Chapter Fifteen
The End of the Line

VINCENT AND I WERE DONE with a delicious lunch he had made. Nobody made onion soup like Vincent Van Gogh, a fact very few people know. We were both tripping out nicely on a bottle of absinthe I had brought. The time had come to bring up the subject of our big idea.

"I have put together a group of formidable artists as you know. They have been making scrupulous copies of your work."

"*Oui*. Yes. To swap out in the houses where my work is held captive."

"Well. It turns out things are not so simple as I had thought. Do you remember the art students who would sit on stools in the Louvre back when you were in Paris?"

"Of course. They were making impeccable copies of the masters to put the mastery into their own hands. It is, in my opinion a fine and democratic way to learn to paint. Free from the pompous world of art conservatories."

"I agree. It pre-dated the mass creation of what we call reproductions which are actually done on paper, not canvas, and are silk screened or photocopied."

"More soup?"

"No, I am full, thank you. Vincent? I was just in a man's house where one of your originals is hanging. He is a hugely wealthy Russian art dealer. And all of his dealings are black market. Totally illegal."

"So?"

"These people take forgeries and originals and interchange them for sale. The customers have no idea that they could be paying millions of dollars for a perfect replica of a painting."

"It is my voice? My words. I am not painting for the money. I paint to make my voice heard. You know all this."

"I do, so what would you think if we changed our plan a little?"

"How?"

"We would take every canvas you are now creating. And you know you are creating at a rate of speed you have never accomplished before. Anyway, what if we took these new paintings and created perfect replicas and sold them?"

"For what reason?"

"We could distribute your magnificent images all over the world to small museums that would otherwise not be able to afford them. We could use the money to create the kind of painting academies or societies or clubs that would take in talented people and give them training for no cost. We could help thousands to become better artists. It would literally raise the aesthetic in the world if learning was not a privilege but a possibility."

"Who would choose? The students, the way of teaching, the actual buildings to work in where the light is conducive?"

"You. And Berthe Morisot, Matisse, Picasso, maybe Gauguin."

"NO!" Not Gauguin. He is an immoral man who has abandoned his wife and children for his own enjoyment."

"What about the idea? Getting together some brilliant, well-established painters who are no longer walking the earth, and bring them here to make your paintings and your aesthetic become the groundwork for new painters?"

"Have you met Picasso? His ego is the size of a small planet."

"But do you like the idea?

"No."

"You don't want other painters copying your work?"

"I am not the last painter who will live. This idea

cements my work the way earlier painters are cemented in conservatories where people who know nothing influence young artists. No."

"There may never be another innovator like you. Transitioning from impressionism to…."

"NO."

"All right. But you will allow me to replace the paintings in the houses of the very rich with copies by Morisot, Manet, Fernandez?"

"Yes, the paintings should never have been sold to these people."

"Then we will proceed with our work, and soon only forgeries will sit in marble bathrooms."

"*Bien*, thank you, and now I have company about to arrive, so if you could come back tomorrow?"

"Yes, tomorrow. Would it be rude if I ask who you are about to entertain?"

"I have met two charming young men who are fascinated by my work, it is a joy to watch them watching me as I paint."

"One of them carries a pistol, is that right?"

"Yes. He is proud of it. His grandfather fought in the revolution with this pistol, but how did you know?"

"Please be careful. Pistols are dangerous, and I know you and the boys will be drinking. Please Vincent, be very careful."

"Of course. *Bien*. Now go my sweet friend. I hear them arriving."

I could hear voices, and the crunching of the leaves underfoot. Soon I saw two teenaged boys approaching. One of them carried a large pistol in his belt. With great reluctance I kissed Vincent and walked through the garden for the last time, into the kitchen, then the bedroom and then—out of the painting.

Once on the museum floor, I leaned against the wall, my

heart was beating very fast and I feared that leaving him was a mistake. Some part of me thought that maybe if I stayed, I could prevent the disaster I knew was coming.

And then I heard it. A loud pop. The kind of sound that comes from an old pistol. I could not help myself, I knew I was not allowed to interfere, but I tried to crawl back inside the painting. It was no longer possible. The canvas was just canvas, the magic of my entering by stepping up onto the floor in the bedroom had evaporated.

I put my head in my hands and wept.

Back at home. I walked slowly up the stairs to my apartment, and as I did, I heard jazz coming from inside. I wondered who the visitor was.

I opened the door to find Tim smoking something that was not a cigarette. I hadn't smoked marijuana much, once or twice and it did nothing for me, but now that it was virtually legal in New York, I had it around me more and more. Tim was sitting in the chair in my bedroom listening to a CD he had brought with him.

"Hey."

"Hey."

"Is that pot?"

"Yes. It goes with the music."

"What is it? It sounds familiar, but I can't place it"

"This is New Orleans funeral music. The pot is an essential component of our pretend trip to Louisiana for the Memorial I have created for us."

"Is this for Van Gogh?"

"Yes. I knew you would be in despair, I figured it would be good for you to grieve."

"And you figured that would be good foreplay too."

"Life and Death, Deborah, they are one. Sex is good, but the essentials are just Life and Death and the circle that brings people out of one life and into another. Here."

He handed me the joint. I took a tentative puff and nearly died coughing. When I was back to breathing, I finally understood why pot is so popular. I was less concentrated in my sorrow, more mobile inside my own spirit. I could see Vincent clearly, lying in a hospital bed, a large wound in his abdomen, hooked up to an IV.

"He's not dead yet."

"No. But he will be in a few hours. No need to wait to memorialize him."

"You know it wasn't a suicide, right?"

Tim tossed me a bunch of yellowed newspapers. I tore through them, they all came from European presses, they all carried the headline that Van Gogh was dead.

"Is this real? I thought he was an unknown. Why so much ink on his death."

"No, they are not real. But I had them made up for you because they condense the way his death was reported once his brother spread the news."

"They all say he committed suicide."

"Yes. Until a few months ago that has been the standard story."

"But this new book —"

"It's 900 pages long. They have done extensive and slightly boring research and they have pretty much proven what all of us knew all along: he did not shoot himself. Some kid showing off his pistol shot him by accident. Van Gogh lied on his death bed to protect the kid. "

"Was he in love with the boy?"

"No."

"What was going on with him and these boys?"

"You're his friend, you should get this. He was scared the boys would be prosecuted if the truth got out. He knew the boy had not meant to shoot him, and he did not want him in jail or worse. He made a dying declaration. Clever. They're considered to be unassailable in almost every court anywhere. So he died the way he lived: on his own terms."

"But it's not fair. He was so young. He could've painted hundreds more canvasses."

"Did I hear you say 'Fair'?"

"Shut up, Tim."

"Where have you seen a preponderance of Fairness?"

"All right."

"Want to have some connubial bliss? Eros and Death go really well together."

"I want —"

"Yes?"

"I want to just this one time create fairness or justice where there was none."

"No es possible, Chica."

"Because this happened way back in Time and Space?"

"Yes. And any way a new book has just come out that sets the record straight. So why don't you rub your grief on my body and see if we can accept the truths of life while we get ecstatic."

"Give me back that joint."

He had smoked it down about half way. I took it and finished it. This was more pot than I had smoked in my lifetime. I was very stoned and I found it quite similar to absinthe without the hallucinations. It made me want to cry. I turned off the New Orleans dirge and turned on the CD Tim had given me on our way to Russia. I listened over and over again to the sad but strong sound of the Men's Chorus singing the Russian National Anthem, and soon I was sobbing and rocking back and forth in a little ball on my bed. Tim stood up and ambled towards me. He turned off the music and lay down next to me. And the phone rang.

I could hear my daughter's voice on the machine. She was crying, but I couldn't make out the words. I couldn't talk to her

right now because I knew it would be something mundane—
Bodhi hurt her feelings, the pregnancy was getting difficult, her
husband wanted her back and would give her anything she
asked for.

I felt sad that I didn't want to help her. Having said that, I
began to undress and as I did that, Tim took off his clothes.

We crawled under my covers and did not begin our usual
frantic groping. Instead, we talked as we very lightly rubbed
our hands over each other. We talked about Life. Death.
Fairness. Justice. Guilt. Shame. Somewhere between Justice
and Guilt, I heard my window rattle and saw Ricky and Louise
jump from the window ledge and land inside the apartment.
They scampered past us without a sideways glance. Apparently,
they had an agenda of their own.

For some reason this made me laugh. Here I was in bed
with an immortal man, my houseguests were two tabbies with
seemingly supernatural capacities. My dead mother would visit
later with my mentor who was 50 million years old.

Was this the pot?

Tim began to move our touching to a more specific activity
and I found it soothing. Soothing and thrilling. Eros and Death.
Pot. This whole new turn my life had taken was breath taking.
Even knowing that Vincent was going to be misrepresented
began to feel like a gift. It would take most people a long time
to know the truth, but because of Vita, I had been given a
crash course. As Tim and I joined forces in the practice of
pleasure, I came to accept more of the world than I had been
able to deal with in my whole life. I came to accept that Life,
with all of its anguish, gives the living many compensations.

After bed with Tim, I realized I was hungry. And I had to
call my daughter back. Tim said he would run to Carbone's and
get us some food, and I could make my call while he was gone.
Tim had absolutely no interest in the day to day of the world
of mortals. For whatever reason he found me special, he did

not care a bit about my daughter or her child or anything else about her. This was helpful.

As he left I dialed my daughter.

"Hello sweetheart."

"Did you listen to my message, mother?"

"I just came in, heard your voice and dialed your number. Tell me."

"It's Bodhi. Son of a bitch phony f*cking yogi."

"What happened?"

"He found the bonds you gave me. They're Bearer Bonds. No proof of ownership necessary."

"And?"

"And he's gone and so are the bonds."

"All of them?"

"Yes. Apparently, he found them, cashed them in and headed home to New Hampshire all within a couple of days."

"Well. I'm sorry for your hurt feelings, but I have lots more of those bonds and I will replace them for you. No worries."

"No worries? He has a wife in New Hampshire. She has three kids. Everything he ever told me was a lie. He never lived in India, never studied with the Yoga masters he blabbered on about. He was a dentist. Got bored, grew a beard, took some community college yoga and came to the Big City to deceive some of the dumbest women on the Upper East Side."

"You think he's done this before?"

"Yes."

"You've spoken to other people in your class?"

"Yes."

"And nobody has ever called the police or tried to get their money back?"

"No."

"Because they were all married women?"

"Yes."

"Clever little Bodhi."

"It's not fair."

"Nothing ever really is."

"You don't care? It was your money?"

"If you want to send somebody up to New Hampshire and try to get him arrested I suppose you can do that."

"Don't you think I should?"

"I think you should be glad he's gone. The money can be replaced, and now you can re-unite with your husband if you want somebody to help with the baby."

"I already have."

"You are back together?"

"We had sex. It was better than I remembered. Better than sex with Bodhi or whatever his real name is."

"That seems like it's worth more than money. Good sex with your own husband?"

"Didn't you have good sex with your husband?"

"Yes, I did. But then he died."

"Have you had sex with anybody else since daddy died?"

Choice point. Do I tell my relatively straight daughter that I had been raped by Set the Egyptian god while my immortal lover listened to it from a couple of flights above us? Should I tell her that since her father's death I had seen my own deceased parents and that my mother and I were now working on a caper to steal back the extraordinarily expensive Van Gogh paintings that the Idle Rich had bought? Could she handle these things?

"Yes, Sweetie, I have had other lovers since becoming a widow."

"And?"

"And life goes on. Sex is one of the great compensations for all the misery of being human."

"So you're not disgusted by my affair with this phony Yogi?"

"I am delighted for you. It means you have balanced the situation that your husband caused with his affair. I think it will make it easier for you to love each other again."

"Mother?"

"Yes, Sweetheart."

"I never had an orgasm with Bodhi."

"Oh."

"But now that I'm back with—my husband, I have to stop myself from practically ejaculating all over my lovely upholstery the minute he gets home."

"Really?"

"It was never like this before. Maybe it's the pregnancy?"

"Yes, that could be it."

"Have you ever felt that way? So desperate to have your lover inside you that you almost burnt the house down leaving the stove on?"

"I don't cook at home. But yes. I know what it is to want somebody so much that it makes you lose all reason."

"So maybe Bodhi served a purpose."

"I would say so."

"Do you want to know why he never helped me over the edge of an orgasm?"

"If you want to tell me."

"He had one of those banana shaped penises. I think there's a medical term for it."

"Peroni's disease?"

"Yes! Sex with him was like sex with very old fruit."

"Ah."

"I'm sorry. That's too much information isn't it?"

"Not at all. It helps me understand the situation. You took a lover, he turned out to be lacking—to be polite—and now you appreciate the father of your child more than you ever have."

"So all I lost was some money."

"And money doesn't really count unless you don't have enough. But you do. Your father left me a huge pot of gold, and I am delighted to give you more."

"Mother?"

"Yes."

"I have never felt so close to you. Never. I always thought you put up with me but had very little interest in me. Now we share stories of lovers and multiple orgasms and the real meaning of what matters and what doesn't."

I heard Tim re-entering my apartment with the food. I was very happy with this conversation, very hungry, and for no reason I could figure out, very horny again.

My daughter and I bid each other a sweet farewell, and almost tripping over Ricky and Louise who were lying in a yin yang wrapped around each other sleeping on my floor, I ran to greet Tim.

Chapter Sixteen
Work Hard for the Money

I WAS IN THE BACK room of the artists' workshop. Work was going beautifully and almost all the forgeries were now in the stage of being framed.

My mother, Vita and I sat together coming up with specific plans for the gala. The thefts themselves were being worked out by a group led by Tim. They were assessing as best they could where each painting hung in the myriad houses of the competing billionaires who had purchased them. They would figure out how to use the four huge Egyptians and how to deal with the security in each home. Now came the really hard work of coming up with an event to which most if not all of these owners of Van Gogh's paintings would attend.

We had already gone through and discarded the idea of some mega-fundraiser. These people already gave hundreds of thousands of dollars to causes. It eased their guilt. My mother was speaking:

"So you understand, the cause cannot be a duplicate of any existing charity, and it must not only be sparklingly new it must also be a "testimonial" to the social consciences of these billionaires."

I asked a naïve question: "Do they have social consciences? They walk past hundreds of homeless people in every city they live in or travel to."

"And they feel terrible about it," Vita chimed in, "on a DNA level." She might have sounded more sincere if she hadn't been sucking down a Moscow Mule and chuckling.

"If they don't consciously care about the injustice of their wealth in a world of so much poverty—how do we appeal to them?"

"Deborah my little darling, we make them believe they do have a social conscience."

"Your mother is right."

"We frame the event and the people invited as something hugely important—something that will equalize the balance of them having billions while billions have nothing."

"It's all about the lie. The lie is soothing to the very wealthy. Thanks to Marie Antoinette it became unpopular to seem callous towards the masses."

"Is lies all we have? You think a just society is not ever going to be possible?"

"This planet is very young by cosmic standards. But still, it's had millions of years and it seems at a very infantile stage of consciousness. The decision has not been made,, but I wouldn't put my money on longevity for the Earth."

"Maybe we should say that. Tell people that as the wealthiest among us, they have the real chance to change the fate of the planet by showing their goodness and generosity."

"Religions try to control the innate human emptiness, but they haven't done well."

"All the more reason to come up with something that might light a candle in the darkness of the human soul."

"An acorn of an idea: you, the wealthiest and most powerful can save the world."

"Boring." Vita poured herself the last of the Mule, before commenting, "you should really try drinks on other planets." Then she returned to the task at hand.

"All right. How about we get astrophysical: the world is on the edge of the Event Horizon. Only you, the chosen, the masters of industry and wealth, can pull the planet back from falling into a black hole in space."

"Proof?" I asked.

"A panel of spiritualists and physicists."

"I'm already making other plans for my evening." Vita

laughed.

"It was your idea. So how can we prove that what you said is true? That you wouldn't put any hope into the long-range survival of this planet?"

"If I knew that answer, I would have tried it. Instead, I look for good human beings and hope that you will find the answers for the others." Was Vita's reply.

"Can I bring out some of those who no longer live in the present?"

"No. We aren't allowed parlor tricks."

"What if we caused a catastrophe of such huge proportion that we frightened everybody? Then we go to these uber-rich people and suggest they can solve the catastrophe?" I suggested.

"Go on."

"How much power do the Lost have? Can we put sink holes into Manhattan, Moscow, the Amazon?" Me.

"Not if you mean real sink holes. But we could certainly create the illusion that some kind of ecological disaster was happening."

"We have already had massive fires, floods, earthquakes, flesh eating bacteria. Nobody really gets scared anymore." Mother was, of course, right.

"What about a miracle?" I knew this would be nixed.

"Miracles are useless on the filthy rich who own Van Goghs!"

"No, wait, Deborah may be onto something."

"You mean like a visitation from Christ?" My mother was very unimpressed with the Abrahamic religions.

"Of course not. Obviously people don't care what he stood for or what he said." Vita replied.

"You knew him?"

"I knew many men of his time. Most of them yearned for kindness, most of them got killed for their efforts."

"Vita's right, my dear. Religion is utterly useless. We need something new."

"What if we created an Event Horizon here in Manhattan. A special space where you step into it and actually see—a black hole. But instead of it being a bad thing, it is a glorious example of a world where everybody lives in peace and plenty?"

"Like a diorama at the Museum of Natural History. Please, people are not easily fooled, they have seen it all, tasted most of it, had sex with the moist parts. They aren't easy to entice." Vita closed down my idea.

"What if we steal a page from the neo-cons: call this a Caucus for Thought Leaders. We are inviting this group because they are so powerful, so concerned for the world. Neo-cons use Thought Leaders like sports stars: they are meaningless until you are on the 10 yard line. And even then— but—people like to be near sports stars, so you can talk them into things if you produce a few at the event." Mother sounded right.

"We word the invitation correctly: make it clear the champagne and food will be the finest, we play to their egos, we might have a chance at getting them. Obviously we aren't using sports stars, but thinker stars. No matter how stupid they actually are. A Pulitzer Prize winner doesn't have to be smart. That's the real trick." Here's where my abhorrence of phony professors with bloated egos and tiny brains came in handy.

"All right, let's work on this. We completely re-tool the rhetoric of the guilty billionaires who pretend they want to bring about a new world order. We ask them to join us because their wealth proves their capacity to successfully traverse and help heal this world of poverty and ignorance." Mother was warming to this. "Yes. 'Join us for an evening of brainstorming as only the powerful can brainstorm.' Play to their guilt, but make it easy for them to assuage the guilt by participating in a caucus of people like themselves who are masters of the universe, with master sized ideas and huge hearts. It's pure bullshit. But it just might work.."

"Mother, you raised millions of dollars. You gave hundreds of fundraisers. You should work on the wording for the invitation."

My mother stood up and smiled at me.

"All right Deborah. I will develop an invitation that makes our guests drool to be invited. Often the trick is to make the extremely wealthy feel ignored and unimportant if they are not invited to an ego stroking event."

Chapter Seventeen
Empire State

THE OBSERVATION DECK of the Empire State Building gave our guests a 360-degree view of the city they rule. Tables with umbrellas, heaters, lights on poles that looked antique but gave off an eerily otherworldly glow. We had decorated the Gala for its theme: "Those of Us Who Oversee the 21st Century, Own the Future."

It was a "caucus" of "Thought Leaders" who could best address the pressing issues they had no real ideas about: homelessness, global climate change, illness among the poorest, gun violence, a lack of plumbing in what they call "shithole" countries.

These Very Rich Guests, among whom were the owners of every Van Gogh painting that had been sold at a legitimate auction, were to be feted with the finest of everything they already had at home, while discussions (none too long or too disheartening) would go on among the Thought Leaders with room for the dull-witted ultra-kleptocrats to ask questions and make suggestions.

Anything that would massage their guilt, allow them to be sure their image was one of sincere social concern, and of course get them into their limos or helicopters in time to be home or at an airport boarding private planes to take them home before boredom set in.

Every table had screens at each place setting so that all could see the dais in the area around the entry way that held the speakers. Our Thought Leaders were mostly members of the Lost. Some of them were "good" some of them were "bad." We had also brought in several "real" thought leaders from the United Nations and Wall Street. Vita had done a little smoke blowing just like our invitation to the guests: if you were a member of the elite Lost 100, or an elite business leader, a cyber master, a hedge fund genius, this event would put you in a lavish environment with others of your class, and would be an interesting diversion from whatever you did all day.

The Lost, who had been on the planet since its beginning, could out bullshit, out charm, and out chic all of the wealthiest guests. When asked questions about history that related to the issue being discussed, these Lost could answer from memory. As natural shape shifters, they were all at their most stunning for this event. After all, they were powerful, but they were also bored with the planet earth. Compared to other planets, earth was a bloody drag. So here was an event where they could completely fool a bunch of powerful moronic humans into thinking they were actually here to change the world.

There was not a single empty seat. Endless tankards of every conceivable alcoholic beverage were provided by the serving people who did a non-stop stroll through the tables to make sure everybody was getting soused. We wanted them to stay to the end of the event so that the thieves tasked with stealing all the real Van Goghs, had time to snatch and replace every painting on the list.

For the first hour, Deborah her mother and Vita circulated and chatted as people were gathering. Everything ran smoothly until Vita's phone went off.

"Hello? Yes I hear you. What?!! Why would she do that?"

"What's happened?" My mother and I asked this simultaneously.

"Well, tell her to get back there and return it," Vita said. "He plans to return to Moscow directly after the event. Yes, I know how many hours that trip takes, I also know Isis can be stubborn, so let's get this done right now."

Vita switched her phone off. She smiled enigmatically and swigged a large amount of her martini. Then she turned to answer our question. "Whoever chose to send Isis to the house in Moscow with the bathroom that houses a gorgeous Van Gogh, neglected to mention that there is a door stop there—a lovely small sculpture of her beloved Osiris. In *Faince* and gold, the real deal, stolen by Belzoni in the 1800s."

"And?" I asked, looking from my mother to Vita.

"And," Vita replied, "she's pocketed it and is refusing to put it back."

"Where is Osiris?" My mother looked confused.

"They're trying to locate him. He'll convince her to put it back, but there is a lot of security to get around, and Isis, in her current state of self-righteousness is getting a little careless. She pushed one of the security guards over the balcony and now an ambulance has been called and she is just standing holding the stolen statue."

Vita's phone rang again."Yes?" she said. "Ah! Glad you called. My darling Isis, you know very well that you have to put the statue back. And you need to do it without mauling any more of Mischa's security staff. The goal is to get the painting out and replaced. Well, that is good news, but you still have to return the statue." She put her hand over the phone.

My mother asked: "Have they finished the painting exchange?"

"Yes. But that made Isis feel like her obligation to our little plan is now accomplished and she really wants the statue of Osiris. She believes it would make a thrilling birthday gift for him to see it back in Egyptian hands. Probably anticipates a very special "thank you" from him when he sees it."

She returned to the phone. "Fine. I will promise you a replica. Yes, one that will satisfy his inspection. Good. Now vacate the mansion you are needed at the next destination which is Tokyo. I understand that's a three second hop for you, but we really do want things over and done with within the next few hours. Please my dear. I will find many ways to make this worth your—hello?"

She turned off the phone. "One problem solved. She is on her way to Tokyo."

The phone went off again. Vita was annoyed that she had to put her drink down to deal with it. "Yes?" She listened. "Why wasn't this part of our intelligence? Never mind. Where is Tim? Please get hold of him, explain the situation and get him over there. I believe he and she have met before. Tell him to wear his best tux and nothing underneath."

Again she clicked off her phone. This time she downed the rest of her martini. "Seems one of our guests is here with a companion for hire not his wife. The wife was in the mansion when our people entered to take the painting. They were quick witted enough to explain their break in, she must be very, very drunk and not too bright. But now she is insisting that they leave and the painting is still hanging in her back bedroom."

"Are you sure Tim can fix this?" I asked.

Vita chuckled. "The poor woman's alone. She's not a great beauty. She hasn't had sex in ten years with anyone but her husband who is a natural wart hog of a lover. Lots of snorting in bed, lots of his clumsy paws mauling her, not much joy for anyone but him. Yes, I am sure Tim can fix this."

This time when the phone rang, I reached for it, I knew it would be Tim. "Hello? Are you there with her yet? Is the painting in our hands? So fast? How long have you been there?"

Tim laughed and hung up. He called to inform us that due to his swordsmanship, the blowsy wife was now snoring contentedly in her massive bed. The Van Gogh had been exchanged with a forgery, and Tim was on his way to the next job.

The event was half over and we could count eight of the fifteen paintings on their way to our warehouse. The last seven paintings were on a strict time clock.

When Isis called the second time, things were not so

smooth. By now we had thirteen of the paintings and our guests still seemed transfixed by the absolute treacle being bleated at them from the dais: the wealthy are the shepherds of the planet, they have proven their leadership abilities and now have the all-important job of remaining wealthy. To me this sounded like the kind of crap I had heard in college, not the same words, but the same stupidity and lack of substance. To our guests, it was like the Pope, Moses, Buddha and Jesus had each kissed them on the forehead and assured them safe transit throughout their lives.

"Hello?" Vita said. "Yes, my sweet where are you? Why? I thought we had straightened this out several hours ago. So what!! When was the last time you listened to Set about anything?"

Vita covered the phone and whispered to my mother and me: "F*cking Set talked Isis into keeping the statue. God I would love to kick him just once in his huge, ridiculous testicles."

"Should you try to get Osiris?" I asked.

"No. Let's assume that Mischa is not that invested in his statue. He probably won't notice that Isis replaced it with a very good fake."

"But…"

"Yes, I know. How many other little fakeries has Isis pulled under Set's guidance?"

Vita returned to her call. "Isis? Am I safe in assuming that all the other tasks of exchanging real paintings for forgeries have been carried out as planned?" Vita listened to the answer and grimaced. "Why?" She gestured for another martini just as the waiter walked by. She grabbed it, downed it and spoke to Isis. "All right. If you're sure. But please remember you are a myth, and I can have you re-written in a less flattering light if I find out you have lied to me."

Vita hung up and began to laugh.

"What?" I asked.

"It's not a problem. I just find sibling rivalry disgusting, albeit amusing. It's not like the Egyptians have never read Cain and Abel."

"Did Set try to sabotage our efforts?"

"Yes. Tried but failed. He is still incensed that Isis put Osiris back in one piece after Set cut him up three thousand years ago. Beyond furious that she found his penis in shape to re-attach it. Set had hopes of being the Big Man in the Myth."

"Why doesn't Isis see through him?" my mother asked.

"Who knows?" Vita said. "She's mythic, not subject to Freudian interpretation or any other form of explanation for bad behavior. Anyway, from what I can tell, almost every one of the original Van Gogh's is now in our hands. Our event is a huge success, and all that's left is to give our guests their bag of treats and send them down the elevator."

"The paintings are safely stashed?" I asked.

"Yes. That was Tim's dominion, the safe storage of the real Van Gogh's."

"You really think these people will take their gift bags?" I asked.

Mother nodded.

Vita pulled us to the exit door. The speakers had left the dais and were mingling with the crowd. You could tell who the Lost were among them. They had a hard time not laughing in the faces of the wealthy sycophants who approached them with comments or questions, or compliments intended to charm them.

As we watched the party scatter and the guests head to the exit, I saw that to a person, the gift bags were taken. I watched several guests grabbed up two or three bags, after all, the event had cost $25,000 a ticket.

Within 15 minutes the guests were gone, the Lost had flown off, and the "real" experts had been given their handsome payment for their time and were in the down elevators.

"What did you put in the guest bags?" I looked at Vita.

"First class airline tickets to Paris in time for the new installation at the Louvre. With accommodations at various palaces and hotels of distinction in the area. And a thank you letter written with great sincerity by your mother. We have puffed up their egos, stuffed their stomachs, and packed their head with total lies about their place in the world order."

"So now we just wait to see if any of them notice that their Van Gogh's have been replaced with forgeries?"

"That was never an issue. The big deal was just to distract them for a few hours. They will not notice anything about their paintings."

"Are any of them smart?"

"I have met one or two smart billionaires, oligarchs, whatever you call them. Mostly they are shrewd. Cruel. Easily deceived by flattery. And I have noticed a peculiar smell among the men. Stale, unpleasant, like the minute their cologne touches their skin it begins to smell like pee."

"Is this why you don't feel sure of the future of this planet?"

"I don't answer questions like that Deborah. That's for you to figure out."

With that, Vita grabbed her handbag, kissed my mother and I on both cheeks and left.

"Where do you think she's going?"

"To the warehouse to check the paintings. From there, back to a conversation she told me she'd been having with some members of Marat's party from the French Revolution. I think she said it was an argument about the relative cruelty of the guillotine."

"Oh." I tried to take that in.

"Good night my girl. Grab yourself a cab, I have an assignation with your father, I am a bit late for."

"You still see him regularly?"

"When we are in the same time frequency. Of course."

"Are you still in love?"

"Yes, Sweetheart."

"Still lovers?"

"My lovely child, lovers is such a relative term once your body has been through its first life and moved on."

"Were you lovers with Tim?"

"Deborah. The beauty of not living in one Frequency is freedom."

"That's your answer?"

"No. My answer is that I love you more than I ever could when I was just a human woman. Now I belong to the universe, and love comes much more easily to me."

The elevator arrived and we got in and descended the hundred floors to the lobby. I felt totally confused. I had been given this tremendous gift from many people who had come together to get back Van Gogh's paintings. I should have felt exhilarated. But I think my real concerns were about where I would go from here.

Chapter Eighteen
Sitting on Top of the World

TIM WAS HOLDING my hand and showing me the wondrous sights in the little world we were in.

"Where are we?"

"I can't tell you."

"Why not?"

"Because I'm not allowed to bring you here."

"Why not?"

"Look around you.

I looked. There was a white sand beach with a sea beyond it. The color of the water was emerald green. Trees rose out of the water intermittently, incredible tall, twisted trees. On every branch was something living, small creatures, like squirrels but not, like birds but not, just little living things I couldn't identify.

"Did we take drugs?"

"No."

"Why are you so enigmatic?"

"You haven't really thanked me yet for my huge part in the success of your Van Gogh switcheroo."

"So we're heading to a bed?" I looked in his eyes.

"No."

"Please just tell me."

"This is a discard planet that we used a million years ago to do some experiments with. They did not work out so we archived the planet in case we ever need it."

"What was wrong with it? It's stunningly beautiful."

"This is all of it. We only built the big water and the sand in front of it.

"What was the problem?"

"No Yin, just Yang. Or if you like it better, no Yang, just Yin."

"Are you saying it was all one note?"

"Yes, Deborah."

"What's wrong with that?"

"Without any friction, the place was totally static. Nothing great could happen here."

"Couldn't you have created music, literature, paintings?"

"Right."

"There is none?"

"No." He sounded slightly annoyed.

"Because there are no contradictions to create from?"

"Partly."

"What else?"

"No problems to solve."

"I would love that."

"You didn't." He was really annoyed now.

"When?"

"What were your problems as a rich woman in Connecticut?"

"Boredom."

"That's not all."

"An inability to figure out why I was alive."

"Right."

"Is this some lesson about why people need conflict in their lives?"

"Want to see the planet we tried where there is nothing but conflict?"

"No. Thanks." Now I was feeling a little stupid.

"There too we only built one large area. It turned red with blood very quickly."

"What is your point?"

Tim and I sat down in the sand. It was like sitting on the most wonderful cloud, soft, but easily supporting our weight.

"Have you decided what your talent is?"

"You spoke with Vincent?"

"I was there when he asked you."

"No, you weren't."

"I was there every moment you spent with him."

"Why?"

"We aren't supposed to let people roam around through Time and Space until we know it won't overwhelm them, and before we know they will make use of the awareness."

"What the hell are you two doing here?"

Tim and I both jumped at the sound of Vita's voice. She almost never sounded annoyed, but she did now.

"Sorry. I thought it might help speed up her progress."

"That's not your decision to make Tim."

"Wait, am I not learning fast enough? Not growing into something I should already be?"

"We gave you the Van Gogh swap meet. That was unusual for us."

"Why?"

"Haven't you noticed we don't answer certain questions, we don't give you certain information. There is a reason for that."

"I get that."

"Do you?" Vita was looking different.

"Yes."

"Explain it to me please. Tim has put me in an awkward position by this little diversionary trip he has taken you on."

"You mean I should not know you have had experimental planets that failed?"

"All experiments have their merit. But so far we haven't gotten what we are looking for. Not anywhere. Earth is actually one of our best chances."

"You want to see how much a living organism like a human being can learn, is that it?"

"An elementary school version of it." She tried to soften.

"Are you waiting to see if people can grow out of their cruelty, their ignorance, their greed?" I asked.

"You tell me."

"You want to see the human soul? See if there is such a thing?" I continued questioning.

"Now you've gotten to junior high."

"It looks to me like human beings are born a certain way and don't deviate much from their early training."Tim chimed in.

"Then it's time to put the experimental planet earth into an archive." Vita snapped at him.

"Were you counting on me to change this?"

"Among other people. Yes."

"Why choose a disengaged housewife from the suburbs? Why not take a kid who lives in poverty and injustice and rises above it?"

"You would have had to make a bigger jump." Vita said.

"Because I had everything and it meant nothing to me?"

"She's not going to answer that Deborah."

Tim had so far stayed mostly out of the conversation. I noticed now that he looked very intently at me. Different from all the times we had been in bed or crawling towards the bed. This was serious even to the carefree Mr. Carbone.

"Is this supposed to be my talent? To become a thinker, a leader, a person of courage and integrity after having no reason at all to do that?" I sounded scared and I didn't want to.

"What's your favorite Bible story?" Vita looked at me closely which prevented me from laughing at the question.

"None of them. How could I have a favorite story in a book so filled with lies?"

"Billions of your fellow creatures count on the Bible, the Koran, the teachings of Buddha."

"But they're getting bad information." I sounded whiny.

"Really?" Vita sounded sarcastic.

"Yes, of course. You've shown me the real workings of life. Time and Space, death and re-birth, the need to love people without the shackles of too many rules and regulations."

"Go on." Tim was goading me.

"Go on what? I am not an intellectual. I still go to Bloomingdale's four times a year for my Free Gift with Purchase."

"Exactly." Tim laughed.

"Exactly what?" I didn't like either of them right now.

"You know enough to smell the lies you have been subjected to. We watched you go through your entire education with a thrilling disregard for the stifling misinformation you were given." Vita now sounded pleasant.

"You chose me because I am rebellious?"

"We chose you because you are not too normal. And you are not psychotic." Vita tried to make this complimentary.

"Thanks. I guess."

"Did you want to have your daughter?" Tim asked.

"No."

"Why did you have her?" Vita followed his question.

"Because."

"Yes." Vita stared at me.

"Because as a woman, if you don't have a child, people question why you are alive. My mother had me for the same reason."

"But you were both kind hearted mothers? Gave everything you could to a child you had felt compelled to have?" Vita was asking but also telling me.

"Yes."

"Why didn't you become some profession that could've excused childlessness?" Tim seemed to be genuinely curious.

"I wanted to make my husband happy. He loved our daughter. He wanted a child."

"Since Deborah had no children, assume that's not why we chose you. Tell me the images of her you have seen." Vita instructed me.

"She's always fierce, Warrior, Judge more even than Prophet, although there's lots of paintings of her under a palm tree offering prophecy."

"And we find in you a fierce Warrior and Judge of anything phony, ignorant, untrue. You killed a brown shirt with a dinner fork when pushed to your limit. That was a happy moment for me. Exactly what Deborah did—although she killed the Canaanite with a tent pole through his head. But you are fierce, and judgmental in the best way. Also, Tim tells me you are an enthusiastic participant in sex."

I turned to Tim, but he was not sitting where he had been.

"Where is he?"

"Back on earth."

"I was going to yell at him for the sex remark."

"Yes, that's when he left."

"So you want to see if a smart but unaware human being can become something better?"

"There are seven billion human beings. Earth cannot sustain them the way things are right now. People will have to make major changes or the planet will be judged a failure and the Boson particle will return and you will all be gone in a billionth of a billionth of a second."

"What should I do about this?"

"Ah. This is where I stand up, take you by the hand and return you to your apartment."

The sunlight on the beautiful sea went out in a split second. I heard the sound of a breezy wind, I felt tingly and when I opened my eyes I was alone on my bed on Thompson Street.

Not completely alone, my two feline roommates were there.

"Where you been Deb?"

"She likes to be called Deborah, you know that Ricky."

"Sorry. Where you been Deborah?"

"I have no idea."

"You were gone. We've been here all day and you were not."

I got up and walked into my kitchen. My husband was there smoking a cigarette.

"You don't smoke?"

"I like the taste. It's not going to hurt me is it?"

He laughed gently and put out the cigarette, then asked me:

"You okay Deborah?"

"I don't know."

"You'll do well. I know you will. If anybody can meet the criteria you can."

"How do you know? All I did in our life together was what every other woman in the suburbs does."

"You're a very smart woman. Very smart. Fair minded. You'll figure out the answer to their questions."

"About whether the planet we live on can be saved?"

"People believe a lot of impossible garbage. The parting of the Red Sea, the impregnation of a virgin by a dove, the gift of 44 virgins if you die after a sinless life.

"But none of that is true."

"I know."

"So what do I do to change things?"

My husband took me by the hand. His body was still very light and almost not fully filled out, but I felt his hand take mine. He led me into the bedroom and on my desk there was a laptop I did not own.

"Write Deborah. Write the truth. That is your weapon, your judgements, your prophecies all wrapped up in one."

"How can you be sure I can do it?"

"I slept next to you for 25 years."

With that remark, my husband simply evaporated right in front of me.

"Wait!"

He did not answer, nor did he return. The cats heard me calling and came running into the bedroom.

"We should not have eaten all the chicken, but you left it on the counter."

"What?!"

"Oh. That wasn't what you were yelling about?"

"What chicken?"

"Never mind."

I watched the two of them saunter innocently away from me, onto my bedroom window and down the side of the building. I was completely alone.

Since the amazing gala and the exchange of Vincent's life work I had not had a minute to really sit and think. I could tell that I would do that now for several days with nobody to engage with except Ricky and Louise.

I lay down on my bed and as the incredible sunset overwhelmed the light in my room, the birds from many months ago flew into my window and perched all around me. I fell asleep to the sound of their laughter, and I slept for the next 24 hours.

I woke up to a bright sunlit day. I ran out and got my usual double latte, added a healthy muffin which I tossed in a garbage can almost immediately, and went back upstairs.

The laptop my husband had given me was open. I sat down and looked at the desktop which had a few folders on it.

One said: "What I think about….?" Another "What I have learned and how I could teach my new understanding ….?" The last one said, "Just for fun!"

Of course I opened the "Fun" folder. In it, there was an impressive array of photos of me with Tim, me with Osiris, me in Weimar in full cabaret garb. Obviously my mentors or masters or manifestations of my insanity, had been watching me from the moment I had entered Bloomingdale's and first met Vita.

As a child, I often fantasized that everywhere I went, unknown people were watching me. They weren't spies they were more like admirers. In my late teens I thought I should force myself to stop this imaginary documentary on myself. I had read enough psychology in my high school class on "personality" to know it might be a sign of neediness, narcissism, or loneliness. So I cut out the people who had never been there to watch me anyway.

Once I was sexually active I would've had to eliminate the ongoing videotape of ME. I am not shy sexually and in fact, I liked people to see me naked, but still. Time to stop.

So here I was at 50 with the absolute proof that everything I did was now under the watchful eyes of who knew how many people, mythological or not. It gave me a little bit of a scare, but I very quickly accepted that this was what my life was about right now, and of course they would be watching me. The fate of the earth was in the hands of some number of humans (non humans too) who the Lost felt had a chance of saving the planet.

I closed the "Fun" folder.

With the desktop open, but the folders closed I should have known something would happen. The background (I believe it's called the wallpaper, but I've never been sure) changed. First there was a photo of Tim, at his desk, pouring over some papers and speaking to somebody I couldn't see. I turned the sound on the computer up but I couldn't hear him. I could just see his lips move. I thought I might practice lip reading but within seconds the photo of Tim slid away and there was Vita, speaking to an audience of 50 people in some small auditorium. Again, I couldn't hear her, but I could tell she was amusing those in front of her because they frequently seemed to chuckle.

The final slide stayed on my screen. It was a picture of me at about 12, each parent was on one side of me, and we were dressed up to go out to dinner. On my feet, were the beautiful white patent leather shoes they had not bought for me. I could tell the slide show was over.

I dialed up a search engine and began frantically searching through psychological papers and parts of books. I was looking at definitions: Dissociative Identity Disorder. Paranoia. Delusional behavior. Early onset dementia. Luckily, none of it quite explained the experiences of the last several months. Not without shoving some of what I had seen into a shoe that didn't fit. Like the chubby little girl at the shoe store where my father had bought me the white shoes—back at the beginning of this journey.

I dialed up the Bible. I read about Deborah. There were four or five sentences only. So I just started at page one. "In the Beginning…" I thought about taking a quick trip to my local synagogue to try and find a rabbi. Somebody who could explain to me why Genesis evolved into the story of Adam and Eve. Why was Eve forbidden curiosity? Was Adam really so great?

I had read enough in college to know that Adam had a wife before Eve. Lillith, he didn't want her because she demanded to lie on top half the time when they had sex. G-d had succumbed to Adam's misogyny (it wouldn't be the last time!) and threw Lillith and her 24,000 offspring (called Lillim) out of the garden. Some people think Lillith and her children are evil spirits who try to kill women when they are in labor. I thought that was just more sexist mythology. But what would a Talmudic scholar say?

Looking in my search engine for Talmudic Scholars provided me with a mass of information that I had to boil down to current scholars who were reachable by phone or maybe a short train ride. I found the name of a woman who worked at Radcliffe College, now called Harvard. I called the switchboard at the school, asked for her and was, to my amazement, immediately connected.

"Hello. I'm sorry to interrupt what you are doing…"

"Then why did you call?"

"Oh. Well, I'm curious about something in Genesis."

"No, it was not an apple, it was probably a pomegranate, apples were rare in Mesopotamia where the Garden may have been."

She hung up. Who cared what fruit Eve ate? I wanted to know why scholars would think she was forbidden knowledge. Wasn't that a kind of stupid way to start people out? I called her back. This time she sounded more pleasant.

"That wasn't my question. About the apple."

"Good."

"I want to know why this book is so restrictive. Why would the early writers start right off with making women to blame for everything?"

She started to laugh.

"Somebody has to be blamed."

"Why?"

"By the time the Bible was written, it was clear the human being has some very unappealing limits. They couldn't blame God."

"Why not?"

"Come on. He had to be All Knowing or he wouldn't have been God."

"He gave some lousy advice. In almost every page of Genesis, the rules and ways of being are reactionary, stupid even. Cain and Abel?"

"I tell my students the Bible was a metaphor."

"I'm not your student."

"When you need to build control over a species, especially one like humans who ask questions and come up with no answers, you need to give them answers, so they did."

"Why couldn't Adam have taken the hit?"

"Pregnancy?"

"What does that mean?"

"The men had to hunt, fight off invaders, protect their

homes."

"So they couldn't have faults?"

"I have a class to teach. I would love to hear more of your questions."

"Really?"

"Are you Deborah?"

"Yes."

"Come up tomorrow. A car will pick you up at Logan Airport and bring you to me."

"What time?"

But she had hung up. I knew her, Professsor Jean Lesdeux, I knew the switchboard that connected me to her. I called it one more time to make sure it really existed. I asked the operator where this woman taught her classes and she said, "the driver will know where to drop you off. And by the way, it's very cold up here right now, so bring a warm coat."

Then she too hung up.

I went online to a commuter airline, booked myself a ticket for noon the next day and went back to my search for meaning in the Book of Genesis.

The plane ride from La Guardia to Logan is short. But it was very turbulent. A couple of times a passenger screamed during a big bump. "Oh God!." I thought this was funny. For me, with my new knowledge of how things really are in the astrophysics of the earth's creation, screaming for god seemed appropriate during a particularly fun sexual eruption. Asking for his help in a plane going through rough air was sad.

I got off the plane and felt an immediate blast of frigid air. I stopped midway into the terminal and put on my coat, my gloves and was starting to search in my bag for my knitted hat when a man approached me with a cardboard sign that said "DEBORAH."

"Hello."

"The car is right out front, I've got it nice and warm, you

can forget your hat."

This journey through the land of the mysterious Lost was always surprising, sometimes shocking. I hadn't ever gotten the hat out of my bag. How did he know what I was looking for?

My driver guided me to a large, black SUV that was literally blocking the sliding doors into the terminal. Nobody seemed to care. I crawled into the huge back seat and felt like a little child. The car was too big for me.

He jumped in the front and we took off. I had been to Boston with my husband several times for conferences he was addressing. We drove through the familiar territory that led us into the Callahan Tunnel then onto Storrow Drive. The wind was making the Charles River choppy. I shivered remembering winters in Connecticut when our huge house was hard to keep warm. I would wrap my daughter in blankets and pretend she was a burrito. Rocking her in my arms and telling her it would be warm very soon.

We crossed the river and were in Cambridge. You could almost smell the learned pomposity of this Very Prestigious University. The driver had taken a call on his blue tooth so he had closed the window that separated front from back seat. I couldn't hear much of what he said but caught a couple of words.

"She is in the back…..Yes, I know which one…maybe five minutes…directly to your office or…."

He got his answer and swung the car in a U-turn.

"Not going to the Schlesinger Library?"

"No."

"Where are we going?"

He rolled the window between us down.

"I asked where are we going?"

"I heard you."

He continued driving.

"Mind if I smoke?"

"No. Go ahead."

He pulled out a huge joint and lit it. I wasn't sure if pot was legal yet in Massachusetts, but I was sure he didn't give a damn. The Lost and their servants can be incredibly arrogant.

He took a few hits and then handed it back to me through the open window.

"No thanks. I need to be on my toes."

"You don't like it anyway, am I right? More of an absinthe enthusiast?"

"How does everybody know everything about me?"

"Everybody? That's a little grandiose."

He pulled the car up in front of a huge Cape Cod style house and stopped. I had been in houses like this all of my married life in New England. White with black shutters on the windows. This one was huge, with a brick pathway that led from the sidewalk right to the two steps up to the front door.

"I'll be back when you're ready to go home."

"My plane leaves at—"

"Really?"

He smiled at me kindly. It was the first time I actually noticed his appearance: he was a stunning black man who could've been a movie star instead of a limo driver. His skin was almost bronze, but not. He wasn't as big as the Egyptians, but you could feel a genetic connection to a past that went all the way back to whatever Egypt was before it was Egypt.

I got out of his car expecting to be hit by freezing wind, but the temperature had risen to a fairly comfortable 40 degrees and the wind was gone. I grabbed my bag and got out of the car.

"Thanks, see you later."

"Yup."

"Am I in West Cambridge?"

"Yup."

"Did you just turn into a New Englander in the last 30

seconds?"

"Nope."

"Okay. Goodbye."

"Hey, Deborah. What are you, a wise guy or a Chelsea cop?"

Before I could answer, he pulled away from the curb chuckling. I had heard this expression but could not remember from whom, or when. The point of it was that it was the same thing; a wise guy or a Chelsea cop. I remember laughing when people said it. I watched as he pulled away, he had removed his hat and looked like a wealthy, hotshot with dark skin.

I stood on the sidewalk for a moment and the front door of the house opened. A slight but sturdy man was coming towards me. He was not much taller than I am, with dark brown hair cut very suavely. I couldn't tell without staring rudely if he had a mustache. He waved, I waved back.

"Hello Deborah."

"Hello, are you here to take me to the meeting?"

"Yes. We'll just go into the living room, get comfortable and talk. So much cozier than the Schlesinger."

"Are you also a Talmudic scholar?"

"Also?"

"Yes. I spoke to a woman yesterday, I thought I would be meeting with her."

"You are."

This man was not a cross dresser, he was not transgender. The only other implication was that he was the she I had talked to on the phone. The voice was similar, but I know yesterday the voice had belonged to a woman.

"Did I speak with you yesterday?'

"Don't you remember?"

"Yes, of course. Forgive me."

"Here we are."

He had swung the large entry door open and we walked into a beautiful old New England home. The first place to put my feet down was a fine Persian rug of reds and blues with unusual streams of green running through the more traditional part of the design. The center of the room had a long oak table with a vase of flowers at both ends. Everything in the room was old. The rocking chairs, mirrors, additional rugs, and plenty of deeply cushioned chairs and sofas. This was clearly a well used room.

"Are you warm enough? I can turn the heat up."

"No thank you. I've already adjusted to the cold. It's kind of pleasant."

"All right, let's take our seats."

He walked over to the back of the room where two beautiful old chairs were covered in an ancient chintz that was in perfect condition. A smaller oak table stood between the chairs, on it was a genuine Tiffany lamp. We sat down and got adjusted.

"So you don't like the *Bible?*"

"Well. No. I find it limiting."

"You have a better suggestion for taming a civilization comprised of totally wild and badly behaved creations?"

"Were we that right away?"

"Unbearable. From the moment the first cell became two cells."

"Why?"

"It happens that way sometimes. Other times our new creations are so dull and pleasant we decide to shelve them."

"You think it might be atmospheric? Like the earth makes its inhabitants difficult to control?"

"We can control you. But what's the point of that?"

"Is that why there's so much emphasis on Free Will?"

"No, that's just an argument some of us lost."

"When?"

"Oh my. Millions of years ago. As soon as the cooling process of the planet was complete, we began to vision who would live here, who we hoped for, how to get that."

"Are there planets that are better than earth? I mean in terms of who you have built to live on them?"

"Would you like some caffeine, I have an espresso maker or good tea?"

"No thanks. I'll stop asking questions like that."

"Good. Let's get to your real questions. She has a class to teach in an hour."

"Fine. The *Bible* is, in my understanding an early effort at telling stories that would help people understand how to live. Is that right?"

"No."

"Can you help me out then?"

"No."

"Can you tell me if I get close to the truth?"

"Try."

"All right. I thought you were a Talmudic scholar? Shouldn't you just be lecturing me on the fact that the *Bible* is a series of metaphors?"

He smiled. As he did, I began to notice that very subtly he was losing some of his more masculine characteristics. By this time in my knowledge of the Lost, this meant to me that he was going to slowly morph into the woman I had spoken to yesterday. The one with the class to teach.

"Why are the metaphors so dumb?"

"We were young. We didn't all speak the same language."

"You mean Aramaic, Hebrew, what else?"

"Neither of those was in existence when we began our conferences on what to say about creation."

"So even that is a lie? That the earliest *Bible* was written in Aramaic?"

"There was no such thing as what you're describing. From the minute the planet was cool enough to have anything live on it, we wandered around, we saw what we had to work with.

Our first steps were not to try to keep women from eating apples you know."

"Good. You're telling me the *Bible* and then presumably all other religious texts were less important than figuring out what the planet was made of?"

"Obviously. If the air was unbreathable or the sun was going to set every two hours, we had a problem. Once we figured out the timing, the circadian rhythms, we already saw Pithic Anthropis Erectus running around clubbing their females."

"Human's earliest instincts were violent?"

"Not just humans."

"Did it start at the first two cell things?"

"Of course. As soon as there was more than one of anything we noticed a tendency for grabby-ness, jealousy, even destruction of an organism if it would prevent its competing organism from getting ahead."

"Were there no peaceful living entities?"

"None that survived."

"Oh."

"Do you see the problem?"

"I think so. You had finally built a planet with complex organisms capable of massive growth and creation, but they were not nice."

"Not nice? I love that. Not nice is a whitewash."

"You think earth born creatures were created to be violent?"

"Cruel."

"All species or just the two-leggeds?"

"Only the two legged animals were given the tools to change their jealousies and pettiness. It's called language. And it didn't make much difference. I'm sure you remember the two cab drivers in the block above Bloomingdale's? They were emblematic of the Tribalism that created cruelty."

"Why couldn't you help? Lead the way to a more

cooperative planet? We have suffered terribly from war, violence at every level, mean-spiritedness. There was nothing you could do?"

"We tried: Buddha, Jesus, even your namesake, Deborah."

"Wait, wasn't that all sequential, first testament, second testament, Buddhism?"

"I hate this kind of question, but since our time is up I will tell you. We actually tried the New Testament first. We didn't call it that. We just wrote it up. Then along came some wise guys in our group who stuck in the crucifixion and the differing prophets, the lie about being the son of god, how Mary got pregnant. Let's face it, they were drunk, and we told them it would never fly, but we were wrong."

"So then you created the Old Testament because it was more disciplined? There were more rules? You were hoping this would help?"

"No. The Old Testament was a bet originally. How many mean spirited things could we tell people their God had imposed on them before they would abandon him."

"A bet that the story of Job, Cain and Abel, Abraham, would turn people off and they would seek something more palatable?"

"Yes."

"And why Eve? What was the point of telling women not to seek wisdom? Didn't that cut out half your chances of people becoming something kinder?"

"Women? Kinder?"

"What does that mean?"

"We knew right away that some means of procreation was necessary. We couldn't grow anything as complex as humans like we grow squash. So somebody had to gestate the new things. We chose women because men had no appropriate opening a child could swim out of."

"Then why not give the men that opening?"

"Some of us wanted to make it so either sex could procreate. In the beginning, it wasn't such a big deal, it was just practical: how do we get new humans on the planet?"

"And then?"

"Again, a little too much drinking one night and a vote was taken. Childbearing would be the domain of women."

"And then?"

"And now you see what a mistake that was!"

"Are you speaking specifically about me?"

"A little narcissistic, don't you think? No, I'm saying that we mistakenly thought one sex would prove better at nurturing, patience, teaching, etc."

"You think you chose the wrong sex?"

"I think making it a one-sex-creates-all-children was a stupid mistake. Some men would make better mothers, some women make better astronomers."

"But now we're stuck."

"Yes. For the planet earth."

"Are you already moving on? Do you have another planet you favor?"

"We've never stopped looking at literally thousands of game plans for other planets. Anything where we could sustain life. We don't move on by the way."

"You archive?"

"I have to go. And anyway, you know plenty to fulfill Vita's plans for you."

"What plans?"

"Would you like the driver to give you a little tour around Cambridge before going back for your flight?"

"No thank you. I've lived in Connecticut, I know New England. I'm ready to go home."

"Yet you hate that movie?"

"What?"

"Don't you hate it when she insists on going Home to

Kansas?"

"Yes. Who the hell wants to live in Kansas during the depression when you can hang in the Emerald City?"

"Ah. You have become a real New Yorker."

"I was always a real New Yorker."

"Well, perhaps one day when I'm down there, we'll have a latte and you can show me the West Village, I literally haven't been there in centuries."

"Who are you?"

"Don't you smell the slightest bit of smoke?"

"What?"

"Sense the slightest bit of fragility and maybe even a little anger?"

"What are you saying?"

"Next time we'll meet up in Salem. I'll show you where they drowned me to prove I was a witch. Idiots. Total idiots. But, no time for bitterness, I love my work and that's where I'm heading right now."

The little man left the room. I was stunned. This was a woman who had been burned during the Salem Witch Trials!!!! And now a Talmudic scholar? Or had the death and resurrection of her body turned her into a brilliant thinker?

As I stared at my hands, s/he re-entered. The face was the same, but s/he sported a professorial pant suit, the hair had grown ten inches and hung easily from the head, s/he wore no makeup, but her eyes somehow sparkled more. S/he carried a large handbag stuffed with her papers for her class.

I stood up and we walked to the door together.

"What do you teach?"

"The role of women in the Boston Tea Party."

"I tried to research that once. For school. I found almost nothing but a couple of magazine articles. What was the role of women?

"Everything. Who the hell do you think put the Indian war

paint on those men? Or made their buckskin skirts and jackets? Sewed their moccasins? These Bostonian men were so drunk they could barely throw the tea in the harbor without falling in themselves. Oh look, my car is here. Goodbye Deborah. Do call if you need me."

My host/ess ran out the door to a waiting Prius s/he jumped into. My black SUV was behind it and the driver was holding the door open. I had to pee, but clearly that was going to be my problem. I jumped into the car, I heard the door to the house close behind me.

"Do you think we could stop at a restaurant for just a moment?"

"You hoping for some fried clams?"

"I'm hoping not to wet your back seat!"

The driver laughed, lurched the car into traffic and took me to the nearest Howard Johnson's where I could empty my bladder. I learned when I got home that no Howard Johnson's still existed anywhere but Bangor, Maine.

The flight home was uneventful and New York was much warmer than Cambridge. I say that as a weather report as well as a metaphor. Something about being up there so close to Harvard made me feel like I had eaten bad clams. But I had only gone into HoJo's to pee and had eaten nothing before Logan Airport and the return to New York. Back in my apartment, I lay on my bed pondering.

I wondered why I felt so unsettled. In high school, I had been accepted to Radcliffe but had been advised not to go by my guidance counselor. I was a legacy from both parents being alumni so I was sure to get in.

But I never studied and I had day dreamed through my entire four years in high school, and still managed to get disturbingly good grades and good scores on the various tests for college. My guidance counselor was going on his opinion that I would take a spot away from one of the girls in my school who worked their asses off to get A's and who desperately wanted to go to Radcliffe, (now just an adjunct to Harvard). I on the other hand, he had decided, would just get married and live a suburban life. I hoped he had choked on his tongue by now, but he had assessed me as being a nobody, with no ambition and just a good brain.

How was it that Vita believed in me?

The phone rang. I was hoping it was Vita, certainly not my daughter or anybody who would need me to be in good spirits.

"Hello?"

"Hey, it's Tim."

"I know that."

"Somebody take a bite out of your ass? You sound cranky. Not your usual texture."

"Why do you think a trip to Cambridge would make me so uncomfortable?"

"You want to give me a hint?" Tim asked. "Like why you went there?"

"I thought you would know"

"Been out of this Time Frequency for a few days. I do have other loves in my life you know."

"I'm happy for you."

"Oh, you are off the rails a little! What happened?"

"I went to meet a Talmudic scholar who was not that at all. But that didn't bother me. We had a very educational talk about the real genesis of the Bible. Sorry. Not trying to be witty."

"Witty?"

"Anyway, it wasn't the person I met with. It was the place itself. I spent my married life in Connecticut near Yale. The whole academic charade seems to piss me off."

"Good thing you didn't go to Radcliffe. You would've ended up in prison."

"Or burnt as a witch."

"Yes, I can see that too."

"So what is it about me, why do you want my opinion on anything?"

"You are the CEO of the Campaign to Cut the Crap. You don't like the patriarchy much, you chose a college with little structure, and you probably didn't want to have sex with any of the men you met from Harvard. I bet they wanted you though."

"Why?"

"Good looking, smart, totally unaware of who you were. A nice white boy's dream wife."

"And I ended up becoming exactly that—a dream. The saving grace was that my husband wasn't a pretentious asshole and he actually used his learning to save lives."

"You want to go back up there with me and burn the place down? I'm free for the next few days?"

"No." I couldn't help my annoyance.

"Well, that's what you feel bad about. You don't want to play with them, but they do just fine without you."

"Shut up." Oops, too annoyed.

"Okay. Should I come over and sit next to you with my mouth closed?"

"No." I meant "yes."

"Mouth in use, but not for talking?"

"No." Now I really meant "yes."

"See you later, my grouchy little bitch buddy."

"Wait."

"You want me to try harder?"

"I'm sorry. I haven't really thanked you for all you did for Van Gogh. I know a lot of the planning and execution were your ideas. Thank you."

"I didn't do it on my own. I can't. A big deal like that requires a vote. A lot of us wanted to see you pull it off. For Van Gogh but also for the principle. All the principles: it was a good thing to do."

"How soon can you be here?"

"How soon can you open your front door?"

I put the phone down and went to my door. I opened it to find Tim standing there with a bottle in his hand.

"Why didn't you just walk through the door like you usually do?"

"Your mood. I could feel it the minute I rounded the bend onto Thompson."

"I just hate the academic mecca with its old Cape Cod mansions and its sense of satisfaction."

"The road not taken?"

"What?"

"You didn't go down that path. You could have. Not doing it turned out to have its own limitations, like 20 years as a housewife and mother. But the point really is, you can do whatever the f*ck you want now. And it's a better time in life to really find yourself."

"No bullshit please."

"I mean it. You don't belong in a big New England house filled with chores that require nothing from you but a warm coat. You belong right here in this room with your weird little room mates and your weird lover, and your even weirder other lovers, and the whole truth about the planet opened up for you."

"Am I getting it?"

"Magna cum laude, my little brainiac."

"Who are my weird roommates, you mean Louise and Ricky?"

"Yes."

"Weird?"

"More accurately your blood sucking roommates. Last time I left my steak here in a little bag for a late night snack, I found it covered in slobber with a telltale whisker or two stuck to the remains. They're pigs. And they don't pay any rent or ever contribute to the household."

I watched Louise and Ricky climb in the bedroom window as Tim started his diatribe. They both circled his ankles the way cats do. Many people interpret this as affection. Tim knew it as the implicit threat of urine sprayed on his ankles.

"Hey you two!" I called.

"Hello Deborah."

"How about me?," Tim said. "No hello?"

"Maybe after the sting of what you said wears off."

"Or maybe I order in from Carbone's. You like your steak rare am I right?"

"Very rare, no onions, no garlic. A side of mash potatoes, ditto no onions and garlic."

"Deborah? You hungry?"

The cats ran off into the bedroom tails up high. Tim smiled at me.

"It's not going to be so easy to buy me off with a steak. I still feel like shit after my trip."

"How about pasta? And a thorough examination of your body to make sure you didn't pick up any deer ticks while you were up there. New England is practically a deer tick resort these days."

"No pasta. But please order your own dinner. I'll take a bath in preparation for your kind offer to rid me of insects."

He was smart enough to let me walk away without demanding a hug from me. I wasn't ready for that. But I was cheered up to be at home with my freaky cats, my immoral and immortal lover, and a sense of who I was going to become now that I was taking the right road.

Tim came in while I was soaking in a hot tub. He brought me a glass of red wine which he put on the table next to the tub.

"See you when you're done."

"No. Please stay and talk to me."

"Okay. Why?"

Tim sat on the small chair I kept in my bathroom. He was too big for it, but he was clearly in a very accommodating mood. This worried me.

"Never mind. You must be totally uncomfortable in that chair. I'll be out quickly."

"I'm fine. What do you want to talk about?"

"I think I've come to the end of my journey."

"Wrong."

"Did the Van Gogh thing mean anything?" I asked.

"You tell me."

I took a gulp of wine. Then another. By now the hot water, the smell of New York, and the sight of Tim had lifted my spirits.

"Of course it meant a lot," I said. "We did something wonderful for a tortured soul whose talent may never be replicated in the world of painting. A complex man who understood the importance of art in civilization."

"Sounds right."

"Vincent had delusions of being in love with many women, but his real love was painting the possibility of a different world."

"Meaning what?" Tim asked.

"A world that is bright and filled with beauty. It posited the existence of a whole different way of life than the one we are restricted to: he was very moral and concerned with living in a principled way. He was enraged at Gauguin for leaving a wife and children behind to go frolic and paint in Tahiti."

"Keep drinking. I'll go get the bottle."

He left me in the tub. I finished my glass of wine and continued to float in the water turning on the hot tap to keep it really cozy. When he came back, he poured more wine into my glass and sat back down.

By now I felt like serious talking. "Vincent was a spiritual man who found religion failed to help people get an understanding and acceptance of mortality. He painted all those yellow stars to give humans and anybody else looking, the sense of a cosmos filled with more than the chicken on your plate. He believed in kindness, he was not interested in institutions of painting anymore than I would've survived the phony intelligence at Harvard. Vincent allowed two boys to kill him accidentally and insured that they would not be punished for it. He was at his most basic soul, a kind man with a terrible progression of psychological monsters in his head. And in spite of all that, he believed the universe is benign, and there is always the possibility for calmness, pure harmony and music inside the human soul."

"And?"

"And he taught me the value of art as one of the most important parts of mortality."

"Art, sex, and animals," Tim said. "That's my list."

"Really? Animals?"

"If you don't count the human animal, the others that have come into existence are some of my favorite parts of this planet."

"Even with the killing, the eating each other alive?"

"They don't have grocery stores, Deborah. Killing is their survival gig."

"Of course, only humans kill for sport."

"Not entirely true," he said. "There are a few tough guy species where the fathers eat their cubs. Almost like they've read Oedipus."

"But mostly other than humans, animals kill because they have to. Do you think there could be a planet where that wasn't necessary?"

"We've tried it," Tim said. "I've shown you two archived planets. From what we can tell, killing for survival is built into the deal. At least in this solar system."

"Then what's the point of me writing? You already know this planet is stuck in a cycle of life that is bloody, competitive, greedy, and very occasionally generous and full of beauty. End of story."

"No."

"So what is the end of the story?" I asked.

"I didn't say there is an end. But the fact is, the end is in your hands."

"What does that mean?"

"Get dressed. Come out and we'll talk in the bedroom."

"No, that's not called talking."

"Come on," Tim said. "You need to listen to me this time. I'm not going to bullshit you. I'm ready to tell you what your job is. And by the way, from a distant exploration of your body, you don't have any ticks."

Tim got up and walked out of the bathroom. I washed quickly, grabbed a towel that would wrap me up completely and joined him. He was lying on my bed, but there was no sexual vibe coming off of him.

"Have you lost interest in me Timothy?"

"No."

"Are you tired? Sated by an earlier encounter, hungry? What's wrong with you?"

"I'm here to work. After that, we can both explore the mysteries of life by rolling around on this bed."

"Work?"

"Yes."

"Please," I said. "Don't be enigmatic. I'm too confused already. Work at what?"

"I'm here to tell you why Vita chose you. Why we all voted on her choice. Why we came to agree with her about the role you would play."

"Do I really have to hear this tonight?"

"Yes."

"Go on then."

"You are a woman of exceptional intellect. You spent many years of your life ignoring that fact. Although that was boring for you, it means there is an empty space in your brain where a lot of thinking can go on for the first time."

"Are you saying this is my recompense for throwing away high school and college?"

"Yes."

"I don't understand."

"You understand that Vincent had stories to tell through his paintings," Tim said.

"Of course."

"You understand that most conscious beings have a certain amount of experience that they could express if given a chance."

"I don't know." I tried not to sound sulky.

"You were alive and living your life for the eight years you did not study. You walked the earth, you made observations that you didn't bother to catalogue or even pay attention to, but they are inside you. And since meeting Vita, and me, you have been given a unique vision of how life moves on this planet. What happens after death, what is important and what is not."

"I still go to Bloomingdale's four times a year for a free bag of makeup I will never wear. I am not a scholar, I have gone along for the fascinating ride you have given me, but I have not created it."

"You have enough information to write a closing argument."

"Of what?"

"Of this planet, Deborah."

"For whom? Is there some Federation of the Lost that need to hear my opinions?"

"Yes."

"Tim, are you sure this is not some subtle bullshit you are

feeding me?"

"For what? A nice time in bed? I'm about to get that anyway. What exactly would I be lying for? We are friends, we are lovers, we each have the freedom to have other friends and lovers. We like each other. We talk a lot. What else do I need if I'm not telling you the truth?"

"What is the closing argument for?"

"Analysis."

"Of what?"

"Of how much more time to give this experiment," he said.

"You want me to make a judgement on the fate of this planet?"

"Deborah: judge, prophet, warrior. Why do you think Vita named you after her?"

"Where do the prophet and warrior fit in?"

"You will make a written argument. It will include your judgement of what you have seen, your vision for what could exist."

"And the warrior?"

"Many of us who hear and read your argument will disagree with you. Some violently. It will be up to you to defend your judgement."

"Why me?

"Who would you suggest?"

"Vincent, or Einstein, or Nelson Mandela."

"It has to be a woman."

"Why?"

"Because."

"Because why?"

"Because of the decision made by a bunch of drunks, millions of years ago, a decision that only women would birth and raise children. That not only relegated women to a role some can barely stand, it also eliminated the men who wanted to play that role from doing that. It was an unnatural divide like Isaac and Ishmael to quote your favorite religious lies."

"You're saying that by dividing the roles into mommy and daddy, you also divided people into tribes, took away any sense of commonality among humans that might have prevented wars and maybe even violence on this planet?"

Tim nodded his head emphatically. "Yes. Divide and conquer. I'm sure you've heard that said. Even if you weren't paying attention."

"This explains my mother's antipathy towards me being in the way of my father. It explains my own disinterest in being a mommy. And we were both women with ample help, and loving husbands. I cannot imagine what the world is like for women forced to have multiple offspring and live in poverty, and get smacked around if they complain about it."

"Okay. I've told you as much as I can. You need to take some time and think about what we've said. Vita will come by. Your mother and father will weigh in. Your daughter's baby will be born. These events will help you to figure out whether or not you want to take this on. You have the right to say no."

"I just wanted to come back to the West Village."

"That's a lie, clearly a lie that you believe, but still a lie."

"You think I came back to use the 8 years that my brain was dormant?"

"I think you yearn for spring. I think you always will. I don't know why you never did something with your yearnings and your very deeply buried feelings about life, but we want you to share them with us."

"Everybody yearns for spring."

"I yearn for nipples. I yearn to touch your skin. I yearn to stop talking and start having fun. Want me to rub your breasts for a minute?"

"How will that answer this huge question you've placed in front of me?"

"It won't. But it feels good. There's a lot to be said for

beginning a project, especially one as important as this one, by having a nice time."

Now the pheromones were in the room again. The lighting changed, the two cats came through and went to curl up somewhere, the evening was here and my lover was taking off his clothes.

"I don't think I can do this, Tim. I am confused and not sure you're telling me the truth."

"Okay. I can go."

He began to get dressed again.

I started to cry. "Don't go."

He took everything back off and hopped onto my bed. He patted a place next to him and I sat down.

"You want Osiris?" Tim looked into my eyes.

"You mean right now?"

"Sure. If you need somebody mythic to validate your feelings we can be in ancient Egypt very quickly."

"I need reality right now. I need not to travel back in time or to another planet. I need…"

Tim began to pull the towel off of me. When my upper body was free of it, he drew little circles around my nipples.

"I can get him to come to you. He's available." He continued to draw his little nipple rippling circles.

"I don't want Osiris. I will again one day. Maybe after I decide what to do."

"Fine. Good idea. Take some time, this is a huge decision. Eat well, rest well, visit your daughter as a reminder of time wasted. Then decide if you want to try writing for us."

"Why are you being so sweet?"

"I like you Deborah. I've been around since the beginning of time. I've known millions of creatures, millions of humans, slept with many of them. I like you."

The lights in the room were now the most intensely beautiful of the sunset colors. The room felt warm, although it was not warm outside. I looked at this man who I had alternately trusted, hated, not trusted, lusted after and spent time with. At least this much of my decision could be made right now. As he continued to manipulate my breasts, I reached down and grabbed his erection. This was a lot less shallow than buying two lipsticks to get a free gift. I decided to let myself have some wild and uninhibited time in bed as I dropped his offer way into the deep recesses of parts of me I never access. He didn't need to drop anything.

Chapter Nineteen
Baby I Need Your Loving

I GOT THE CALL FROM MY DAUGHTER'S HUSBAND right after Tim left. I was just drifting off to sleep after an Olympic sexual sprint. I really wanted to curl into my warm bed and let the great sex, the strange and frightening offer he had made, and the odd trip to Cambridge settle in without me paying attention.

But my daughter was in labor. She had told me weeks ago that she had decided on giving birth at home with a midwife on hand. My husband and I had had a brief discussion about this. I could guess his opinion before he opined it.

"Please tell her that can be a disaster. She should go to the birthing room at Beth Israel or Lenox Hill and do a natural birth but inside a medical facility."

I had told my daughter all of this. Not the part about discussing it with her dead father. But pleading in his name for her to do her birthing where any emergency could be taken care of fast. She refused. By now she and her husband had found a depth of feeling for each other that surpassed anything they had before. She wanted to have the baby in their bedroom, with only a minimal group of people with them.

When I was pregnant with her, my husband's doctor-hood precluded any wild-eyed choices I could make about giving birth in our home. I also was not a huge proponent of pain and decided on an epidural before I went into labor. My husband was with me not only as the father of the child, but also as a respected doctor who the other doctors would not screw around with. I got the best advice, the best treatment, the birth was relatively easy, meaning less painful than being questioned by the Spanish Inquisition. Now my child was refusing these comforts and the safety net that goes with them.

I asked him to put her on the phone, but he said she was already at the stage of screaming and chortling and she didn't want phone calls. She wanted me to come up there.

In minutes I entered the world of New Life. My daughter had not asked me ahead of time to be at her birthing, but I had been very pre-occupied for months with Vincent's event and if she did ask me, I didn't remember.

I came into the room she was in quietly. She was sobbing and screaming and calling the midwife a pig.

I took her hand. She looked at me like I was something from Star Wars. A strange creature she barely recognized. Then the contraction passed and she looked like herself for a minute.

"Sweetheart, maybe it's time to go to a birthing room at —"

"No!" She squeezed my hand convincingly.

I hoped she hadn't broken any tiny bones as she gripped me.

"Listen to me, your father would want you to be in a hospital."

"Did he tell you that?"

For a split second I felt like my daughter knew everything about the journey I had been on since meeting Vita. But that was impossible. Wasn't it?

"He expressed that opinion many times as many people we knew had their children."

"No, mother. Not what I meant."

Another contraction seized her and she held my hand in a crushing vice grip. Her husband came to my side to reassure her that things were going well. She told him to f*ck off. More accurately, she screamed at him to f*ck off. And a few other choice things that went back to his infidelity. The midwife turned her back and pretended to be checking some chart she was keeping.

My daughter pulled me close. "Please get him and the

midwife to leave for three minutes," she said. "I want to talk privately to you."

"And then you'll go to a hospital?"

"Yes. Call the ambulance now."

She directed this at the midwife who nodded and picked up her cell phone.

I gently pushed the woman and the baby's father out of the room as per my daughter's request. "All right. We're alone. You'd better communicate quickly."

"I know, mother."

"Good. Then talk."

"I know what's been going on with you."

"You mean my return to the west village? My meandering through life figuring out how to live now?"

"No. I mean I know about the Lost. I know about Vincent. I know you have been to ancient Egypt many times. I know you are lovers with Osiris."

I was so shocked that I dropped her hand.

"I know how you felt about me, how you think I feel about my own child, how my grandmother felt about you." She grabbed my hand again and let out a guttural yell as the baby began to enter the world.

The midwife stuck her head in. "They'll be here in four minutes. May I just take a look at where the baby is?"

"GET OUT!"

The midwife retreated. What could go wrong in four minutes?

"I need you to know that I am not like you and my grandmother. I love you both and honor how you dealt with having a child as a prerequisite to being acceptable as women in society. But I am different. I really want this child."

A really quick flush of red filled her face as another contraction hit her.

"This f*cking child! Where the f*ck is the ambulance?"

Her husband came in. "Downstairs, getting the gurney into the elevator."

"Go away."

He did.

"Please mother. I obviously know what you're going through, and I would like it if you would share it with me to the extent you are OWWWWWW!!"

"You need that epidural now, Sweetheart!"

I nodded my head to the EMTs who entered the room and within seconds got her onto the gurney and removed her from the house. Her husband was with them in the elevator along with the midwife. There was no room for me so I went back into her apartment, made sure all stoves and heaters were off, then pulled the door locked behind me.

Although the weather was now cold, I decided to walk part way to the hospital they were heading for. She wasn't going to push this child out in the next 15 minutes.

I stopped at a fancy pants East Side bar and eatery for a very quick shot of absinthe. I tossed it back, made a silent toast to my soon to be arriving grandchild and headed to Lenox Hill excited and less scared than I had been before the drink. I had examined my new taste for alcohol with Vita and was assured that I was not an alcoholic. I had replaced avoidance with something to make reality easier for me to tolerate.

My son-in-law had pre-arranged for my daughter to have one of the luxury private birthing suites at Lenox Hill. I walked in and could barely see my daughter because of the number of serving people (not medical) who were there serving food to the father and offering my daughter services I couldn't get easily anywhere in New York. It seemed dumb to me, but when I did get past the crowd of caterers, etc., I saw my daughter lying in her bed looking much more relaxed than she had been at home.

"They serve wine, mother."

"Oh, do they?"

She seemed really calm, I tapped her husband and whispered: "Is she on some drugs?"

"Yes. They did an epidural."

"Good."

He smiled and returned to his wife and emerging child. A waiter walked by and offered me a glass of wine. I saw no reason to refuse now that everything was under control. I drank a glass of red wine and ate some lobster salad. It was ridiculous eating three feet away from a wet, emerging baby, but I had a thing for lobster salad.

In the next two hours my granddaughter was born. I hadn't known what the baby would be since my daughter and her husband wanted to be surprised. As soon as the baby was presentable, the cord cut, my daughter propped up a little and washed off, I went over to her.

The baby was a baby. She looked like a very big raisin or a very elaborate old doll. I loved her immediately and enjoyed watching my daughter's joy as they handed her this accomplishment and her husband rushed to her side in genuine bliss.

I stayed only one more hour. I was exhausted and so was everybody else in the room. As I was tiptoeing out, my daughter called me to her bedside.

"Thank you, mother."

"You did all the work."

"No. Thank you for being somebody who got chosen to save the world."

"That's not what I'm doing."

"Yes. It will be."

My daughter dismissed me sweetly by returning her attention to her newborn and helping the nurses with the next step in the process. I waved, blew a kiss, and left.

I took a cab home. Once inside and moving downtown on

Lexington, I could reflect on the timing of this child's birth. She was actually a week early. Unusual for a first child. But perfect timing for my daughter's announcement to me that she was aware of the astro-spiritual turn my life had taken.

And the child itself. New life. Genetically linked to me, but that didn't seem to be what got to me. New Life. This is where the human being begins. Although very few have such an elaborate place to enter. Lenox Hill had cornered a market on women who wanted birth to be like any other party except with less clean up on their parts.

The room had hardwood floors, the bed sheets were more like the Four Seasons hotel than a bloody hospital bed. The food and wine were actually delicious.

I wondered why these empty thoughts were filling my head. New Life. But so few people could do what my daughter just did. For many, a new baby was a disaster either economically or physically or emotionally. This was not my normal path of thought. Something about Tim's offer was taking hold.

I climbed slowly up the steps to my unit and opened the door to find both of my parents, my husband, Tim, Vita and the two cats waiting for me.

My husband spoke first. "So?"

"She's a little girl. They haven't named her yet."

"Is she cute? You were cute the minute you were born." That was my mother.

"No, not cute. She looked wrinkled and wet. I didn't stay long enough for them to gussy her up."

My father came and gave me an airy hug. His smell was distinct as always, but it seemed like his corporeal self was still slight, not completely reconfigured. I wondered briefly how he and my mother had an assignation if both of them felt as insubstantial as air?

"Congratulations! I'm glad things went smoothly."

Vita hugged me and then went to the kitchen where a lot of

food and drink was on my counter.

"Let's grab a bite, you hadn't eaten all day when you left here."

Tim took me by the elbow steered me into the kitchen. Obviously my mother and Vita had collaborated on the spread.

"Do you guys think about the disparity between how we're celebrating and how some people have to deal with a new baby?"

Vita and Tim smiled at each other.

"You're already taking us up on our offer?"

"Yes. It was noticeable to me that my daughter's experience was so much easier than it might have been."

Vita and Tim toasted each other which I found annoying. But before I could make a nasty comment, my mother, father and husband came to say goodbye. Their visit in this Time Frequency was up and they had gone a little past their return time to wherever they were supposed to be. My husband hugged me with the same anemic grip as my father's, but his smile was like the sunrise and clearly being a grandfather, even a dead one, was making him very happy.

After the family left, I sat with Vita and Tim and we snarfed up everything that had been ordered to eat and drink. I left a big piece of fish for my cats. As I did this, I was reminded of a photograph I had seen somewhere recently. It was a Greek fishing village on a small, beautiful island. Along the waterfront there was a semi-circular sidewalk where the fishermen stepped out of the water with their days' catch. Along this piece of curved concrete, several dozen cats were spread out waiting for the fishermen. Obviously, they did this every day. It was a splendid way to live and the cats all looked fluffy and well fed.

I thought it would be a good idea to travel. To see what life has to offer in places in the world I had only heard the names of. It seems I had decided to write an argument. And to do this, since I was by no means a student, I thought it best that I experience life on this planet in as many ways as it existed on every continent. Greek islands seemed like a gentle entry point.

I told Vita and Tim my idea. Of course, they loved it. Both offered to meet up with me when they could, and when I was some place they would enjoy.

I asked what the limits were. I could go back in time ten thousand years to study. That was when they had heard the last argument for or against this planet.

"You can still have sex with Osiris."

"But it's irrelevant to my work."

"This report is due, and you don't have time to wonder through the whole fifty-million-year history of the planet."

"What is my due date?"

"We've allocated you two years. It could have been eight, the Lost Years of Your Brain, but we've shown you so much we think two years is sufficient. And there is a certain amount of rush to a decision about the future of this planet."

"Two years?!"

"Yes, you don't need to use it all. But that's your limit."

They both wanted to stop talking about specifics. I dropped it for now. As I did, a wave of fatigue came over me. Vita and Tim saw it and were polite enough to leave. This was not a moment for sex. This was the last time I would spend as myself.

In the coming months, I would be tasked with working vigilantly on my opinion of the world I live in, the only planet I have any knowledge of. That seemed overwhelming right now. As they closed my door, I went into my bedroom and passed out peacefully on my bed. Within a few minutes, I sensed eight paws at the foot of the bed. It was a peaceful sleep for me and Louise, and Ricky, the deli cat.

Chapter Twenty
My Way

I NEVER WORKED HARD IN SCHOOL, but I was good at organizing my thoughts, keeping different colored tabs on the pages of my notebook. I looked, to anybody not too observant, like a diligent student. That was a good thing for my new life's work. My first life's work consisted of making Halloween costumes and dinner for three in Connecticut.

"LIFE'S WORK:" I wrote that down on the folder I had opened in my new laptop.

"LIFE'S WORK:" all capital letters with a colon. Then I sat and stared into space. I guess I was waiting for inspiration. But of course, that doesn't work.

When Louise jumped up on my desk, she read my heading. Then, without a word, she put herself into the position she liked best for cleaning herself after using her litter box. She was licking and talking which made it hard to hear her.

"Could you either wait to talk to me or postpone your bath?"

She looked up at me. Obviously, I was an idiot, or I could have heard her with her face buried in her ass. But she knew I was under pressure so she sat in a different circle on my desk and began to talk.

"I'm excited for you Deborah."

"Really?"

"Sure. You've been on Thompson street long enough. And of course, it will be your launch pad and home base."

"Meaning?" I asked her.

"You have to travel, don't you? Not just to other Time Frequencies but to each of the seven continents. At least the ones you've never explored."

"I hadn't gotten that far in my planning."

"Well, you can't sit in the West Village and decide if planet earth is worth keeping on with."

"No. Of course not."

I realized with some embarrassment that this cat had done more creative thinking so far than I had. Maybe she should dictate the argument to me.

"I have explored North America most of all."

"Ever been to Arkansas?"

"No."

"The Russian River in northern California?"

"No."

"Any other borough in New York City?"

"No. Why would I?"

"Wow."

"You mean to see the disparity economically?"

"I mean this is called the Empire State, and New York is the seat of that empire. You need to learn about more than Carbone's and Bloomingdale's." A sarcastic cat!

"I could jump on a subway and go to Coney Island."

"Good."

"Do I need to do all of the boroughs?"

"Deborah!"

"What?"

"Use your time wisely so you can make as strong an argument as possible."

"Yes."

"And," Louise continued, "as Glinda says in the Wizard of Oz, 'it's always best to begin at the beginning.' Which for you is the city of New York. Then the upstate parts which will be as foreign to you as Slovenia."

"Upstate?" Louise smiled at me as I said this.

"Grab Tim and go to Albany, Buffalo, Croton on Hudson."

"Maybe I'm not up to this Louise."

"When I talk about hard places to get to, you can decide."

She was done with her list of suggestions for now. I got this message loud and clear as she renewed her lower body licking and cleaning.

I knew she was right. Any shame I felt at getting this project started by talking to Louise was more than compensated for by the fact that it is a rare privilege to talk to a cat. Or dog. And as dumbfounded as I was by the task at hand, she believed in me. She had also given me a starting point to think about.

How much of the world should I actually visit? How much of my time should be spent in the world of Now, as opposed to say the world of yesteryear? How could I codify and categorize places that would give me a balanced view of our world?

I decided to look at a good world map. I went to a search engine and pulled up in sequence, several maps. Some showed topography, some were easier to read than others. I chose a brightly colored National Geographic map and stared at it.

Counting the number of countries, counties and states I had been to was sobering. But I had plenty of time to travel. And if this report was to become a discussion point for the fate of the planet, I had to do the work.

At this moment I understood exactly why Vita had chosen me. I had avoided serious scholarship so desperately when I was in the prison system known as high school, that I was filled with an exuberance now. Sure, the Bronx had never been on my itinerary, but there were great things to see and taste and learn almost everywhere I looked on this map.

The whole thing was exhausting. But for once I didn't just run out for lattes. I ordered them in, along with some chocolate pastries and for some reason, cheese, two of the major food groups.

I left the map on my screen as the order arrived. I started with the latte and a chocolate croissant and by the time they were finished, I was only about halfway through my on-the-map inspection of New York state.

This project called for organization. I was good at that. Mostly, my organizing had been done around my husband's schedule, my daughter's schedule, my housekeeper's schedule, and my hair dresser's schedule. This time the organization was all mine.

I did not want to use up all my energy moving around or I would have no time to write up an argument for or against what I had seen. I arbitrarily gave one year to travel and study, and one year to analysis, questioning, and finally writing my thesis.

This felt stiff and I knew it. But I had to start somewhere. I decided, in spite of Louise's advice, to do New York last. I looked at the map and California caught my eye. It was as if the map on my laptop was actually pulsing on the state of California. I had been to Los Angeles and San Francisco on trips with my parents when I was 11 or 12. In fact, it was in Los Angeles that I had first felt my longing for a spring time that I couldn't describe.

If I started at the farthest point west on the continent where I was, I could zig zag up and down the states all the way back to Thompson Street. Given my lack of experience as a traveler, I figured I should go someplace, and then come home and write up my notes. Then head out again. This seemed like it would yield the most comprehensive results.

I began to feel the pull of visiting places with vast economic disparities since that was the part of life on earth I had come to understand with the Vincent experience: there sat a man whose talents were intergalactic, but who could barely afford to eat. And his work, his masterpieces, were bought up by people who could have just bought the country of France if they wanted to look at something extraordinarily beautiful.

Wasn't that a big part of what Vincent tried to teach me?

Money is not the goal. You cannot buy a soul. You cannot buy somebody else's gifts and talents, but you could pay money and seem to own them.

I switched off the map and searched for charts about economies in the U.S. Where were the poorest of us, the richest of us, those in between? The charts were startling and it was all beginning to make me yearn for the cosmetics counter at Bloomingdale's.

I walked around my apartment for a few minutes. Sitting is the new cancer according to all the latest information. And before my husband had fallen over dead, he had encouraged me to walk with him every weekend no matter the weather.

A lot of good it did him. But he knew it was a vital thing to do. Walk. Get up and go. Look around, smell the river that ran about a mile behind our house.

I ate another pastry. I drank my second latte. The phone rang. For once I didn't look at the caller's ID. I just picked it up.

"Hello? Mother?"

"Sweetheart! How are you? How is the little one?"

"You mean Deborah?"

"She's named after me?"

"Yes."

"Fantastic." I was delighted.

"She is a natural nipple sucker by the way. They took to each other like you and Tim."

"Sweetheart?! How much of my life have they filled you in on?" I sounded unusually concerned.

"All of it."

"My god. I wish they hadn't done that"

"Why not, mother?"

"Because I am your mother. You shouldn't know about my sex life, should you?"

"It seems like we've been involved in a cosmic reality that

goes far deeper than who you play with."

"True." I nodded my head. "Sweetheart,
I am a bit worried about this task I've taken on."

"If you're wondering if you're up to the task at hand, let me assure you I have never met anybody as smart as you. Or as generous. I believe you were chosen because of your genetic strength, and because you have tried so hard to play by the rules, even though the rules really didn't fit you."

"You knew that as you were growing up?"

"Absolutely." She assured me.

"So when did you develop this opinion of me?"

"When I got pregnant. The minute I felt little you as a real thing inside of me. I realized that it is a huge choice to have a child. It's clear that you did not have any choice. But you still gave me many moments of wonder and a constant sense of being loved. That's heroic, mother."

She started to cry.

"I'm sorry. I wish I had been more joyful about parenting."

"You did a beautiful job. You seemed delighted with me even when, in retrospect, you must have felt very empty."

"I didn't even feel it. The emptiness. Did you know my whole life that I was missing my contract with creation."

"Who told you that? That expression?"

"I just said it. Why?"

"One of the nurses at Lenox Hill. She is a Yoruban priestess, the only woman ever ordained in Nigeria."

"Yoruban?" I thought I knew a lot. But not this.

"The slaves we brought over," my daughter continued. "Many were Yoruban and Ebo people. They were forbidden to practice their religions for fear they would rebel against their kidnappers in a fever of their memories of freedom."

"You learned about one's contract with creation from one of the nurses?" I was stunned.

"Yes."

"Is it possible I could meet her?" I sounded shy.

"I have told her all about you."

"When will you see her again?"

"Tomorrow."

"What is her name?" I asked.

"I don't know her name. But her appellation as a priestess is Yeye. It's respectful to call her that."

"Do they call her Yeye at Lenox Hill?" I asked.

"No."

"Is she treated with any sort of dignity?" Influenced by my mother and father who were still activists for social justice, even dead!

"It is impossible not to treat her well. She is tall, powerful, kind, and all the newborns grab for her as if she smelled like chocolate breast milk. That's why we began to talk. I noticed that whenever she entered the room, the baby would stop what she was doing, Yeye would say a very quiet hello and the baby would reach out her little arms to be held by her."

"Even if she had been nursing?"

"Yes, mother."

"I will be there tomorrow at two. Promise it won't embarrass you if I ask her some questions that I should know the answer to."

"Like what?"

"Why were her people singled out for slavery? Why did the leaders of the villages let their people go?"

"That's not embarrassing. Embarrassing is why Nigeria has let history repeat itself. Why didn't anybody stop the men of Boko Haram from grabbing hundreds of girls and dragging them off to be their slave wives? You know this story don't you mother?"

"Didn't the UN try to stop them?"

"Now that is an embarrassing question, mother. Please read up on this before you come. Nobody did anything to retrieve these girls. Some of them escaped, and some of them were freed by a group of men in the forest where they were kept captive."

"Men?"

"Yes, men who chanted and put out incantations and spells on the members of Boko Haram."

"Yeye told you this??"

"Yes. She told me that Boko Haram members heard the chanting and knew they were dead if they did not release the girls."

"I have to talk to Yeye. Should I bring food?" Still using my mother's strong suit: party planning.

"Yes, do. Yeye eats organic, she eats healthy, she eats a diet that could sustain the earth if we all gave up eating so many cows and pigs."

"I will bring stuff. I will bring enough for her to feel respected by me. I am feeling so renewed sweetheart. Thank you."

With that we hung up and I went straight to my computer and read for hours about Nigeria. About the Yoruban and Ebo people. About the work of spirit in their lives.

When I was done, I printed up my notes. Copied everything onto a little black thingy Tim had given me to back up my material and grabbed a glass of wine.

My head was spinning as I read, and for the first time, I understood the gift I had been given by Vita, by Tim, even by the ruthless Set. Louise and Ricky came and went, and I was glued to my reading. Entranced by my studies. For the first time in my whole life.

At two p.m. sharp I walked into my daughter's room at Lenox Hill. It was the first time it had occurred to me to ask why my daughter hadn't gone home yet. The baby was three days old, usually a new mother is booted out by then.

"Hello, Sweetheart." I said.

My daughter was dozing with her child. They had obviously been having a feeding session and both had passed out.

"Hello!" She woke up, took the sight of me in with delight.

"May I hold her?"

I reached out my arms and gently took my granddaughter and held her close to my chest. She remained sound asleep. This reminded me of my daughter. She had been an enthusiastic eater and a wildly cooperative sleeper, often sleeping for four or five hours at a time even as an infant.

The baby was little, but she was beginning to take human form. We were staring at her when Yeye entered the room.

"You must be this baby's ancestor."

"Yes, and you must be Yeye?"

She was dressed in a nurse's uniform but had the most colorful piece of cloth wrapped as a turban around her head. She was as described, tall, powerful, compelling.

I spoke. "Thank you for the care you've been giving these two."

"I'm a child of Yemaya. It comes very naturally to me."

At this moment the baby's eyes opened and I handed her back to my daughter who was fully woken up.

"Mother, you and Yeye should sit down and talk, as long as she's in here, she's considered On Duty. I am her main charge. So just close the door and we will be in our own little expensive cocoon." My daughter took back her child.

The nurse priestess smiled and closed the door. We went and sat together on one of the many pieces of furniture my daughter's birthing suite provided. I pulled out a bag of food and asked if anybody wanted to eat. Nobody did—we just began to talk.

"I am writing a paper on the situation in our world. Saying it sounds strange. Like I'm the judge of the planet. Which I am not. But I have been asked to write up observations, and I know nothing about Africa or the Ivory Coast or the Yoruban people."

For the next two hours, as my daughter and her baby slept, this woman gave me a capsule version of the African slave trade and the capture of the Yoruban people, coming mostly from Nigeria. It led me to question her politely about the current existence in Nigeria, of the Islamic terrorists known as Boko Haram.

"Yes. Of course that story was all over the western press. But not for long."

She didn't sound bitter. She smiled graciously as she explained her understanding of exactly what had happened there.

"Boko Haram is a group of Muslim insurgents. They are not really Muslim any more than your Fundamentalist Christians actually follow the teachings of Christ as described in the Bible."

"Do you think of the Bible as a book of true stories?" I asked her.

"No."

"So your reference?"

"I believe in a very different way of looking at the world than anything in the Bible or the Koran. Yoruba does believe in a Divine Spirit, but s/he is not the only divinity, and certainly not the only important guide."

"Your tradition is pantheistic?" I asked.

"Yes. But let's not waste time on things you can research. If it is suitable to your interest, let me tell you that there is a reason why Boko Haram being in Nigeria is so important."

"Please."

"I know you are aware that several years ago these men kidnapped several hundred teenaged girls. They needed wives. They needed breeding material and they assessed correctly that the capture of black girls in Nigeria would not stir the world's rage."

"Because these children were black?"

"Yes."

"Is that why you think the world did nothing to help the girls to escape?" I felt very sad.

"Yes. That and the corruption of the man in power at the time in Nigeria. A man unfortunately named Good Luck Jonathan."

"His real name?"

"Let me go on. I need to be out of this room very soon."

"Please."

"So the girls were taken—some of them escaped on their own the first year. Most did not. And the world stood by clucking their tongues. Few people know the history of Nigeria as a great source of sale priced humanity when the British, Dutch and Americans were grabbing slaves. But for those of us who knew this to be true, this terrible kidnapping could not stand."

"Did you go to Nigeria?" I asked.

"Yes."

"And ultimately all the girls were set free?" I was hoping so.

"Not all. Some were dead, some were so entrenched with small children they could not be saved. But the vast majority, I am proud to say, we liberated."

"How?" I stared at her.

"Boko Haram was in the Sambisa forest, where they brought their new wives. The Nigerian army is afraid of this place."

"Because?"

"Deborah, go home and study. I will just give you the pieces to the puzzle.

"Thank you."

"Many of the slaves who landed in the American south came from Nigeria, hundreds of years ago. And unresolved history is unresolved. So when Boko Haram took up residence in Nigeria, particularly in the Sambisa Forest, there is a link. Find it yourself."

"I will."

"Here is the outline of the story: Good Luck Jonathan would do nothing to save these kidnapped young women. They had been taken from a boarding school where they were getting educated and would eventually have contributed to great things in Nigeria. This did not interest him. What he was afraid of was the Sambisa forest and trying to talk the army into an assault on what they knew was the Boko Haram stronghold."

"This is when you went over?" I asked.

"Yes. I am the only woman ordained in Nigerian history as a Yoruban Priestess. With this honor comes the responsibility to care for my people."

"Were the girls who were taken part of Yoruban culture?" I asked.

"No. But they were children, and as a daughter of Yemaya." Her eyes pierced mine. "Please look her up," she said. "I am always obligated to save children. I went to Lagos and gathered a group of Yoruban men. They were fearless because they knew how to defeat the Muslim insurgents. Or any insurgents for that matter. They know the history of Nigerian slavery and will not allow it to happen again."

"Did you have armaments?" Deborah the ignorant.

"Armaments were not our main weapon."

"What was?"

"A group of us agreed on a ritual we would perform. We agreed on what chants and incantations would be most effective. We went, under cover of darkness to the forest and waited until Boko Haram was gathering for their evening meal. We began to chant. They could not see us, but they could hear us. They could not understand our words, but our spirits came through very clearly to them."

"What kind of spirits?"

Yeye looked keenly at me.

"That, Deborah, you won't find on your computer. And unless you become an initiate into Yoruban tradition, you cannot know how we do what we do. I can tell you that we began to chant and, after several hours of relentless sounds hitting the ears of these cowardly 'rebels,' they took off running out of the forest leaving their wives and children behind."

"Did you run in and save them?" I asked.

"They needed no saving."

"The girls saw their captors take off and left with their children?" Me, smart for once.

"Yes."

"How far did they have to travel?" Me, not so smart.

"Once they were out of the forest, they were greeted by the Nigerian army who had gotten news of our success. Happy to take credit for freeing these girls, they took them and returned them to their families."

"Boko Haram did not follow?" I was surprised.

"I am going to let you hear the sounds from that night. Then you will understand many things that now elude you. Are you willing to come with me to the Sonrisa Forest?"

"Yes."

YeYe looked over at my sleeping daughter and grandchild. When she turned back to me, she was a different woman: A Nigerian woman with powers as great as anyone I had ever met. She took my hands in hers and looked directly into my eyes. "Please close your eyes, and just listen inside your soul."

I closed my eyes. I felt awkward. I was afraid that this was where I would find out that I could not complete what the Lost expected of me because I had no interior life.

Then, from deep in the recess of the universe, a drum began to beat. It got louder and louder as more drums joined in and soon, I could hear men's voices. They were chanting in unison and it was overwhelming. The depth of their intensity, the repetition of their words, the intention in their voices, all became crystal clear to me as my body became covered in goose bumps. Yeye held my hands more tightly. I kept listening. After ten minutes, or maybe two hours, I could no longer tell what increments of time went by, the men stopped chanting and there was a silence. Yeye was watching me. She gently let go of my hands and led me to a chair which I fell into. I wasn't sure I could speak, but when I opened my mouth words miraculously came out in the right order.

"You defeated their violence without having to confront them?" I was shivering from the sounds I had heard.

"We did confront them. They have no spirit, we brought out ours. There is nothing as frightening to an empty soul as a person with spirit."

There was a quiet knock on the door. My daughter woke up and called out and her husband entered.

"They're ready to release you!"

"Now? Right now?"

"Yes. I think they are receiving a celebrity in labor and don't have a suite for her and her entourage. Don't you want to come home?"

"Of course she does," Yeye assured him.

Then she helped me out of the chair and we embraced.

"I can't thank you properly, I can't express anything right now. I wish I knew more." I bowed slightly to Yeye.

"There are endless histories of people doing what we did. Overcoming an enemy with spirits. I think it is more important for your report than statistics on rich vs poor or any other comparison. There is nothing that can defeat or suppress a person with spirit."

"Should I just read about —"

"I'm leaving now. You'll find these answers easily."

She walked over to my daughter and kissed her gently on the cheek, then she smiled at the baby and rubbed her hands on the baby's stomach. She said something to the baby, who gurgled happily, then she nodded to my son in law and left the room.

He was packing up my daughter's things. I began to help. In twenty minutes we had the baby in a carrier with all her baby things packed.

I told my daughter to go home with her family and I would pay the bill and follow them.

I went to the administrative offices and wrote a large check for my daughter's stay and all the care she had received. I thanked them and then went back up to the birthing floor. The suite we had occupied was now inhabited by somebody who looked familiar to me from the movies. I went to the nursing station and asked if Yeye would be caregiver to this woman, and if so, could I leave a note for her.

"I'm sorry madam, but the woman you describe has left."

"Well, can you give her this note tomorrow or whatever day she returns?"

"She isn't a regular nurse here. We brought her in for your daughter."

"Why?"

"I have to look in the file."

She clicked the computer and brought up my daughter's file. She looked at it and turned back to me.

"Is this your signature?"

I stared at a letter that had been scanned into their computer. It asked for a woman named Yeye who had been my daughter's nurse and who we would appreciate them hiring for my daughter's birth. It was signed by me. The signature was mine.

"Yes. Yes, it is. I'm sorry for any confusion, this whole

process is so new to me. I guess I'd forgotten that I made this request. But thank you, may I just grab her contact information, I can put it in my phone in case we need her."

The nurse was clearly rushing to get rid of me, but she was cordial as she let me copy a phone number off the letter. The big check I had given her was very big.

"Here at Lenox Hill we go the extra mile to keep our new mothers relaxed."

"Well. I'll be going."

The woman jumped up from her computer and ran to the suite now occupied by the celebrity and her entourage. She had been signaled in some way.

I sauntered to the elevator. Then my phone rang. I grabbed it—it was a text from Tim. "All went well?"

I began a text conversation. "Yes."

"Was she helpful?"

"If you mean the priestess, she was invaluable. Gave me insights I would not have known to look for and saved me weeks of research already done by every economist, sociologist and historian in the world."

"Good. Glad it worked out."

"She was your idea?"

"Do you want to meet later on?"

"Was Yeye your idea?"

"I was thinking Carbone's at 8."

"Will you tell me then?"

"No."

"Please order me the usual for starters. I will see you at eight."

"Good."

"Tim? Thank you."

"Gotta go."

The text stopped as it had started, the elevator arrived, and I was on my way to my daughter's place to see them get settled in. My mind was crystal clear. The way to look at the planet earth was to evaluate whether the spirit of its inhabitants was strong enough to overcome all the inequities, injustices, and environmental crises.

Quite a big job for a girl who had passed her high school French exam on Camus' "L'Etranger" with the final words: "Who cares about this man and his mother? We all have mothers." Of course, my French was perfect, so they had to give me an A.

Chapter Twenty One
Got The World On A String

IT WAS HARD TO DEAL with the idea of travel: where to go and what to look for. I began to conclude that travel was not the point. The theme of my work had taken shape. It was not my job to duplicate existing research on the earth. Climate change, income disparity, tribalism, the struggle to let patriarchy die and be replaced—these had all been studied and written about by scholars. That wasn't my job.

I tried to accept that Vita had seen something in me that included an understanding of the magic in the world. I had not been confused by travel on the Space Time continuum. It seemed a lot easier than transferring subways from the east side to the west. And certainly easier than going to another borough on the train.

When I had lived in Connecticut we traveled by car. You had to—everything was miles away from our house. The seasons came and went and I was taking my child to school, my husband to work on days when he was riding home with a colleague. I went to the grocery store. I yearned for something connected to Spring that I never understood. What was the hidden clue in that?

Why couldn't I look deeply at Van Gogh's Arles series without crying? What did a pair of white patent leather shoes mean to a child who could have whatever she asked for?

For a few minutes, my mind fell into a hamster cage and all I could see was me getting in and out of our Audi going and doing the errands of the suburban housewife.

How many times had I gone into the cleaners my arms filled with clothing and upholstery. How many times had I come out of the local market with a cart filled with slightly bloody packages of meat (sealed in a plastic bag, but you could still see the blood). How many supermarket plastic bags had I struggled to open to stick something inside it? An onion. Some broccoli. I was swimming in this tediousness.

And I had swum in that tedium for decades. Why had I done that? Why hadn't I thought my way out? By the time my child was four I was totally redundant. We had a nanny. My child went to pre-school and then into the classy public school system.

Why had I done nothing?

Did I have any spirit that was finally free to express itself? The meeting with YeYe had been reassuring but not conclusive.

This was the key to the larger question I had to answer.

It is an abstraction to say "does the human being have enough spirit to save the world?" I needed to ask if I have enough spirit? And if I do, what the hell had I done to bury it for so long?

My whole life I had been exposed to intellect. Art. Culture. Ideas about a better society. We had spoken to intelligent people and my parents had run a small but significant human rights organization. It was their lives.

I knew instinctively that something about my parents love for each other made me a beloved but peripheral part of their lives. They had never failed to be caring, but I was secondary to Them as a couple. I had no siblings and the few cousins I had lived far away. They never got me a pet, but if every kid who grew up pet-less wasted high school and college, the world would be even worse off than it is now.

Did I ever ask for a pet?

I liked the creatures behind the house when I moved to Connecticut as a young wife. I showed my daughter the squirrels and hares and foxes that lived nearby. And now remembering that, I remembered that they brought about the same fear that looking at Van Gogh's paintings had brought about. A fear of? Life? Because there was Death?

I had suffered no traumatic losses to death. My parents were atheists, but because their organization worked internationally, they had certainly dealt with church people. They had no negative attitude about religion. It simply meant nothing to them.

I tapped my fingers on my desk. My mind was snagged on something.

If nobody close to me had died until I was a grown woman, if my parents neither lauded nor condemned a wide tent full of people of different beliefs, then the subject of Death, of Spirit, or even of the purpose of existence might never have come up.

Did I sit in high school and try to comprehend the world as I now know it? With Einstein's physics as my starting point, the Higgs Boson particle something to wonder about? And the Spacetime Continuum, did that cross my mind while I sat not listening to my high school or college teachers?

I know I thought about sex. My friends over at Our Lady of Pompeii. I thought about these boys anatomically: mostly about their hands and really about their fingers. Was I just so sexually obsessed that the rest of me lay dormant? Or is there no rest of me?

One of the squirrels was killed on the road in front of our Connecticut house. I didn't look at it closely, but I began to feel something strange when I saw the little creature dead. I made sure my daughter never saw it. But I never forgot it. Is that what I feel when I look at a Van Gogh painting?

I needed to find an organized way to ask and answer these questions before I tried to write up a description or critique of how human beings show their spirit. Or lack of spirit.

Death. The most poignant of all human realities. Was that the Thing that Could Not Be Named or even Thought About?

I had seen Romeo and Juliet on a TV movie channel when I was about 10. I had never read the story, so I was enjoying how pretty everybody was until the death scene.

After that I began to remember lines of poetry: "A glooming peace this morning with it brings, the sun for sorrow will not show its head. For never was a story of more woe than that of Juliet and her Romeo."

When I finally read the play, I realized I had seen Zefferelli's edited version of this last speech. I liked the edit better than the full speech. Did this mean anything?

After a school outing to see Macbeth, I came home and repeated to myself:

"She should have died hereafter. There would have been a time for such a word."

But then I got called to dinner and with the lines running constantly in the back of my soul, I ate my dinner and even participated in my parent's conversation about their latest fundraiser and whether the dinner menu had to be expanded to include a choice of salmon.

And it wasn't only Shakespeare I muttered to myself. These couplets or poetic portions seemed to sear very deeply into me. I can remember the extreme complexity of how they made me feel. But for some reason, I was not moved to read more Shakespeare or to write anything myself. Why not?

Louise entered the room, she was on her way out the window when I called to her.

"Louise? Do you think of me as somebody shallow?"

"Could I answer you if I do?"

"Yes. Please. Answer me, it's important."

"No. Nobody could think of you as shallow. You're too withdrawn inside some deep space inside yourself to be shallow."

"Do you know I love having you here. You and Ricky? Am I at all expressive?"

"What's wrong with you, Deborah?"

"I'm trying to figure out if I have a human spirit. And if I do, why haven't I done more with it."

"Oh."

"It's okay, you were on your way out. Go on with your plans."

The cat stared at me and then came closer and sat down next to me. "Where's this question coming from?"

"I don't know."

"Yes, of course you know. You're a very smart woman."

"I think this task I've been given is making me question myself."

"Whether you're up to doing this argument thing?"

"No. Whether I am exactly what I am beginning to think is the fundamental question I need to answer."

"Are people shallow?" Louise asked me.

"Do people use their spirit to overcome things? Or does the human spirit just languish around while people continue their same old patterns and the world spins endlessly but goes nowhere."

"Wow. Do you have any sardines?"

"I know. I'm sorry. These are not questions to spring on somebody on their way out for the evening."

"Deborah. You have been more than generous to Ricky and me. Why not just open a can of tuna and we can sit and talk."

I went into the kitchen and was shocked to find the larder full up. I don't shop for food anymore. Who had done this?

"Louise?"

She tinkled her little paws into the kitchen.

"Yes?"

"Who filled my kitchen with this food?"

"I have no idea."

I opened the tuna, put it on a plate, and we went back together into my bedroom.

Louise was a delicate eater. She would pull a piece of tuna to the edge of the plate and eat it. She didn't eat like a dog who would just stick her face into the food and gobble it up as fast as she could.

"So talk." The little cat's mouth was full but her words were clear.

"I think the question I need to present in my report is about spirit."

"Uh huh."

"And I'm not sure why I have been so shy of dealing with my own spirit all my life until I met Vita."

"Does that matter? You're dealing with it now."

"Yes, it matters."

Before answering me Louise worked on a big chunk of the albacore and pulled it apart enough that she could bring a piece of it to the plate's edge. "You really think most people just land on their deepest spirit like it was the most obvious thing in the world?" she asked.

"I don't know."

"You think Joan of Arc was born waiting to be burnt at the stake for her beliefs? You think Marie LaVeau knew that being a voodoo queen would help her free more slaves than anybody else?"

"Who?"

"Marie, Marie the Voodoo Queen, Marie Marie La Veau!" If a cat can giggle, Louise did.

"Who are you talking about?"

"I'm surprised your talks with Yeye didn't get into this. Anyway, go to your laptop. Put in Marie La Veau freeing slaves. You'll have to rifle through a lot of crap about her, racist crap. But you'll see through it and learn about her."

"Racist and misogynist crap? Is that more accurate?"

"Read it. We'll talk tomorrow. And thanks for the tuna."

"Are you going to meet Ricky?"

"Yeah. And I'm already late." She walked to the window, crawled down the bricks, and was gone.

I was hesitant about this instruction of hers. Of course, Joan of Arc was always Joan of Arc. Wasn't she? But a voodoo queen? Wait. Hadn't Yeye mentioned in passing that Yoruba became morphed in America into several traditions, one of them voodoo?

I ran to the laptop and opened it up to Marie LaVeau. By the time I had finished reading it was very late, and I was very excited.

I called Tim.

"You in the mood for some rolling around?" He laughed.

"In about an hour."

"Okay, I won't need food. So eat before I get there if you're hungry." Unusual for Tim.

"Are you working?" The kind of question I knew better than to ask. But I asked anyway.

"Yes."

As he hung up I heard a woman's voice in the background. "Working" was a nice euphemism for what he was doing. But as long as he showered on his way over, I genuinely didn't care.

I sat waiting for Tim and finished the scraps of tuna Louise had left on the plate. My mind was simmering. I had looked up Marie La Veau and the story, even on Wikipedia was captivating. If anybody had taught me this kind of history in school, I would have become a scholar.

Tim walked through the door and into my bedroom where I was hunched over my laptop on the bed.

"You know about Marie La Veau?"

Tim grinned. "Intimately."

"She was beautiful."

"Still is."

"Yes. I forgot."

"You want to talk to her?" he offered.

"I think I can get what I need from you, but let's see."

"Who turned you on to the African diaspora?"

"Yeye, the woman you sent to my daughter's birthing suite."

"Daughter of Yemaya."

He said this so casually that it didn't register how much knowledge he had accumulated in the millions of years he had been on earth.

"You want some wine, there's an open bottle on my counter."

"I'll bring two glasses."

He went into my kitchen to get the wine. I yelled in to him: "Did you stock up my kitchen with food and drink?"

"Yes."

He came back in with a little tray I had never seen. On it were two glasses, the bottle of wine, and a piece of something that looked like pale orange pudding, with some pita bread next to it.

"What is that?"

"Tarama. I'm in a Greek mood."

"You were just in a Greek woman?"

"None of your business. But yes."

I stuck a piece of the bread in the orange glop. It was fantastic.

"Is this smashed-up caviar?" I asked.

"Yes."

"Are you too tired to talk?"

"Never."

"I am trying to figure out what the hell I'm doing For my closing argument." I stuck more bread and tarama in my mouth.

"I know. That's why I sent Yeye."

"Because?"

"Cut through a lot of the sociology bullshit that we know all about. The charts of income inequality, the dire warnings about global climate change. The acceptable ways of analyzing this species of yours."

"I should cut right to the spirit?"

"That's why you were chosen."

"Because I have spirit?"

"Your yearning for spring time. Your fear and hope of getting stuck inside a painting, your inability to tolerate the insignificant teachings of most schools."

"Couldn't that just mean I'm a chapter in the Diagnostic Manual of Mental illness?"

"We've been on this planet a very long time. Some say too long. Some of the Lost believe we should vacate and let you all die off. There are a lot of other places we can investigate."

"But?"

"Vita has a theory, and over the millennia, I have come to agree with it."

"Please?"

"Certain things happened on this planet that killed off a lot of peoples' spirits and left them instead with religion."

"Is that the reason people are so cruel?"

"When was the last time you went to a funeral?"

"My husband died a few months ago."

"I was there, all you did was cremate him and have a little event in his honor."

"So?"

"You didn't wait to see his spirit leave his body. You didn't know it would."

"Will you come with me?"

"Where to?"

"To Riverside Chapel. They have funerals all day, every day."

"You go yourself."

"Why?"

"Just go. I'll stay here and catch up on some crap on TV. I'll be here when you get back. Then we'll talk."

"Why am I going, Tim?"

"Didn't I just tell you?"

"To see the deceased's spirit leave the body?"

"You need to go now, it's getting to be bad traffic."

Tim grabbed my TV remote and turned on some crap. He passed by the news, the documentary channel, the one or two intelligent procedurals that are on all day. He went to the Real Housewives of New Jersey.

"What are you doing?"

"Laughing."

I heard the sounds of the women, high pitched and drunk. I turned back and Tim was sipping red wine and watching as they screamed hysterically at each other over pathetic things.

"Did you have a hard time with whomever you were with who gave you the Tarama?" I shot back to Tim.

"Athena? No. We had a fine time. She's just a bit of a bore."

"Born from her father's head with no mother. That's tough."

"The real point is she has a lot of the qualities of Deborah. But she can't get out of the Greek mythology and do anything in the real world. That's why we chose you."

"We were supposed to talk about Marie LaVeau."

"You have to really understand spirit for that discussion."

"Why?" Did I sound as dumb as I felt?

"The African traditions are not like the Judeo-Christian-Islamic stuff. But you don't really know much about that even."

"Marie is a real woman, right?"

"Oh yes. She birthed 15 children!"

"Is that some kind of snotty remark about my one little vaginal birth?"

"What?!" He had no idea what I meant.

"Never mind. 15 children and she's still beautiful?"

"Stunning."

"And you will tell me about Yoruba and all that when I get back?"

"Yes, my one and only Deborah."

"I'm leaving now Tim. I have a funeral to spy on."

I hopped a cab on Sixth Avenue and was at the Riverside Funeral Chapel in minutes. I walked in trying to look appropriately bereaved. I looked at the names of the family funerals and chose one that was currently in session.

There was a chapel full of people, I stood at the back. The service was almost over, the people in the pews were weeping and some were calling out to Margaret, the poor dead creature on display in the open casket. Subtlety was not the objective for embalming. The deceased looked like a candle that was missing its wick.

As the service concluded, the mourners walked by the casket on their way out. There would be no procession to a cemetery because the body was to be cremated. Passing the open casket some of them spoke to the dead woman, some broke down, but soon they were gone, and the lid of the casket was closed.

The coffin was moved very quickly after the chapel emptied out. I followed it to the crematorium and hoped nobody would ask what the hell I was doing there. For a few minutes the big box was left on its base while they were either heating up the crematorium or stopping for a cup of coffee. I walked timidly up to it.

When I got within a few feet, I felt something strange happening. The lid of the casket raised about a half an inch and a bunch of what first looked like smoke began to pour out of it. As I stood and watched, the smoke formed itself into the image of the woman I assumed was in the casket. Only it was Margaret when she was younger. I watched as the young smoke thing rose above the casket and flew to the ceiling of the crematorium.

Once up high she began to make small noises. She was chuckling and talking to herself.

"I guess they couldn't afford the good makeup artist. Did you see the shit they put on my face? And blue eyeliner? What is this, 1956?"

She continued to mutter and chuckle as she pulled a cigarette out of thin air and lit it with her finger.

"And the hair!! That must have been my sister's choice. Cheap and ugly, always her specialty where I was concerned."

I looked up at her and she caught sight of me.

"Who the hell are you?" Margaret's spirit hissed.

"Oh. No. I walked into the wrong space. Forgive me."

"You walked into the room with the cremation chamber by mistake?" She sounded incredulous.

"I wanted to see if the body inside the casket had a spirit." Oh no. She's going to get really mad at me now.

"Well, now get out! I look like shit."

"Are you scared of the cremation?"

"Are you?"

"No. I'm not being cremated."

"Neither am I! Didn't you see me leave my body behind?" She blew smoke rings as she ridiculed me.

"Yes, yes I did."

"So now what do you want?"

"How do you feel?"

"Young. Pain free. Ready to move on."

"Do you believe God did this for you?"

"No." She chuckled, but not maliciously.

"Do you believe in reincarnation?"

"Haven't you read anything about physics? Matter can neither be created nor destroyed. I'm matter now."

"Where will you go?"

"No idea."

At this moment, the official cremators entered and while the lively spirit of the deceased watched from on high, I left.

I stood outside the doors which had little windows in the top, and I peaked in. The body in the casket was dumped unceremoniously into the cremation chamber. The door was slammed shut, and a thermostat was set. The workers then lit cigarettes while the body was burned to ash.

I looked up at where the woman's spirit was. She was looking on with a combination of curiosity and annoyance as her body was disrespectfully dropped off and burned.

I wanted to talk to her some more, but that was impossible. So I ran out of the funeral home and walked over to Broadway where I could get a subway going downtown.

Tim was still on my bed. Louise and Ricky were with him. All three were watching the movement on the TV screen. Tim had switched to one of the reality shows where people do moronic things to see if they can survive. A woman had a boa constrictor wrapped around her neck. She was crying and screaming for help.

The two cats were almost shaking with laughter, and Tim was close behind.

"Why are you watching this?"

"It's my daily dose of human dumbness."

That was Tim. The cats said nothing but tried to look ashamed of themselves. Cats do not pull this off very well.

"I've just been to a funeral. It was very educational. Can we talk, please?"

Tim turned the TV off and the two cats scampered out the window.

"I want to talk about Marie LaVeau."

"Why?"

"Wasn't she a Voodoo practitioner?"

"Yes. Also, a hairdresser." Tim tried not to be condescending but failed.

"Why?"

"To make money to buy slaves and set them free. She sent them all to California. She and Mary Ellen Pleasants. Read about her, too."

"The message is in here right?" I pointed to my head.

"You should've gotten it by now."

"Okay. All humans have spirits. But not all humans actively use their spirit during their lifetimes."

"Friendly amendment? Is that all right?" He smiled.

"Yes."

"Most humans have spirits. Not all. This is part of the complication of whether to call down Higgs Boson and blow this place away."

"Why can't we work on getting the spirited humans to be better?" I didn't mean to sound accusatory, but the Lost had been here for 50 million years.

"You go on and try."

"Tell me about Marie?"

"She was raised in New Orleans during the height of the slave trade. She figured out the spirit of every slave was being killed. She also realized that those slave owners who had a spirit, were also being destroyed by their own cruelty. But what could she do about it?"

"What?" I felt three years old.

"She became a hairdresser to the most powerful wives in New Orleans, learned their secrets, gained their confidence. By doing this she was able to bribe or convince them to allow her to run Congo Square."

"Where the slave auctions were held."

"Very good. Yes. And after every auction, Marie would have a festival of freedom with drummers beating out the rhythms of the Orisha, the gods of the Yoruba tradition. These drummers summoned the gods to Congo Square to clean off some of the indignity and bloody greed that had gone on during the auction."

"But they still held the auctions."

"Yes. And that was why Marie got hold of Mary Ellen and formed an interlocking directorate with her. Together they made enough money to buy so many slaves that I believe they outdid the Underground Railway."

"They sent the freed slaves to California? Why?" Oh yikes. If I had only read a little in school, I would know this answer.

"There was no law protecting slavery in California. So they sent newly freed women there. These women opened nightclubs and bordellos and made money and bought more slaves their freedom. By the time they had worked this for a while, the Fugitive Slave Act was passed in California."

"To send the slaves back? But how, they had been paid for." Stupid. Stupid. Stupid me.

"Yes, and we all know that bounty hunters and slave traders lived by the law."

"It's practically the same today isn't it? Slave trafficking girls, slave trafficking children who are sold into a life exactly the same as the slaves on the plantations."

"Yes."

"Meaning nobody learned anything?" I looked down at my hands as if they had an answer.

"The point is to try to bring justice to the planet. The point is not how successful you are."

"Then why do your fellow Lost question the viability of earth?"

"Because you take up a lot of resources, and we're not sure the percentage of people who are bothering to try is worth it."

"How in hell can I prove that?"

"I guess that's where Vita played a little trick on you."

"What does that mean?"

"She watched you for a long time. She has impeccable instincts and when your husband dropped dead, she was nearby and you came into her sights. From there she watched how you navigated widowhood, how you treated your kid, how you got the hell out of the suburbs and returned to where you are now."

"This is the West Village. I didn't go to Congo and work at

AIDS clinics."

"No, you returned to where you had unfinished business, Deborah."

"You mean my whole life?"

"Yes."

"So am I the experiment?"

"Yes."

"Come on Tim. Don't bullshit me."

"You have a nascent, one could say dormant, brilliance. And you were using it to pick out Gift with Purchase at department stores. But Vita believed if we showed you what the real story is, that you would prove a powerful advocate for our side."

"The side that says change is possible. The human race might be worth keeping alive?"

"Yes."

"What do I do now?"

"I can't tell you that. And you don't need me to. Vita introduced you to Vincent, and you did something really meaningful, not just for him but for the world."

"You mean I uncovered the largest fraud and money laundering scheme there is: the art market?"

"No. I mean you returned to this tortured, brilliant man the work that belonged to him. You showed him the effect he had made on other painters, and on everybody who looks at his paintings and sees what he is saying."

"He was saying the stars are the real god. He was saying yellow is a way to see genuine spirituaity, not the squared off version people get in religious institutions."

"Yes."

"What about Yeye and Marie and the whole tradition of Yoruba and how it got dispersed and sometimes distorted."

"All part of your education." Tim nodded as he spoke.

"Because I never listened in school?"

"Because you resisted the unimportant education offered to you. And when you were offered meaningful information, you gobbled it up, Deborah."

"But look at my daughter. She couldn't be more suburban, sweet, uninvolved, materialistic. That's what I've spawned."

"She isn't dead yet. She just began a new life. You don't have to change nappies, but you can influence your daughter and her daughter to join the fight."

"At that rate, the human race will be extinct before I can even weigh in on my observations."

"That's totally wrong."

"Then please Tim, tell me what is right."

"Deborah: Learn. Fight. Learn more. Stand for something. Have some sex. Try new foods. Fight for justice. Learn about completely new things. Like how's your knowledge about plant medicines grown in South America?"

"Nil."

"But these natural medicines could cure all the diseases the pharmas can't touch."

"Is that true?"

"Yes, Deborah. "

"How?"

"My lovely friend and sometimes sexual companion: the beauty of this planet, the main reason we have let it live this long, is that for every rotten behavior, for every hideous disease, there is a cure right in the earth or in the minds of the living creatures. Not just humans."

"Then why don't you—the side of you that wants to see the earth survive—why don't you just tell this to people. Prove it."

"Like magic acts? Medicine shows? The Lost bring you Burlesque with a Theme?"

"No."

"Then how? You see the stories that humans have

swallowed, mostly unbelievable and total crap. The other side of the potential for an informed group of living creatures on earth, is the potential for unbelievable stupidity."

"Like the dove that impregnated Mother Mary?"

"That's the least of it. How about favoring one child over the other? That worked well for Cain and Abel." He was angry.

"Is it just the Bible?"

"Deborah, it's time you read the Koran, Tibetan Book of the Dead, the teachings of Buddha."

"All the same?"

"Packaged differently, but none of it has done a thing to show humans how to live."

"Which is?"

"You will be born, given a lifetime and then die. After you die you will reconfigure into a shadow of who you were, but you will exist. And everything you have ever done, said, or experienced is all on the Space Time continuum forever."

"That sounds like New Age stuff."

"Wrong. Over the centuries, many groups have embraced a description of Life and Death that is closer to the truth than you get in a church, or mosque, synagogue or Ashram." Tim looked annoyed.

"Have we talked enough for today?"

"You have a lot to think about. Why are mythic figures different than humans who have mythologies built around them? What's the difference between Mother Mary and Joan of Arc? One of them was real and died for what she believed in, one of them was a fabrication who has more statues and buildings built for her than God itself. Why?"

I put my head in my hands.

"I thought this was going to be like a thesis. Hard work, lots of research, then some writing. But you want me to figure out why human beings do or do not fulfill their destinies. Why some people waste their whole lives being lumps and some people paint the most beautiful images ever created and die poor, hungry and with a bullet in their stomach."

"That's what we need."

"You still think I can do this?"

Tim could see my frustration and in an unusual moment of plain kindness, he nodded "yes." Then he reached out his hand to me.

"And now, what you never got for doing your homework!"

"You mean sex?"

He laughed. Then we both got on the bed, turned the TV back on to one of the dumbest shows we could find, and continued our conversation in physical form.

Chapter Twenty Two
The Show Must Go On

I MET WITH VITA AT CARBONE'S. We hadn't spoken since my last conversation with Tim and I needed some clarification from her.

"Why did you warn me off of Tim when I first met him? And now, he's like half of my guide through the discovery I am trying to make."

"Tim is not a simple man. And although it has its advantages, his extreme emotional sensitivity has, at times, made him a liability to our cause which requires total objectivity. You don't bring in Higgs Boson and eliminate 50 million years of development without a damn good reason."

"Are you saying he is so emotional that he sometimes thinks the earth is not worth the oxygen it takes up?"

"Yes."

"Can you give me an example?"

"Of course not." She smiled at me.

"All right. You aren't going to get specific. But do you feel like my relationship with Tim is somehow artificial or opportunistic on his part?"

"No."

"You think he cares about me?"

"I think Tim has seen you the way I did the first time I laid eyes on you."

"You don't mean he's in love with me?" It sounded desperate as it came out of my mouth.

"Am I in love with you? Or does my hope for a changed world reside somewhere inside your potential?"

"Oh." I hated that I sounded disappointed.

"Do you want me to say Tim is in love with you?"

"No." I tried to sound centered.

"So now you're not going to answer my questions?"

"I am glad for the faith you and seemingly Tim have in me. It is very heady and exciting. It is also very frightening."

"It should be. There are seven billion lives at stake, not to mention a very elaborate planet."

"But I'm not casting some kind of final vote?" I asked.

"Of course not." Vita dusted off her mouth with her napkin which muffled her response.

"That doesn't sound sincere."

"I hope that before you go much further with the fascinating research you are involved with, that you will realize that you have been entrusted with something very powerful— the response of a human being to the question of the world you exist in."

"Are other human beings weighing in as well?"

"Yes."

"I don't believe you."

"Well, that's a little narcissistic of you Deborah."

"Can I know any of my counterparts?"

"Answer that question yourself." Vita chuckled.

"I just did. So before I order a bottle of absinthe and drown my confusion—Tim really thinks well of me?"

"Yes."

"And you believe that and don't think it's a trick?"

"You need to go see Osiris as soon as you can."

"Why?"

"Because you are too connected to Tim. And I don't say that because he means to slow you down or somehow throw a monkey wrench in your work."

"You think I'm in love with him, Vita?"

"I think you have grown into the kind of evolved woman who knows that whether or not he has sex with millions of other women, or sheep or even well-shaped topiary, he still cares for you in a special way."

"That sounds good. I like that."

"You've been married. You've seen hundreds of relationships, you don't need to be the one and only. You need somebody you can love and be free of. Your task is huge, and you need to keep your focus broad and not narrow it down to any one creature." Vita was done.

"Except for you?"

"Yes. Because I am your handler."

"All right. I appreciate this conversation. You have made me feel centered. Would you like a glass of absinthe?"

I waved to the waiter who came immediately.

"We'll have the absinthe and two glasses, please."

He smiled at me and went off.

"Shall we get crazy drunk in honor of what you just learned?" A strange question from Vita, who never got crazy drunk except that one time in Weimar when the Nazis turned the nightclub into a butcher shop.

"Not now. I finally feel capable of my task. I still hope there are others working on it as well, but my own judgment will be strong and fair."

"And you know you may have to fight for your opinion to prevail?"

"I can fight."

"Can you see a different future for the world?"

"Yes."

"One that you can articulate to me?" Vita smiled.

"No. Not yet."

"Then Deborah, let's drink."

The waiter arrived with a brand new bottle of absinthe and two glasses. He poured for both of us, and we raised the glasses in a toast.

"The faster you figure this out, the faster we can enjoy a bright future."

"I know." I raised my glass, "To you Vita, for giving me the world!"

We clinked glasses, each took a big swallow, and I realized somewhere down inside my stomach, that the final chapter of the incredible journey I had been on since that day at Bloomingdale's, was now in full swing.

Chapter Twenty Three
See You In My Dreams

I WAS HAVING A HORRIBLE NIGHTMARE. I woke up scared and turned on the light on my bedside table. I looked for the cats, but of course, they were not there. Tim hadn't come over after my dinner with Vita, so I had gone to sleep alone. And then came the nightmare.

I was at the funeral parlor where my favorite uncle, Frank, had been buried when I was quite young. He was sitting up in his casket and screaming at me. "How stupid are you?"

"Why, Uncle Frank?"

"You need a colony of people to explain death to you?"

"Nobody ever talked about death in my family."

"So why didn't you go to church like everybody else who's scared of dying?" Uncle Frank was snarling.

"I don't believe they have the answer for me."

"Well, aren't you the big shot. Seven billion people seek solace from death in some form of religion. But that's not good enough for you."

"I'm sorry, but you are wrong, Uncle Frank. Not all human beings look to a church or a mosque or an ashram for this answer. And for many who do, they don't get any comfort, they feel more scared."

"Then tell me the answer Miss Smarter Than Everybody Else. Tell me. Go on. I know you, you never did your homework, you got by on native intelligence and a lot of coca cola. Now all of a sudden you know the meaning of death and you don't need Jesus, Mohammed, Buddha or Moses to guide you."

"You only mentioned men."

"Please, my little niecelette! I'm dead, I'm not arguing

feminism with a snotty nothing like you."

"I loved you. You were always my favorite uncle."

"Big deal."

"Why are you so angry Uncle Frank?"

"Because you think you're going to solve the Big Problem in the world for your dumb ass friends, the Lost. And boy are you all in for a big disappointment."

"What does that mean?"

"The years since I died have not been good to you. You didn't become anything, you lived off your fancy husband's fancy money. You squeezed out one kid and you didn't even grow things in a garden behind your mansion in the woods. You're a big zero. Why these elders of the planet have put faith in you is a howling mystery to me. You have no spirit and you know it."

"You have no faith to lose, and you know it."

"That's not what I said, Deborah. Or whatever your new name is. You can't even quote somebody who's sitting in a casket right in front of you."

"It's a line from a song. I use to sing it when I was younger."

"Who cares?"

"Look. I am sorry that you have such a low opinion of me, but I am going to prove to the world that I do have a spirit. I am going to give every ounce of my energy to bringing my spirit to its fullness."

"Sounds exciting, maybe even full of shit."

As he said this last demeaning line, the walls in the dream began to move away and soon Uncle Frank in his casket, and I were in a wide, open field with a group of people walking towards us chanting.

"She is stupid. She is empty. Spirit zero, sex drive high."

I recognized teachers and friends from my school. They seemed to really hate me, and worse, they seemed to know my little secret: that I hadn't worked hard in school because I didn't like the material being taught. They were scornful and almost violent in their disgust for me.

"She is stupid. Come and fuck her. She is empty but she likes to hump."

This was strange. I had not been the most sexually active of the kids I grew up with. I had my boy friends and we had experimented, but some of the girls in the mob approaching me with disdain, really had sexed out their whole adolescence. I started to scream back at them.

"You're talking about yourselves. I am not stupid. I have been chosen. You are the ones who never did anything with the spirit you were given."

The air in the dream began to darken until I was in a place as dark as the basement where Set had raped me and I hadn't felt it. The wind began to howl and my uncle reached up and pulled down the lid of his casket. As his last words he yelled through the wind at me:

"Figure it out for yourself. This is a dream. A nightmare. You get to decide how you feel about what we said. Goodnight."

The casket was shut, Uncle Frank disappeared inside it, and the casket flew high into the darkness and was gone. The crowd that had been walking towards me evaporated and I was suddenly alone in a dark place that felt like planet earth's destroyed remains.

Then, I woke up.

I got out of my bed and went to the phone and called my daughter.

"Hello? Sweetheart? It's me. Have you got a moment to talk?"

"Sorry, mother. The baby hasn't stopped screaming all day and we are about to take her for a ride in a cab where she will drift off to sleep."

"Oh. Of course. You go."

"Are you all right?"

"Yes. Fine. Go, I can hear her screaming."

I hung up before my daughter responded. And I wondered why I had called her. Was I going to ask her if I was a good person? A person with spirit? Ask my own child? What were the chances that she would say "no"? Anyway, I had already asked for her reassurance and gotten it.

I wished I could find my husband, or one of my parents. Somebody from my past who could wipe away the cruelty of the people in the nightmare—reassure me of my uncle's love.

But I knew that was not the answer.

It had always been clear to me that Uncle Frank loved me. We used to play Jotto, a word game that required smarts and deductive skills, and I usually won, although my uncle was a brilliant man, a professor at Columbia, a real linguist.

Every time I won a game of Jotto against him, his lovely warm smile filled his face and he would take my face in his hand and lean in close and say: "This is a smart family, but you my little one, you are the smartest of us all. Just wait, you'll see."

Then he would kiss me on both cheeks and pick up his pad and pencil to resume the next hand of Jotto.

When he died, I was in my early teens. I was grief stricken and terrified from seeing him in an open casket. This was all occurring to me right now, for the first time.

He had been at Riverside Chapel where everybody from the West side goes, and at the time of his death, the funeral entrepreneurs had been experimenting with some classier caskets: lined in a traditional pink satin, the top of the body could be elevated in the casket as if the person was on a lounge chair sleeping. My uncle had been lifted up, his glasses were on, and his son had put his pipe in the coffin with him.

As I looked—after the first shock of seeing him—the pipe moved a tiny bit. I could hear my family all around me gasp, and many of them popped open capsules that would prevent them from fainting. I didn't have one of those. I think they were filled with amylnitrate. Certainly nobody gave a popper to a teenaged girl. Also, nobody explained to me why there was suddenly a cacophony of poppers popping when my unfortunate Uncle, an experimental body on the altar of funeral practices, seemed to move.

I tried to find my parents. I was sitting between two cousins who were much older than I was. They were both kind but said almost nothing.

After the moving pipe incident, the funeral entrepreneur came quickly to the coffin, adjusted the top down so my uncle's head disappeared from view, and delicately repositioned the top so there would be no more illusion of him lounging or sunbathing.

The funeral ended, we all stood up and formed a line. I had no idea what was next. The first row emptied out and all the family members went to the coffin and either said something to the dead body, or just wept and walked past him.

I realized I was expected to do the same thing. Why hadn't anybody asked me if I had ever seen a dead body? Why hadn't anybody asked me if I was scared to walk by this man I had loved and find him inert, empty of his usual smile and witticisms. Dead.

The queue moved forward and I looked around once more for my parents, but they had managed to get into the lobby where they were consoling my aunt and her children.

I walked toward the coffin in dread fear. When I got to it, I saw my uncle, laid out flat. The pipe had fallen out of sight, his glasses were on but slightly askew. He had been turned into a wax figure by the embalmers. I looked at him and said, "Goodbye, Uncle Frank. I will miss our games of Jotto. Good luck."

I moved on. "Good luck"? Why had I said that? I kept

walking towards the lobby and my parents, but I was embarrassed that I hadn't said something profound. And at that moment, something inside my spirit went dark.

Was I having a nightmare about his death because I was ready to let my spirit breathe again? Was this terrible incident from my adolescence responsible for the dead space in my head for the next two decades? Why didn't I wake from this spiritual narcolepsy when my own child had fallen off a seesaw and gotten a gash in her head?

Why hadn't the terror of my little girl dying forced me to go back to my first experience with lost life to figure out how traumatized I had been, and how much of my life I had slept through?

This had to be the part of me Vita saw when my husband died and she said she had been watching my every move. I refused to allow an open casket at his funeral, and for that matter, the funeral had been brief, and not held at a funeral parlor.

My husband had been in his casket in the hospital where he worked. There was a huge open room they used for special events, his casket along with hundreds of folding chairs had filled it.. I had not cared much about anything anybody was saying to me. I was working overtime to quell the horror I was feeling. And I had no idea that had been happening.

The nightmare had opened up a vein. I began to remember all the times one of my parent's or any other family member had been sick, or in jeopardy. My parents traveled often to dangerous places for their Human Rights organization. I could feel the fright that had stricken me every time. An agony I had ignored.

Was this why I had to sleep walk through the Great Books I should have been fascinated by? Was I so afraid of Death that I skipped over it as an issue? And how did that work when I got the phone call that my husband had died?

Had I blocked out the issue because I had no way to address it? I began to realize that the fear of mortality is probably the only thing all human beings share. Maybe all living creatures share. At least the ones who have enough brain cell development.

Look at Louise. She had killed a rat for no good reason, and been permanently banned from her home in the zoo. Clearly the other animals felt that the Death Sentence she had issued over a nursing rodent was worthy of banishing her forever.

I stared at the cat. She and Ricky were together at the foot of my bed. They must have been there while I was having my nightmare. They must have entered my room and curled up together as I was being insulted and berated by my uncle.

These two had been witness to my realization. Even though I was asleep, I had given myself a message from deep inside: the emotional narcolepsy that had lasted for decades of my life, came from a terrible fear of mortality.

I remembered reading in a magazine that in a small town filled with Evangelical Christians, the writer had met with and interviewed many of the townspeople in an effort to understand their particularly extreme form of religiosity.

The inhabitants, all 2600 of them, believed deeply that this life was a prelude to their real life when they were in heaven. This being their belief, they had spent their time ascertaining the exact dimensions of Heaven. They had concluded that Heaven was 15,000 miles wide. The interviewer was too polite to ask if they assumed the earth was flat, or else why a dimension that was not a circumference? The journalist did ask how high Heaven is, how close it comes to earth.

She asked how people could get up to Heaven if they were not tall enough. The reporter got an answer to the question: if a short person needs to enter Heaven, a ladder is dropped down for them.

Does Heaven have a deal with Home Depot, Ace Hardware,

Builders' Emporium? The question wasn't asked. But the article left me further assured that fear of the unknown Next Step after Death was a driving force for human beings. Including me. It certainly explained religion.

Weeks went by after the illuminating nightmare about my uncle. In those many days, I had seen almost nobody, not my daughter, her daughter, Vita or Tim. I had hugged my arms around my metaphorical self and tried to deal with how much of my time on the planet had been deadened by fears I hadn't understood.

At the same time, my brain, that sits on top of the subconscious discoveries I was making, had kicked into high gear. What was the question that I was being asked to bring forward in my "argument" or more to the point my Judgement for the Lost?

Death, I knew, was part of it. Afterwards the atoms, boson particles, whatever material we are made of, does go on but in a different way. I knew from my parents and my husband that some of the delights of being alive disappeared, but that one still moved through Time and Space. The change involved loss—food, drink, maybe sex (I hadn't gotten real answers when I asked my mother what "an assignation" with my father meant without her full corporeal body, and I certainly hadn't gotten an answer when I questioned Tim's claims about having sex with her).

I had taken comfort from the Spacetime Continuum and the realization that everything that has ever happened is recorded for all time.

Was that the answer they wanted from me? The Lost didn't have the power to make people immortal. They didn't have the power to change peoples' fears of aging and ultimately dying.

But somewhere in my reporting to them, they wanted a judgement from me.

They had chosen an identity for me that involved wisdom,

judgement, a warrior's strength and a seer's prescience.

It was nice weather so I had been walking all over the lower part of Manhattan. From East River to Hudson River, from Canal to 14th Street. This rectangle included where I had been in school until I left for college, it included where I had chosen to hang out on weekends when I was old enough to leave on a weekend evening and go hang with my friends.

Although the neighborhoods I walked had been sold to extremely wealthy people, mostly from other countries, a lot of it felt the same to me. The smells of coffee, of exotic foods, of fresh water when I got near either river.

Music went through my head as I walked songs written long before my teen years. The music in my head was from my parent's generation. As I hummed the music began to pull at a string inside of me that would prove invaluable. If only I could identify it.

I went home, limited myself to one glass of red wine, and turned on my laptop. I dialed up YouTube and listened to the classic songs from the 50s that my mother and father turned on after I had gone into my room. I remembered how I would open my door just a crack and stare at them "slow dancing" to a favorite from when they had first fallen in love. On the coffee table I would see their empty martini glasses, and unfinished cigarettes as if the impulse to hold each other and move together had become overwhelming.

They never noticed me. The music and their need for each other had swept them away. Their hearts beating against each other as they danced. Here was something I had never had. My One True Love.

I had enjoyed my marriage, enjoyed my boyfriends, but I had never felt what I saw when my parents danced. They would press their bodies together, one arm around each other, holding the other hands tightly together and pressing their heads together as they sang along to the record.

We did not listen to much music. They took me to Broadway musicals and I cried as I watched the dancing, especially tap dancing. We had gone to the ballet and I had felt myself lifted out of my seat by the sheer beauty of dancers spinning and jumping high in the air.

But my mother and father dancing was different: These two people felt something for each other that was for all time. They had beaten the odds on boredom or cheating or just becoming encased in anger over their time together. When mother and I were home and my father opened the front door she would forget whatever she was doing so she could run to him and kiss his cheek, taking in that wonderful smell he had. On the rare occasions when my father and I were home alone, he would watch the front door as if the answer to all of Life's questions would be answered when my mother walked in.

I understood what spring meant to me. It was this forever after love my parents had. I never found that. I knew no other couple that had. It was a thing of overwhelming joy, like the wedding in Romeo and Juliet. But my parents had not died tragically trying to save each other. They had lived out a love affair that was something I had been denied. I enjoyed feeling sorry for myself as I reminisced. I wondered if they were the reason I had never had wine with dinner when my husband was alive? It felt like a counterfeit copy of my parents. Alcohol was part of what kept them so in love.

I knew on the nights they drank martinis they would wait for me to go into my room, then turn on their old record player (this was 35 years ago) and play some of their favorite oldies: 45's. They would drink and smoke cigarettes while they talked seriously about their work. Then the stack of 45's would drop down on a song they simply could not resist, and without a word, they would stand up, move away from the couch, and slow dance. I remember exactly three of the songs that had this effect on them: My True Story, To the Aisle, and their all-time favorite, In the Still of the Night.

They sang along, with my father grabbing the high falsetto at the end, and my mother holding onto him as they moved back and forth from one leg to the other.

In the Still of the Night, I held you, held you tight.
Cause I love, love you so,
Promise I'll never let you go
In the Still of the Night.

As my father sang the lyrics my mother would provide the Shoo Doo Bee Shoo Bee Doos to accompany him. At the end of the song, my mother wiped away tears, and my father held her in his arms as if he was holding life's breath and could not live a moment without it.

Then they would laugh and go back to the couch. And I would quietly shut my bedroom door.

Between my memory of Uncle Frank and the memory of my parents' love affair, I was getting a very clear picture of why I was who I was. A woman who loved lightly, who cared, but did so on some kind of auto-pilot. I had never had a Great Love. I had never let myself have a compulsion to be excellent at something hard for me. I was smart enough to get by without much investment. And that had cost me everything.

I was forming a sense of what my mission was about. Why they had chosen me to create it: I am cultured and smart, nobody was ever diabolical to me, I had no siblings who could've filled that gap. My parents were principled and kind and having decided to have me, they took care to give me a well-rounded life.

We traveled to beautiful places, they pointed out to me the poverty in some of these places. But they always made sure to imbue in me the knowledge that I could enjoy the earth's bounty and loveliness, and that privilege came with an obligation to seek justice for those who could not.

I would report on the terrible lives lived by those who had nothing: who lacked potable water, edible food, comfortable housing, medical amenities and of course a good education. But everybody on the planet already knew about the terrible inequities of the planet's population, people knew that we were destroying our planet with toxins and plastics, and terrifying leaders whose greed is worn like a new dress: proudly and with no excuses.

The Lost did not need me to do more than reference the dark and light parts of life on earth. I would concentrate on mortality and the existential questions that lead people to spiritual systems that don't quell their fears or give them any real answers.

I would speak to my new found awareness that the earth could be healed if its human inhabitants wanted to help each other.

Cruelty stayed in my mind as I was developing my thoughts. All forms of cruelty from slaughtering too many animals, and doing it in unthinkable ways, to the way some people treat each other. I was always taught at home that economic inequities could be solved by social systems that demanded a decent life for all people. I was sure that if we stopped burning too much fossil fuels, the ground and the plants and the air and the water would slowly be cleaned if not completely then with great improvement.

But cruelty? I had no answer for that. And the solutions offered from the same religious institutions that failed to help people understand mortality, were useless. They had no understanding of Time and Space, the truth that once you have existed you will always exist in some way, these religions also had no real solutions to cruelty. "Do unto others" had done nothing. "Thou shalt not kill," nothing. Tribal hatreds were thriving even though social scientists could explain that fear of other was no reason to burn down their villages or steal their lands and slaughter whole populations.

Man's inhumanity to Man. I would spend time studying. I would try to create a balanced understanding of where the instinct comes from to slap a child, to kick a dog, or just to tell a friend they look fat in their new outfit. As to talent: Vincent was right, everybody has a talent. But people are capable of stomping their talent into the ground through neglect or just because they (like me) weren't able to find what they loved doing.

I had seen Vincent's joyful compulsion when he painted, often working all night. Creating the forgeries, every painter had the same thing going on inside: a simple dedication to their art. They would get no credit for a copy of a Van Gogh painting, but doing it beautifully clearly filled them with joy. And misery. The twin children of the true artist.

My head was swimming, and I decided to go back outside in the cool night air and walk to Carbone's and try to stop thinking.

As I got dressed, another theme repeated itself endlessly inside of me until I was crying and kept having to re-do my makeup. I had never had a great love in my life. It did not have to be a person, although as I looked back at my parents I realized how much joy they had gotten from the duration of their love affair.

I had never ached for anything, and this was a huge loss. I had no idea how to change that, but I knew that if the argument was going to mean anything to the Lost or to me, I would have to figure this out. I had many years left to me, years of probably good health, although one never knows that for sure. But probably many years of good health. I could not spend it eating bread and drinking red wine. The light went on brightly inside my head: all the things I just said about myself, those were the reasons I had been chosen by Vita and the Lost to make an argument. The light would not ever go out again.

Chapter Twenty Four
Help!

I SEARCHED THROUGH MY PHONE CONTACTS to find the word "Yeye" and dialed the number.

When she answered, I told her who it was, and she remembered me.

"I hope this question won't sound stupid to you, Yeye."

"Ask me, Deborah."

"Why did you become a priestess?"

"I carried a child to term, but I was poor. The fetus was not nourished well. The baby was born dead."

"You couldn't get any government help?"

"The first check arrived the day my child died, inside my body."

"Oh no! I am so sorry."

"I could never have another baby. And I watched the lights around my soul go out. I disappeared from everybody in Oakland, where I lived. I put out the word that I was dead."

"And what did you do?"

"Nothing. For the first year. I sat very still. I was shaking so hard inside I knew I could not move or I would shatter."

"The father?"

"It was another time Deborah. He had fathered several children with several of his women, as he called them. It was a different time."

"He gave you—?"

"A dead little boy."

"After the first year?"

"I went to a friend who practiced the Yoruba Tradition. His name was Ahadi and he was a priest. He told me the way to save myself was to join the tradition of my ancestors."

"Did he tell you how to do that?"

"Ahadi took me to Lagos. There had never been a woman Priestess in the tradition. I talked to many people there and finally they said I could become a Priestess representing a Mothering figure: the goddess Yemaya."

"What did you have to do?"

"I'm sorry, Deborah, that I cannot share. But I will tell you that you have been given the name of a Priestess, a Judge, a Warrior. Find your way to being that woman and you will be your real self."

The phone beeped as if somebody was calling in on my other line. Yeye responded.

"Go, Deborah. I have told you what to look for. And call me to report on your progress please. Oh. And plan to wear nothing but white for at least a year."

With that, she hung up and I switched to the other line.

"Where've you been?" Tim's deep voice.

"Working."

"Want to take a break and eat?"

"No thanks. I think I'll just take a bath and go to sleep."

"Want company?" I could feel him smiling on the other end of the line.

"Yes. And could you bring me something to eat please?"

"I've already ordered for you." He said.

"I am almost figuring out my argument."

"You don't need any input from me, right? Or could you ask me for help? I am 50 million years older than you. Maybe I have an idea or two. About your work."

"Okay."

"No need to thank me.

"Thank you, Tim."

"I got you well-done fries with your chicken. See you in a flash."

I could hear him chuckle as he hung up. I didn't need to tell

him what to bring, Tim and I knew each other very well. I only
hoped he would remember to bring something for Louise and.
Ricky or I would be sharing my dinner with them.

Chapter Twenty Five
The End of the Rainbow

THE DELIVERY OF MY ARGUMENT WAS TO BE GIVEN to the entirety of the Lost and some invited guests.

My work was completed in less time than was anticipated, and I had traveled almost nowhere except inside my own soul and the body of written knowledge accumulated by people who had the time to think about more than what they could catch or harvest to eat that day. And here I was, arriving where I was to deliver my thoughts. Forsaking my New York Woman's uniform of black clothing. I was, as suggested by Yeye, entirely dressed in white. As I approached the entrance to the auditorium I would be speaking in, two dark oak doors opened for me as if they were automated, which they were not.

I walked with deliberation. There were people on two sides of the audience, which led up to a stage that looked like a courtroom. This is where I was to speak.

Vita was in the courtroom on stage, seated on the judge's bench, which had three seats and sat at the back of the courtroom. I looked for Tim and was surprised and uncomfortable to find him in the aisle at the far side of the audience from me. He was talking to Set. They were laughing and it brought back a terrible memory of a night they had obviously planned together to hurt me.

As I stared at him a moment too long, Tim looked up and saw me. He pushed Set away. Set left the auditorium and the doors closed behind him. Tim walked up onto the courtroom and sat next to Vita. There did not seem to be a third judge. An empty witness box sat downstage and to the right side of the judges' bench, the bench was dead center at the back of the stage. There was no jury's box, but there were two tables at the very front of the stage.

Walking straight ahead with my long, white skirt billowing a little, I went up the steps and into the courtroom. At one of the tables sat the woman from Bloomingdale's who had tried on the lipstick the day I met Vita. She was not opposing Counsel, but she was somehow part of this. That left the other table for me. Defense Counsel? Prosecutor? Which was I? The only hint was that next to my table there was a large screen, presumably there if I needed to use it for visuals.

Vita, Tim and the empty seat in the Judge's area, seemed to be complete, I could tell nobody else would join them. Looking up to get directions from Vita, she pointed to the front where the audience was. Clearly I would be given no introduction. I turned to my audience.

I didn't know how to address them. "Ladies and Gentlemen of the Jury?" No. "Good afternoon and welcome." No, worse. Why the hell hadn't I figured out this all-important means of opening my argument?

"If it please the court." This got an unexpected but very welcome chuckle from my audience. "Thank you for the opportunity to look at the world I live in and be allowed to take it in as deeply as I can. Thank you for the incredible books I have finally read, the diversity and depth of music I have listened to, and the lives that have touched me.

Thank you for giving me a reason to overcome my own fears so I could understand my fellow humans, and the nature of this planet. I have seen the earth's beauty with an intensity I could never have found without this 'assignment.' I have witnessed ugliness that sent me home to cry in my bed for days without end.

I have no gigantic scale on which to put these things. There is no blind Lady Justice to cast her judgement. But you have asked for my judgement. You have assured me that my conclusions about the value of the earth, will be one of many conclusions you will consider.

So today, I am ready to give you my thoughts, the judgements I have made. The more I read and watched and considered what I was seeing, the more I realized how little any one person's opinion matters. But maybe some of my thinking is slightly unique, and if so, I hope I can contribute to your ultimate decision."

The woman stood up from the other table and addressed me as she spoke. "How will you know whether we have accepted your conclusion?"

A man stood up from the audience to answer her. "One day she won't wake up ever again, or she will wake up every day until her own lifespan is over."

"Meaning you will not tell me your decision?" I asked.

A third person stood up from the audience. The person looked familiar. I realized it was the trans-neutral Talmudic scholar I had met with in Cambridge. "Meaning we may never make a decision. We may not be able to agree on one."

Vita stood up from the judge's bench and stopped any more cross talking. "Deborah has drawn up her Argument, that is what we are here for today."

Vita sat back down.

I was ready to go on. "I am not certain of everything I have learned. But I am certain I will not spend any more of my life in a state of unconsciousness. I will not waste time because I know my time has limits. I know my time could end without warning. And knowing I have a permanent place in Time and Space, makes the present moment and the present day, matter more to me than ever, for as long as I am allowed to have them.

"It has been ten thousand years since you last came together with a mortal to give their observations about the earth. In that time, previously unimaginable things have happened on this planet. People have waged constant wars, and the earth itself became a flaming hell in two Wars that affected the whole world. The humans used their newly developed scientific knowledge to create weapons so diabolical it is hard to look back on it. Atomic bombs were dropped on civilian populations. Poison gases were sprayed that killed not only people, but also entire landscapes of trees, growing fields, and everything that lived within them. Forgive me, I am telling you things you already know.

"Looking at the violence and brutality people have vented on each other I became very disturbed by those who knew it was wrong and did nothing to stop it.

"In the hundreds of years of the Spanish Inquisition, why did nobody demand an end to the torture and murder? Millions of women were burned as witches, along with them their cats. Why could nobody figure out that this blood fest was not only abusive, but that without their natural predators, the rats would unleash a plague unlike anything ever seen before?"

My audience seemed attentive, even riveted. I continued. "How many people sat at a picnic table and watched as lynchings went on not twenty feet away, while they continued munching on their tuna sandwiches?

"What did the Germans really believe when the smell of burning flesh permeated their towns as ovens with thousands of people in them began to stink? Did they tell themselves it was some huge barbecue they had not been invited to?

"These bystanders, enablers, are part of my dilemma. If you take a side, you are at least part of what is going on. For better or worse, whether you are courageous or evilly intended, you are a member of the species and you are participating in the world. You deserve oxygen, food, water, all the resources it takes to care for a human life, because you are a part of the effort to make a change in human creatures. You have a spirit inside of you. And the rubbing against each other of peoples' spirits makes the hope for change possible. If you are involved in this, conceivably you could learn something that would change your opinion and allow you to be responsible for a bit of human evolution.

"But if you are a bystander, and the smells, the screams, the blood running down the roads where the heads fall with a loud splat to the ground do not move you, then I believe the earth's resources are wasted on you. I believe you have no Spirit.

"Onlookers, whose Spirits are gone, cannot be sustained. They are proudly cruel, the cold and uncaring among us. They create an obstacle to the hard work to be done to free humanity from the pain of being mortal. We cannot sustain those who have no soul. The planet's survival is only possible if we make a clear definition of what it means to be human, if we can teach people to be kinder. That is hard to do because cruelty is the most seductive drug on earth. A person who has stood by and watched the causing of pain, the spilling of rivers of blood, the crushing of others, won't ever forget the enjoyment they have gotten. Meanness is a deeply engrained pleasure for those who practice or observe it blandly.

"Religions of all kinds try to teach people to be 'better' by promising humans a form of afterlife that does not exist. People have the right to know the truth: your life is temporary, but your spirit and what fills your soul is forever. The more you practice being gentle to others, the more wondrous the world will be.

"I asked myself, if we took away cruelty would the people who have never cared about the brutality they witness, become kind? Does cruelty contribute anything? Brilliant art? Exceptional intelligence? Unfettered energy? Does cruelty serve a purpose? I have no answer, and no idea how to extract cruelty altogether, which leaves me with mixed judgements about this planet.

"What I am sure of, is that we are at the Event

Horizon—you must either call on the Higgs Boson particle to
return to earth and end it, or together we must find a way to
do what the ancient Egyptians did: When someone died, the
god Ma'at would weigh their heart against a feather. If they had
not learned enough, become a better person in the life they
were dying away from, they did not move on to a new
existence. They were sent back to become a more profound
part of the world, instructed to try to live brilliantly, and most
of all, to stand for kindness. I do not know if this can be done
any more on this planet. But I will spend my life trying to
accomplish it as I go along. I have been honored by you with
the title, Priestess, Warrior, Judge. I will try to carry on Ma'at's
work in any ways I can. And that is my Judgement: We must all
try, and I will try harder every day that I live out my life. Thank
you."

I took a deep breath. There was a silence in the room.

Tim stood up and began a slow, rhythmic clapping. I
looked at him and saw the man I had loved and trusted. I saw
that Set's friendship was part of him I hoped he would
eradicate. I could see from how he was looking at me, he
would agree with that. I could see that he would try to excise
that ancient piece of the Troglodyte in himself. Maybe only for
as long as I am in human form to remind him. Maybe well
beyond my leaving this frequency.

Tim's clapping produced a beautiful rhythm in the air. The
whole room began to roll gently, the ceiling blew away as if it
was a piece of cloth, and everybody stood up as the sound of
Tim's hands were joined by others and burst into raucous
applause. It was so loud and sustained that I grew afraid that it
signaled the end of my journey and meant I would find myself
back in a state of nothingness. The rolling went on for minutes
as images flashed on the screen beside my table: first, the two
archived planets I had been shown. Then flowers blossoming,
shriveling and dying back, the sun coming up and going down

as the stars came out. Images that were part of the journey I had taken. Part of the planet I had seen in depth.

The Lost had put it all in perspective for me, they had shown me the universe. The Space Time Continuum, the beauty of a death that is not the end, but a transition to a mysterious "other" existence. They had taught me the truth of the earth I live in, and the even greater truth of the Universe the tiny planet spins in. This Argument was a culmination of my thoughts, but I knew it would not be the end of my chance to think, and ultimately grow a deeper knowledge of human life.

Vita stepped up to me, shook my hand and smiled. She addressed the audience.

"Now we must show our gratitude to Deborah." (she turned to look at me). "Within reason, and the laws of this universe, you may have anything you like."

I could hear that Vita was still speaking as I spun out into Time and Space, flying out the top of the room where the roof had been. I could hear Tim commenting on my insights, and other voices I could not identify jumping in to speak to the depth or stupidity of my observations. It was a lively discussion of my ideas, but I had left them behind for now.

Slowly, floating with eyes that saw only colors but no images, I began to smell onions. Sweet, sweet onions cooking in a deep pot. I focused my eyes just as I arrived in the kitchen at Arles. My heart jumped at the sight of Vincent, my dearest friend, alive and stirring one of his soups. On the little table was a bottle of absinthe with two glasses already poured.

Vincent kept working on his soup as he spoke to me. "Please, grab yourself a glass. And one for me too."

I took the two glasses and gave one to Vincent as he put the finishing touch on his creation. He turned to me and kissed me on both cheeks, but we did not sit down at the table. Instead, we lifted our glasses and toasted each other.

"Thank you, Deborah, for your perceptions, and your bravery."

"Thank you, Vincent for convincing me that my talents existed and needed to be found and named."

We smiled and drank from our glasses. A moment went by, and then from out of nowhere, I could hear the sound of a record dropping onto the top of a pile of ancient 45s and the needle moving over to play it.

Without a word, we both put down our glasses and came together somewhat formally putting our arms out and joining each other to dance. As the first bass note hit, my knees weakened with the recognition of what was about to play. Vincent held me so I would not fall. We moved closer together as the music came on.

A line of instrumentation, and then the deep, male voices singing my parent's favorite song, "In the Still of the Night." For people in love in the fifties, it had been the most important love song of all time. Our dance was not romantic, it was deeper: ours was a friendship of mutual enlightenment. The song played and Vincent sang the lyrics along with me. I did not need to ask him how he knew this song.

In the still of the night, I held you
Held you tight,
'Cause I love, love you so
Promise I'll never let you go
In the still of the night."

Vincent was quite a dancer. I felt like a rag doll being dragged around for the first few seconds, but soon, we were dancing as if we had danced together throughout eternity. We shared a love that was devout, not physical, but it was as intense as any love affair had ever been.

Neither of us had ever had a Great Love in our lives, but

we had this kinship, the knowledge of what I had given him, the knowledge of what he had taught me. And we danced to the song holding each other tightly. It was the sweetest three and a half minutes I had ever known. Vincent joined the singer as he hit the falsetto at the end of the song. We were still in a warm embrace. Then the music ended, and I was alone.

—The End —